Vince

by

Peter Lane

VINCE

ISBN 978-1-908090-26-3

Published by: Ragged Cover Publishing

www.raggedcover.com

Chapter 1

The doctor calls them flashbacks, but they seem more like nightmares to me, even if I'm awake. I get some warning because I suddenly start to feel shivery all over. It's a pretty horrible feeling because I know what's coming and there's nothing I can do to stop it. I don't know if I'm seeing them for real with my eyes or just in my mind, but I stop seeing what's actually in front of me, like I'm not there anymore. Some of the pictures that flash up are just like they happened, such as when my finger got caught in the door or the look on the face of the teacher when she undid the bandage and saw the gangrene. Mostly though, the images are mixed-up and twisted round. The things in them did happen, well kind of, except not in that particular way or order. I go down this long, dark tunnel and I come out at a Nazi concentration camp. There are dead bodies lying about and survivors looking like living skeletons. One of the guards and I are eating spaghetti and he denies what's happened to the Jews, even though the evidence is all around. He's wearing a badge that says 'Serial Killer', only the word Serial has been crossed out and replaced with Cereal. Or I'm hanging from this rope and I'm afraid that I can't keep hold and I'm going to fall, but I manage to swing it to and fro until I crash into this window, only it's a cockpit window and the pilot inside is dead and I don't know how to fly the plane. Then suddenly he twitches back into life, grins an evil smile and springs towards me. He plunges his grey hands right into my stomach and twists my insides round and round until the plane somersaults and begins to break apart.

"Get this bloody mess cleared up," is all my parents say as they look at the crash scene.

"Poor thing," cries my sister as she spies my broken, lifeless body in the café. "He never even knew me."

That's how it usually ends; me dead in a café with a sister I didn't know I had. I don't know how long it lasts, either. Just a few seconds maybe, though it takes ages before the images have faded from my mind and I'm myself again. All a bit weird, eh?

The doc says he isn't surprised about the flashbacks, given what I've been through. He doesn't want to give me any pills for them though. He says I'm still young and he's worried I could get addicted. He thinks they'll stop anyway. I'm not so sure. It was his idea that I should write it down. He said that if I work it all out logically in my mind it will help me come to terms with it. We'll see.

The start of it all was just a normal school day, with me wandering about as usual. I get bored a lot in lessons so I like to have a wander about from time to time. Most teachers don't seem to mind. I expect they're glad to get rid of me, if only for a few minutes. This time though the teacher wouldn't let me go to the toilet even when I said it would be her fault if I wet myself, so I had to come up with something else. I took the top off a biro and squeezed the ink out all over my hands and book, so she had to let me go. I got to the bog as quick as could be to wash it off, then I was out looking for empty classrooms. Some teachers don't lock their classrooms or their desks when they're not there and I needed the money to get a bacon butty at break. The first room I went in there was just a chocolate bar in the desk but I took it anyway. The next was a mistake. I thought it was empty but the teacher was actually at a bookcase to the side and I had to come up with a good excuse just like that. I struck gold at the third because the teacher had left his wallet, mobile phone and keys in the desk. I could've got thirty quid for the mobile but I'm not stupid. He'd have reported it gone immediately and they would have easily worked out that I was out of the classroom at the time. Anyway, there was about forty quid in notes in the wallet but I only took a fiver because the chances were that he wouldn't even miss that. I remember that I passed Mr Milner on the way back and he looked at me, suspicious like, and asked what I was up to. I like to tell the truth whenever I can so I told him.

"Thieving, Sir."

"Wouldn't put it past you," he replied, so I asked him if he was thieving as well.

"Horrible little reprobate," he said. I told him it takes one to know one, presuming that a reprobate was something not very nice. I still don't know what it means.

When I got back to the classroom Miss Williams had cleaned up the mess and taken the ruined pages out of my book. I liked Miss Williams even then. She was new and quite pretty and even though she had even more problems controlling us than most of the other teachers, she tried hard to make the lessons interesting. I suppose I felt a bit sorry for her. I mean, Set 6 for English can't be much fun. Some of the kids can hardly write their own names. Anyway, she'd put my bag on my seat and the pencil case from inside it was on the desk. That got me a bit worried because I don't let anyone near my bag. As soon as I could I had a feel inside it to see if they were still there and they weren't. That really set me panicking. I looked under the table and all around but there was no sign of them, so I figured that one of the other kids must have been through the bag while I was away and Miss Williams wasn't looking.

I suppose I should explain that the things that were missing were my big notebook with the hard covers and the fountain pen that I use to write in it. You're probably thinking that this notebook must be full of swear words and obscene drawings and things like that for me to be worried. Well I wouldn't have been concerned if it was because that's just what everyone would have expected. But what was actually in the notebook was school work, just a few subjects but all done as well as I could, in neat writing with headings underlined and that sort of stuff. I'd never shown it to anyone and I didn't ever intend to because it would have made me look a laughing stock. After all, what would they say if they ever found out that Vince Viggors, one of the worst kids in the school, always in trouble and who didn't give a damn about anything, especially schoolwork, actually went away and spent hours almost every evening doing what he should have done in school?

As I was thinking about it I suddenly became aware that Miss Williams was speaking to me.

"Are you listening Vince? I said it's all right Vince, I've got them. You left the room in such a hurry that you kicked your bag over and some things fell out. I've got them. You can have them back at the end of the lesson."

Well that really did worry me. I didn't want her looking in the notebook and questioning me about it. I got quite angry.

"You can't do that," I told her, shouting, "they're my property. I want them back now. You can't just take my things, I could get you done."

"Nonsense, Vince," she said, quite calmly. "I want a word with you at the end of the lesson anyway, and you can have them back then."

I was going to go on arguing but it struck me that if I did, she just might get curious about the book and wonder what was it in, so I mumbled something apologetic and just kept quiet for the rest of the lesson, pretending to work. When the bell went I stayed in my seat while everyone else left.

She didn't say anything at first, just went on correcting the work in the book she was marking. Then she looked in my direction and reacted like she'd forgotten I was there. She opened up the drawer in her desk and took the book out. I was hoping, of course, that she'd just hand it back over but she looked at the cover for a bit and then started to flick through the pages.

"I need them now Miss," I told her, "I'm supposed to see Mr Wills at break."

It didn't work. She'd stopped at one page and was reading it and she had this confused look on her face.

"What's all this, Vince? I don't understand it. This is the work from Monday's lesson and the homework I set. Why is it here? Who did this, Vince?"

At least she hadn't twigged it was me. I was searching for something to say, well more like panicking really and I blurted out the first thing that came to mind.

"It's nothing, Miss. It's my brother's, Miss. He likes to do the work, Miss. I show him what it is and he does it."

She didn't look convinced.

"But you don't have a brother, Vince."

"Yes I do, Miss. He's not right, Miss. He doesn't go to school, so I get the work for him."

"Stop this nonsense, Vince. I know you are an only child. Are you going to explain this work or not?"

"It's true, Miss. It's like I said, Miss. Please, Miss, can I have the book back now, Miss? Please Miss, please."

I could tell I was shouting. It was a mistake to have got so worked up. She knew I was lying and I knew she would want to get to the bottom of it.

"I think I'm going to hang on to this for a while, Vince. I'd like to take a proper look inside. You can come back at the end of the day," she said.

"You can't do that, Miss. It's my property. You have to give it back."

"I'll tell you what, Vince," she answered, this time with a bit of a smile on her face. "Why don't we take it to show Mr Harding and let him decide?"

That was it then. I knew I was beaten. It was bad enough that she'd got to see it, but it would be even worse if the Headmaster read it.

"No thank you, Miss," I mumbled.

"So you'll come and get it later?"

"Yes, Miss, but please don't tell anyone else about it, will you, Miss?"

"We'll see."

I felt a bit gutted after that. I was really concerned that she'd go through it and show it to the other teachers and then it would be all round the school in no time. Instead of finding my mates and buying the bacon roll I just spent the rest of break sitting in a quiet corner by myself. I didn't even eat the chocolate bar. I was pretty quiet for the rest of the day too, so much so that one of the teachers asked if I wasn't well and needed to go to Welfare, and he wasn't being sarcastic either. All though the day I kept trying to think about what I could say to her, how I could make her think that it was someone else's work. It was no good. I couldn't think of anything. I even considered not going at all at the end of the day, but I knew I'd only have to face her the next time I had English. I was dead worried when I knocked on her door at twenty to four.

She was sitting at her desk at the front of the room

and she turned towards me as I walked in. For a few seconds she was silent and her face was blank but then it broke into a smile.

"Sit down there," she instructed, pointing to one of the front row desks and waiting until I was settled. Then she opened her drawer and took out my notebook.

"I really don't know whether I should be pleased or angry with you, Vince."

I started to mumble something in reply but she went on abruptly in quite a stern voice, the smile gone.

"And don't interrupt until I have finished. I have read this book from cover to cover and I think, indeed I am completely sure now, that this is your own work, Vince. I must admit that it is a very pleasant surprise to find out that you really do have a brain after all, and you can use it to produce work of such an excellent standard. All of which makes it equally annoying to wonder why you keep up this pretence of idiocy and are perfectly happy to produce appalling rubbish in class, and to disrupt my lessons and those of almost every other teacher who has the dubious pleasure of taking you. I don't pretend to understand this, Vince, and I don't yet know what I'm going to do about it. But what I do decide to do is going to very much depend on what you tell me now, so it had better be the truth. Well, Vince, what have you got to say for yourself?"

I didn't know what to say. I knew she'd have worked out that I did it. I'd been trying to think of an excuse all day. It was no good. I just stood there, dumb, wishing I were somewhere else, willing the ground to open up and swallow me. I could feel the blood coming to my face. And she just sat there looking at me, waiting. It seemed like ages. In the end I felt the words slip out as though they were in charge of my mind and not the other way round.

"It has to be secret, Miss. Where I come from, with my friends, they think you're gay if you try hard at school. If you look clever, they call you 'boff' and things like that. So I does it on my own Miss, after school, when nobody can see."

I hoped that I'd said enough but she just stayed silent and waited, as if she expected me to continue.

"I never tried, Miss, when I was younger. I always mucked around. I always got in trouble, Miss, I never wanted to be good. Then one day, when I was off school, ill or something, I had nothing to do, so I tried, Miss, on my own. I done the work I should have done in school and it was easy, Miss, when I really tried it was easy. It was easy to write neatly and easy to work out the answers. It felt good, Miss. I wanted to show it to the teacher, Miss. The next time I went to school I took it in with me. I was going to find a quiet moment when the others weren't around to show her. I was excited. I thought she'd be really pleased but when the bell rang for registration and she saw that I was back, this look came over her face and she didn't try to hide it. I suppose that she would have had good reason to be disappointed to see me again, what with all the problems I'd caused in class but it was more than just disappointment. It was a look of... well, I suppose it was a look of hate, just pure hatred. So I didn't show her, I just mucked around even more to make her sorry. Ever since then that's what I do, Miss, I muck around in school and do the work afterwards."

"How long has this been going on?"

"I was in the last year of juniors when it happened, so it's over three years now."

"So for more than three years you've been messing about in lessons but doing the work in your own time?"

"Yes, Miss."

"And why is it just four subjects?"

"I don't have time to do everything. They're the lessons I like Miss, the lessons with…" I remember pausing slightly, a bit embarrassed, "the lessons with okay teachers. Every year when school starts, I wait until we've had all the teachers once or twice and then I choose the ones to do the work for."

I was beginning to feel a bit better, a little more relaxed. She didn't look angry. Then she reached over to the pile of exercise books from my class and searched through until she found mine. She opened it up at no particular page and then took my open notebook and placed it next to it. The difference even made me cringe. One lessons worth in the exercise book was just the questions written out and then a few lines of scrawl that even I couldn't read. Plus I seemed to have spent most of that lesson drawing penises in the margin and practising how to write my signature. And next to it there was a whole page of neat writing in my notebook, just part of an essay I'd done.

"I don't understand, Vince." She was sounding agitated again. "I just don't understand how you could be content to do such rubbish when you could do this."

"It's like I told you, Miss, they say you're gay if you try hard."

"But there are children in the class who try hard. Children who obviously don't have your ability, but still make an effort, while you're content to produce drivel like this. It's difficult not to be angry, Vince."

"But I've always been bad. Even at infants school they kept me in at break so I couldn't terrorise the other kids. It's just the way I am. People like me don't like school. We muck about and get into trouble. We'd look stupid if we didn't. It's expected. We're not supposed to try."

"That's an awful thing to say, Vince."

"I'm sorry, Miss, but it's true. My mates, Nathan and Brad, and the others, they'd think the notebook was hilarious. It'd be all round the school, the whole neighbourhood, in minutes. They'd all be laughing at me. They'd never speak to me again."

Miss Williams went quiet for a bit, as if she was thinking about it. I thought I'd maybe said enough. She'd just hand over the notebook and let me go. Her next question really threw me.

"What does your mother say about it?"

"How do you mean, Miss?"

"What does she have to say about you messing about all day and going home and doing all your school work there?"

I was tempted to lie, to say she understood and was happy about it but then a picture came into my mind of Miss Williams talking to my mum at Parent's Evening and then Mum coming back home and shouting at me, or even worse, my dad thumping me.

"She don't know about it, Miss, I keep it a secret."

She looked confused again.

"But she must know about it, Vince, if you go home and spend all this time every evening doing school work."

"It's not every evening Miss, just some. I don't do it every night."

"But even so, she must see you doing it."

"She don't, Miss, I don't do it at home. I do it in the library."

"What, you mean you stay on in the school library several days each week to work? We'd all know about it Vince. This can't be true."

"No, Miss, not the school library, the one in town, on Duke Street."

She had that puzzled look on her face again.

"The public library? The main one? Why would you do that? Why don't you do it at home? Surely it would be easier to do it at home?"

"I can't, Miss. My mum works late. I don't have a key so I go to the library. I've always gone there. It's warm."

I knew straight away that I'd said too much, let too much out. She was frowning. I knew what was coming next.

"I don't understand this, Vince. Why don't you have a key? Why can't you go home when she's not there?"

"She don't like me in the house alone, Miss. Says she don't trust me. Just tells me not to come home till she gets back. She don't know about the library, Miss. She don't know about the work, Miss. Nobody knows about the work, Miss, except you."

"Where does she think you go if she doesn't know about the library?"

"Just out, Miss. She don't care as long as I'm not in the house and I come back on time. Please, Miss, can I have my things back now? I've told you the truth like you asked, I just want them back, I don't want to say no more. I don't want any trouble, just give me my things."

I was really getting worried by then. I could tell my voice was getting higher. I snatched the notebook off the desk.

"I want the pen, too. It's okay, Miss, I didn't steal it. I saved up to buy it. I like to write with it."

As she opened the desk to find the fountain pen, she said in a more gentle voice.

"This isn't right, Vince. It isn't right that a boy of your age should be locked out and wandering the streets. And you say this has been going on for years, even when you were younger? It's just not right. I'll have to report it."

I didn't know what to think. I really was panicking. She didn't realise what she was saying, what would happen if she reported it. She didn't know our family history, all the difficulties, all the times Social Services had been round. She didn't know the trouble it would cause.

"You can't do that, Miss. You don't know. It'll cause terrible problems. They'll put me in care. Dad will blame Mum and take it out on her. Please don't, Miss. I'm not wandering the streets. I'm not in any danger. It's the library, Miss, the public library. It's safe there. Come along and see, Miss, if you don't believe me. Come along when I'm there. You'll see and know it's all right. Please don't tell anyone."

She didn't say anything for what seemed like ages. I was praying I'd said enough to convince her. Eventually she replied.

"All right, Vince, I'll do that. I'll come along and see. I can't come tonight, staff meeting, they go on for ages. Tomorrow would be better. Will you be there, about six? Will that be okay?"

I was so relieved. I just muttered that it would be fine, that I'd be waiting for her, and I grabbed the pen from her hand and rushed out of the room.

Chapter 2

The police picked me up on my way home. I was walking past the parade of shops down the bottom of the street when the car drew up beside me with its window open.

"Need a word with you, Vince. Get in."

I thought it was because of the ASBO.

"I'm not hanging about, just walking past on my own. You can't do me for that."

The ASBO was to stop me and my mates from loitering around outside the parade. The shopkeepers had complained, said it ruined trade with so many kids outside. Said we frightened off the customers. I've got another one as well, supposed to keep me out of the indoor shopping mall down town. Been caught shoplifting too many times.

"It's not about that, Vince. We just need to ask you a few questions down at the station. It won't take long. You'll get a lift back."

There was no point arguing, I'd only get arrested. I knew him anyway. Everybody did down our way. He was okay, always dead straight with me. I asked what it was about as I was getting in but he said they didn't tell him everything and I'd find out soon enough.

I wasn't really worried. The police were always picking me up. I suppose it gave them something to do. Besides, I'd been trying to behave myself for the past few months. The last magistrate told me they were running out of patience and the next time I was up before them they would have me detained at Her Majesty's pleasure in some young offenders' institution. In other words, sent to borstal for a long time. That was for burglary. The house had a hidden camera and a silent alarm, the sort that only goes off at the police station. I never noticed a thing but they were waiting for me at home. It's not so easy nowadays, breaking in; almost everywhere has some sort of alarm and a camera. A few weeks afterwards me and a few other lads had to attend a meeting with some of the people whose houses had been done. There was this one old woman who lived alone, who was really upset. She started crying, saying that the thieves hadn't just stolen things but wrecked the place as well. Pictures of her dead husband had been broken and torn up. I've never done anything like that and I actually felt sorry for her, but what really made me think was that after we were allowed to go and I was walking out with the other kids, a few of them started laughing about the old woman and saying how they were really going to scare her to death next time they did her place. After that, and with what the magistrate had said, I thought that it was time to stop breaking into people's houses. I wouldn't like it if it happened to mine, not that there was anything worth stealing.

Turned out it was about burglaries after all. They kept me waiting for over an hour before they questioned me but they didn't put me in a cell and I got a couple of cups of tea and some biscuits. They didn't question me in a proper interview room either, like they are supposed to, with a camera filming it all. It was just in an ordinary office. There'd been a spate of break-ins in some of the posh roads near our estate, all during the daytime when people were out working. I suppose they would've had me down as a prime suspect but I hadn't skived off school for ages and they took registers each lesson as well as in tutor time, so it was easy for me to prove to them that I wasn't involved. I even told them it was stupid to have brought me in at all because they could have ruled me out by just checking with the school, but then they started asking all sorts of other questions about local drug dealers and drug houses, and I think that was really why they'd got me down there. I told them that I didn't take drugs or even smoke ciggies, that they were just a waste of money. And I said I didn't know of any dealers or places where they sold drugs. I actually did but I wasn't going to tell the police, was I. Basically I played dumb and after a bit they got fed up and told me to wait in reception till someone was free to take me home.

It was different officers for the way home, one I'd never seen before and the driver who I knew was a real pig. I was a bit worried before I even got in the car. He started off okay, saying that his mate was new to the town and that we'd be driving around for a bit to show him the layout. But when we got near to our estate he turned to the other one and told him it was where all the local 'scum' lived. That was the word he used.

"It's called the Forest Estate," he said, "cos all the roads are named after trees. The Council have been dumping problem families here for donkey's years. People who cause problems wherever they live, except here the only ones they can affect are scum like themselves. Some of the houses are empty but even the ones that are lived in look derelict, windows boarded up, front gardens full of rubbish. They don't care. Look over there, that parade, no proper shops, just takeaways and bookies. It's how they live. Almost all the adults are unemployed, half of them faking sickness or disability. The kids are all yobs, like him in the back, Vince. Fourteen years old, two ASBOs, string of convictions, thick as two short ones. Father's a particularly nasty case. First name William, different surname to the boy, never married the mother. In prison now; habitual re-offender, addict or alcoholic, can't remember which. Gets violent, beats the kid up and the mother. He'll be the same, Vince, in the back. Like father like son. Sandra, his mother, she's a prostitute, works the streets. Had him when she were no more than a kid herself. That's all they're capable of, scum like them: breeding. He's probably started already. She'll likely as not be a grandmother before she's thirty."

I just sat there listening. I could feel myself getting angry but I knew he was probably just trying to get me going so he had an excuse for hitting me.

"The system's too soft," he continued. "The mother's got a council flat, claims on the social, even though she's earning money as a tart, everything provided. Never done an honest day's work yet, his father neither. It costs £40 000 a year to keep a bloke like him in prison and once he's out he'll be on the social too until he's sent back. If you work it all out then this one family alone will probably cost us more than a million pounds over the years and it just carries on, generation after generation."

He was sounding agitated.

"It makes me sick. I don't mind paying taxes but not to

support scum like them. Lad in the back, think we'll have to put him down for the cull. No other alternative, he'd just be a burden on society otherwise. What do you think?"

There was a pause. He'd stopped talking and I could see his eyes in the mirror, looking at me, waiting for me to react.

"Oh, you've got a cull going here too, do you? That's good news. Makes our job a lot easier in the long run." It was the other officer speaking, his face turned towards the driver and smiling.

"What's a cull?" I asked. It sounded a funny word.

"So you were listening, eh? Well laddie, let me try and explain it to you in a way your tiny mind can understand. In Canada, don't know if they still do it or not but in the Arctic, in the far north of Canada, they used to have a cull of the new born seals every year. You see baby seals grow up into big strong adult seals that eat lots of fish. The fishermen don't like it. If the seals eat the fish then the fishermen can't catch them, so they kill some of the cubs just after they're born, when they're helpless and can't get away. Shoot them or bang them on the head. That's what a cull is. That way there aren't so many around to grow into adults. More fish for the fishermen. There are some of us that do the same round here with yobs like you. We know how to do it, dead easy. Simple: tap on the head in the right place. No problem disposing of the bodies, either. Runaways never seen again, bodies mangled up in a traffic accident. Stops them growing up and breeding more parasites like themselves. You're a prime candidate, Vince. We've had you in mind for ages. I'd watch out if I were you. You never know when it might happen. Couple of strangers, no uniform, tap on the head, one dead Vince, one less problem for society. Job done."

He was still looking at me in the mirror. I knew in my mind he was just having me on, making it up, but it was pretty scary nonetheless. A few streets further he pulled the car over and stopped.

"Nearly at your road, Vince. Out you get. You can walk the rest. Remember what I said. You'd better have eyes in the back of your head from now on."

"Give us a break," I said as I was getting out. "I wasn't born yesterday. It's you that better look out. Bloody great ugly fat bastard, it's you who'll need eyes in the back of your head if I ever catch up with you."

He opened his door as I said it and I ran off quick, just in case. When I stopped and turned round to look back I could see them both in the car, turned to each other and laughing.

I didn't go home straight away. It was still an hour early. I just wandered around for a bit and then queued up to get some chips for tea. It was true what he said about my father. He was in prison, he drank like a fish and he did get violent. When I was younger and he wasn't inside, Social Services used to come round every week to check me out for bruises. He was wrong about my mother, though. She wasn't on the streets, she worked from home. When I was younger the men used to give me a pound or two to get lost for an hour or so but as I got older it was obvious they didn't like me being around at all. Suppose they were worried I might see them in town with their wives and give them away, or maybe try to blackmail some money out of them to keep quiet about it. I didn't know if my father knew or not. She only did it when he was inside. I used to worry that he'd kill her if he found out. Either that or he'd take the money off her and drink it away. That's why I couldn't go home till late, because my mum had men in the flat. I couldn't tell that to Miss Williams though, could I? I couldn't tell her that my mother was a prossie.

Chapter 3

The following day, after the detention I'd been given for not having my sports kit yet again, I made my way to Duke Street. The library was next to the Guildhall, part of the same building which had a row of marble columns along the front. I remember that I'd been quite scared the first time I went in because it looked so big and official like, but you didn't have to sign in or register or anything like that, and I spent the first half hour or so just wandering about and finding out where things were. Since then I'd always made straight for the reading room on the middle floor. It was a great, big, long room, with a row of huge tables down the middle and lights that hung down low with one great, long metal lampshade, so that it reminded me of a snooker hall.

I had a regular place, unless someone else was sitting in it. Mostly I didn't bother with the books from the library, except sometimes when I used a dictionary or a thesaurus. When I knew I'd need a textbook to do the work I used to slip one into my bag during the lesson so that I could use it later. I didn't steal it, just used it in the library and took it back to school the next day. I didn't know whether Miss Williams would come or not and I didn't really know if I wanted her to, either. I hadn't had English that day which was a bit of a relief, otherwise I would've been worried that she'd say something about it in front of the class. I'd been sat there for over an hour but I hadn't really been able to settle down to work. Mostly I had my eyes on the door to see if she'd come. When she did I saw her immediately. She stopped at the entrance and looked around until she saw me. Then she smiled. I was so nervous I could feel myself shaking.

She sat down in the chair next to me. I forget what she said but I remember that she had her face quite near to mine because there were these big 'silence' signs and she had to whisper. She was so near I could even smell the scent she was wearing. It was a bit unsettling. She stayed for about half an hour. Mostly she just read through the English work I'd done and made comments about it, but after a while I asked her if she would mark it properly with a red pen and point out the spelling mistakes. She stopped at one place and said that what I'd written showed 'mature understanding' because the point wasn't 'explicit, only inferred'. I had to ask her what the words meant and started a new vocabulary section in the back of my notebook. I was worried all through that she'd bring it up again about me being made to stay out until late and having to report it but she never did. When she finally said she had to go I found myself asking if she'd come again and she said she would, once a week, if it would help. When I asked to not tell anyone, she hesitated for a moment.

"Let's just keep it our secret for the time being," she whispered.

She did come once a week, sometimes more. After a while she stopped looking at bits I'd already done and started setting me new work. She said that some of it was the sort of stuff she did with the top set GCSE group she had for English. That really pleased me. It wasn't that difficult either, you just had to think it through more carefully before writing it down. Once, after she'd gone through one of these pieces of work, she wrote something down and smiled as she passed the book to me. It said 'Well done Vince, A* standard. You must be one of the cleverest boys in the school.' I was dead chuffed and I think I must have gone red. Another thing she did was to get me a library ticket. It happened when she told me to take a particular book home and she found out I wasn't a member. She took me down to the reception and signed the form herself as the responsible adult. After that she used to help me choose books to take home to read. I had to read at least one a week and she would ask me questions about it or make me write a report on it.

Sometimes she stayed longer. She'd set me work and then get out a set of exercise books to mark while I was doing it. We'd usually have a break in the middle and go down to the foyer area where there were some machines for drinks and snacks. She would have a coffee and get me a Coke, and we would share a chocolate bar or something like that. We would just talk about things outside school, such as films she'd seen or music we liked. I was dead impressed with her musical taste; I didn't think that any teachers listened to

Kanye West or the Kaiser Chiefs. I found out that her first name was Karen and that she lived in a house with some other teachers but not from the same school. She never mentioned a boyfriend or anything like that and it seemed to me that she must have been a bit lonely because she said that mostly, in the evenings, she just stayed in her room and did marking or watched TV.

Once, after a couple of months and right out of the blue, she gave me a present, a gift set of men's toiletries, with shower gel, deodorant and shampoo. I was dead pleased because it was a trendy brand that had a good advert on the telly. Then she said that teenage boys needed to be very careful to shower every day, use deodorant and change their clothes regularly. I didn't like to tell her that we didn't have a shower, only a bath. It didn't twig at the time but later on, after she'd gone, I realised that she had been telling me something personal and that's when I realised that I could actually smell myself and I knew that if I could, then she could even more. After that I stood in the bath every morning and washed myself all over, even if the water was cold, especially my feet which always did stink a bit. I only had one school shirt, so I washed it out every evening and hung it up to dry before I went to bed. Sometimes it was still damp in the morning but I put it on anyway. I used the deodorant every morning too and just in case I'd got smelly during the day I used to spray a bit more on, inside my shirt, before she came to the library.

Now you can probably guess that my meetings with Miss Williams put me in a bit of a bind about how to behave in her lessons. I could hardly carry on as usual, given how much help she was giving me. To begin with I cut out the cheek and just kept quiet in class but carried on doing rubbish work or nothing at all. After a while I realised this was stupid and started getting on with the work. When my exercise book was full and needed replacing I even started to produce neat work in the new one. None of this, of course, was missed by Nathan or the others who started to make comments about how I behaved in English compared with my other lessons. Nath said it must be because I had a crush on Miss Williams. When he said that, I punched him in the face a bit harder than I meant to and broke his nose. For that, I got another police warning and was suspended from school for three days. Mr Milner heard about it and told me that the only reason I wasn't punished more severely was that everyone knew that Nathan was an even worse little sod than me and had it coming. Nobody else made any more comments however, except Miss Williams who said that I should be ashamed of myself and that she would stop coming to the library if I did anything like that again. I figured she would have to say something like that so I didn't let it worry me.

Truth be told, I did get quite a crush on Miss Williams. I liked everything about her. There was nothing over the top, nothing rough. She was pretty and wore just the right amount of make-up. Her clothes weren't dowdy like some of the other female teachers. In English lessons I often found myself just looking at her. One of the other lads said he'd been able to see down her top a few times. I was going to hit him as well, until I remembered what she'd said. I couldn't help seeing a few times too when she leant forward during our lessons, but I always looked away quick in case she noticed and thought I was doing it deliberately. I suppose I did daydream about her quite a lot. I used to wonder why she didn't have a boyfriend and if some bloke had broken her heart and whether I could be the person to mend it. I even imagined what it would be like if she was to lean over and kiss me.

Not that anything like that ever happened. Miss Williams was always sort of careful about how she was with me. She never gave me her mobile number even when it could have been useful, like the time when I was sick and couldn't get to the library. Neither did she ever tell me where she lived and in school she hardly spoke to me at all. I didn't realise that she had to be careful until the theatre business. One of the books she made me read was To Kill a Mockingbird by Harper Lee. I really enjoyed it. I told Miss that there was a pop group called the Boo Radleys. When we talked about it I said I didn't think it was fair that the black man was found guilty of something he didn't do and died as well. Miss Williams said that life could be like that. Things weren't always fair; that sometimes they don't turn out like you hope. The following week I found out that there was a play of it on at the theatre in the square, round the other side of the Guildhall and I said it would be great if we could go. I even said I would pay for the tickets as a treat for all the time she'd given up. She said she'd have to think about it but next time she came she said she was sorry but we'd better not. She told me that it was okay for her to give me lessons but that people, especially Mr Harding, might get the wrong idea if they saw us going around together, to the theatre or things like that. I was disappointed but she tried to make it up by getting me a ticket on my own for a matinee performance. I'd never been to the theatre before. It was really old inside and the aisles were much steeper than in the cinema. I enjoyed the play a lot but it would have been much better if Miss had been there with me.

There was only one odd thing about my meetings with Miss Williams in the library. Usually it wasn't very busy, just a few other people at the tables but I noticed that there was always someone sitting at this particular place quite near us. Sometimes it was a man with a beard and a moustache, sometimes someone who was clean shaven and so on. Then one day, just before Miss Williams arrived, a man came in and sat down at the place. He put a case on the table and took out a laptop. It wasn't a proper laptop case, more like an old fashioned leather bag, the sort that gets opened and closed by a clasp at the top. Thing was that the following day I noticed the bag again, in the same place but with a different man. Then it happened again and it kept on happening. When I looked closely at who it was I began to wonder if it wasn't the same man, only dressed differently, like in disguise. I never mentioned it to Miss Williams and in the end I stopped bothering about it. He never seemed to pay us any attention anyway, always working away at his laptop, headphones in his ears.

One day Miss Williams was marking some books while I was working. She stopped and looked at my hand and asked what had happened to my finger. I don't know if she'd only just noticed or whether she hadn't liked to mention it before.

The question made me wince because it brought back the shock of it, and the pain. It came out of the blue because I hardly ever used to think about it by then and the other kids had long since stopped making stupid remarks. It was the fourth finger on my left hand, not my writing one.

"It's nothing Miss. I caught it in the door and they had to amputate it. It's all right now."

It wasn't much of an explanation.

"Don't you like to talk about it?"

"Not really. It caused a lot of problems."

She didn't say anything else and went back to her marking but it had got me thinking how bad it had been and how guilty I'd felt. I'd never trusted anyone enough to tell before but I knew I could trust Miss Williams.

"I was at home, Miss, and my mum and dad were having another argument, and I was crying because it frightened me when they shouted at each other like that. My dad got really angry with her and he turned round and stormed off and slammed the door really hard. He didn't notice that my hand was in the doorway and I couldn't get it away in time and the door banged shut on it. It was bad, Miss, but they didn't realise at first because I was already crying and they were shouting so much. When I managed to make Mum understand she put my hand under the cold tap and held it there and then she put a bandage round the finger that hurt the most. Then she told me to go and watch TV to take my mind off it. Next day when the pain was still bad I showed it to Dad but he just bandaged it up again and told me to stop making a fuss about it. Then they both got angry with me and told me to go and clear up the mess in my room. Anyway, when I went to school the teacher asked me about it and when the bandage was still there after a few days, she said she wanted to take a look. She undid it and my finger was all swollen and green and gungy and it smelt really bad. The teacher looked as if she was going to be sick, She called Mum but she wasn't at home and her mobile was switched off. Then the head teacher put me in her car and took me to the hospital. They gave me injections and told me not to look while they cleaned it up and they kept trying to phone

Mum but in the end they had to get the police to find her, and when she arrived the doctor got really mad with her and they had a slanging match. When it cooled down they told me that I needed to have an operation and they took me up to the operating theatre and explained to me what was going to happen. When I woke up the doctor said I was quite lucky because he thought they would have to amputate the whole finger but in the end they only had to take half of it off."

Miss Williams asked how old I had been.

"Ten, Miss, but that's not all. A few days later, when I was back home, the Social Services came round and said that the hospital had got in touch with them and they had to do a report and my mum and dad had to co-operate and even so I might get taken into care. When they'd gone my dad started swearing at my mum, saying it was all her fault and she started screaming at him and they started fighting, really fighting, Miss, and I was frightened and hid in the bedroom. After a while there was lots of banging on the door and the police came. They took my dad away and put him back in prison."

She had a shocked look on her face.

"That's horrible, Vince."

"Sorry, Miss. It's not nice, Miss. I shouldn't have told you. I've never told anyone before. Miss, do you think it was my fault that my dad got sent to prison that time? My mum said it was my fault. She said I should have shown my finger to her, not the teacher, and then she'd have taken me to hospital and my dad wouldn't be in prison."

"Of course not, Vince. How could you be blamed for that? Perhaps she was just upset because of everything that had happened. Maybe she didn't realise what she was saying. I'm sure she couldn't have meant it."

I thought about it for a few seconds.

"I'm not sure, Miss. I don't think my mum loves me, Miss. She told me once that I'm not really her child."

I could tell she didn't know what to say. We just sat there for what seemed like ages. Then the silence was broken by the man I told you about before. He'd started to pack up his laptop, stood up and banged his head really hard on the metal lamp shade. After he'd finished rubbing it his hair was all messed up. It broke the ice anyway. Miss and I both started to giggle.

Chapter 4

The runner had just delivered a note to the classroom. My French teacher read it, looked up towards the ceiling and smiled.

"Thank you, God," he said, just loud enough for us all to hear.

Then he called out my name and told me to report to the Head's office immediately. I'd already spent half the morning sitting outside the Deputy Head's room because of the incident with Nath and I was a bit worried that there was going to be some follow-up. The last time I'd been up before Mr Harding he had said that the way things were going, he'd have to call a special meeting of the Governors about me and they would have no alternative but to recommend permanent exclusion.

The thing with Nath was only supposed to have been a bit of fun but I have to admit that it did get out of hand. Nath and I set it up together. History had got a bit boring because we were having this student teacher instead of the usual one and he was a bit gormless. Nath had to ask him what hung, drawn and quartered was and after he explained it, I had to stick my hand up and ask him if he could tell us what hung like a horse was. We'd already tried it out, well the second part anyway, with Mr Milner. He said he didn't rightly know what it meant and the only time he'd heard it before was when his wife said it the first time he'd got undressed in front of her. He was good like that, Mr Milner; knew how to take a joke and join in. This bloke didn't, he just stood there looking stupid and going red, as if he didn't know what to say, and the other kids started laughing at him which only made him go redder.

The rest of the class were hooting so much that the proper teacher in the back of the room, who was supposed to be watching things, had to take the student teacher out and after that Mr Wills came in and hauled me down to the Deputy Head. Bloody Nath got away with it scot free but it was looking like the Deputy Head had a chat to Mr Harding about me.

Things began to look even worse when I turned the corner just outside the Head's office and saw my mum sitting there, looking worried and biting her fingernails.

"What have you been up to?" she whispered, just as the door opened and Mr Harding appeared. He looked a bit taken aback to see Mum.

"Oh, are you here as well, Miss Viggors? Did you want to see me? I won't be a minute. We just need to have a few words with Vince. Come along now, Vince."

It struck me that the 'Come along now, Vince' sounded a bit like the nurse when she called you into the dentist's room to let the 'driller killer' loose on your teeth, but the two men sitting at the desk looked nothing at all like dentists. They were both wearing very smart grey suits and they didn't greet me with a welcoming smile and a 'how are you today?' Instead, they eyed me up and down several times before the younger of them said in a rather posh voice. "Certainly fits the bill. He's got the right face, right build. Shame about the hair but we can always do something about that. Could be our man, don't you think?"

I was more looking at him than listening to him. I thought I knew him from somewhere. He told me to take a seat and asked Mr Harding to introduce us. Mr Harding seemed a bit stuck for words.

"Vince... I don't quite understand what it is that you've done to draw yourself to the attention of these gentlemen, but they tell me they are from the... Intelligence Services, and they have come all the way from London to meet you. I'm sorry gentlemen, you did give me your names, but..."

"I'm Perkins," said the one who'd already spoken, "and this is Mr Greene."

Mr Greene started to speak. He had a much more ordinary accent than Perkins.

"You can call me Felix, Vince. This must be a bit of a surprise for you, Vince, but there's nothing to be alarmed about."

I didn't know about a bit of a surprise, more of a great big one really. Still, at least it didn't appear to be about the incident with the student teacher. They wouldn't have sent someone from London to deal with that. I wasn't quite sure what the Intelligence Services were though, so I asked.

"There are a number of them, Vince," said Mr Greene. "We're from MI5, have you heard of us?"

I told him I had which was true but I didn't say that it was only from watching James Bond movies, and that it had never occurred to me in the cinema that MI5 actually existed. Perkins started to explain anyway.

"MI5 is the protector of this great country of ours, Vince. You might be surprised to learn that there are individuals, organisations and even other countries that view us as the enemy, that want to destroy us, that want to change our whole way of life."

I would have told him that I wasn't surprised at all, everybody knew about Al-Qaeda, but it was difficult to get a word in edgeways. He kept rambling on about how MI5 was always there in the background, watching and listening for threats to the country, and how all the people in it were brave and risked their lives without ordinary people knowing. I think he would have rambled on for ages if the other man, Mr Greene, hadn't interrupted him and said they hadn't got all day and it would be better if he did the talking.

"Vince, we are very pleased to meet you. We want you to help us, Vince. Something has come up, a problem. I can't go into details here but it's very serious. Actually, the future of the whole world is at stake. Our files tell us that Vince Viggors might be the very person who can help us overcome it."

I wondered if he was having a laugh, if it was like Candid Camera on the telly where they tricked you into making a fool of yourself. I was going to ask him but Mr Harding started to speak instead.

"Excuse me," he said, "there must be some mistake. Surely you must mean some other Vince Viggors. You can't seriously believe that this miscreant is the answer to your problems. This boy, I'm sorry about this Vince but it is for your own good, this boy is already a hardened criminal and an inveterate liar."

"No I'm not!" I said.

"You see what I mean? Can't open his mouth without lying," said Mr Harding.

"But don't you see, Headmaster, that is exactly what makes him so useful to us. Most of our spies have to spend months, even years, learning how to lie effectively and how to break into buildings or steal cars or pick pockets. But this boy can do it already."

"Come now," said Mr Harding, "the same could apply to any number of mindless thugs up and down the country."

"But Vince isn't mindless, Headmaster, his IQ is nearly off the scale and his work reaches a truly excellent standard."

"I think you must be confusing him with someone else. Have you seen Vince's schoolwork? It really is some to the worst we have ever come across. Now I'm sure we are all busy people, so unless there is anything else?"

"Miss Williams would not agree with you, Headmaster. She is of the opinion that Vince is one of the most able pupils in the school."

Mr Greene glanced towards Perkins as he spoke, who then reached down and lifted up a bag. It twigged immediately, the bag in the library, the brown leather one with the clasp on top. It must have been him there, spying on us. I suddenly felt all shivery with excitement. All kinds of thoughts were going through my mind.

"Ah, Miss Williams, you say," said Mr Harding in a putting down sort of voice. "I think this explains it. I mean, if she is the source of your information. I'm afraid Miss Williams is very inexperienced and, how can I put this given our present company?" he said, nodding in my direction. "Miss Williams came to us on a temporary contract and in the light of her present performance there is a distinct question mark over her future here. I think that will suffice. If Miss Williams has told you the boy is bright then she is clearly mistaken."

At this point Perkins pushed a bundle of papers in front of Mr Harding and suggested he spent a minute or so 'perusing' them. Mr Harding looked at one or two pages and read a few sentences before continuing.

"And what, may I ask, is the point of showing me work

of this quality when we are discussing Vince?"

"This is Vince's work, Headmaster. Work he has done for Miss Williams. This is only a small sample of what he has accomplished in the private lessons she gives him."

Mr Harding sat back in his chair. He looked surprised and started to go red.

"Private lessons with Miss Williams," he muttered. "I know nothing of private lessons with Miss Williams. Is this true, Vince? I have not approved any private lessons. There is some mischief going on here."

"Come now, Headmaster," interrupted Mr Greene. "This is beside the point. Look at the work, Headmaster. It is excellent, isn't it? Vince is just the boy we are looking for, and we have come to borrow him for a short time."

"Borrow him? Borrow him!" Mr Harding had stood up and his voice was getting louder. "You mean you intend to take him away with you? Are you mad, you can't just walk into my school and *borrow* one of my pupils. Who do you think you are?"

"Oh come now, Headmaster…"

"Don't you 'come now' me. What about his parents? Don't they get a say in this? And just who are you anyway? You come into my office, help yourself to my desk, demand coffee and tell me that you're going to borrow one of my pupils. I'm going to phone the police. The whole situation is completely absurd."

"Really, Headmaster, this is becoming rather tiresome. We already have the father's permission, and have his mother outside in order to obtain hers. We have shown you our identification papers. You are aware that obstructing the Security Services in the operation of their business is a criminal offence?"

"I don't care if it's a capital offence! How am I to know what MI5 identification papers are supposed to look like anyway? For all I know your so-called identification papers could have been rustled up on any old computer in ten minutes flat and what father would simply allow strangers to take away his son like that? This is completely preposterous."

"I do understand your concerns, Headmaster. Maybe

we have been too presumptuous. Perhaps we should explain further. Vince's father has had the unexpected good fortune to be facing early release in the very near future, let's say because of prison overcrowding, and he has fully agreed to our requests. His mother is outside and we are very confident that she will agree too when we speak to her. You are right to be suspicious of us, Headmaster, and it is indeed commendable of you to be so. We would not like to feel that you would let just anyone come into your school and walk out with a pupil. The problem is, how to convince you that we are genuinely who we say we are. Let me see now.... how can it be done? Would it help if you spoke to the Prime Minister? Would that convince you?"

Mr Harding looked taken aback. He sat down again.

"The Prime Minister, you mean the Prime Minister is here as well?"

"Not here in person," answered Mr Greene, "but at the end of this line."

He took out a mobile phone and pressed a single key. A few seconds later he began to speak.

"Hello Rebecca, Greene here. I need to speak to the PM urgently. Is he available? ... I think you will need to interrupt the meeting with this. I'm on the Viggors case but we have a difficulty. He's been taking a personal interest so I'm sure he won't mind."

Greene put his hand over the mouthpiece and spoke quietly to Mr Harding, "having to fetch him, shouldn't take a minute."

It took ages. None of us said anything while we were waiting. I was beginning to wonder if I was in bed and dreaming.

"Ah, Prime Minister, Greene here. Sorry to drag you out of Cabinet. Slight problem cropped up on the Viggors case. We're at the school to collect him but we're having a spot of difficulty convincing the Headmaster to agree to release him into our care. I don't think he's confident about our credentials. Perhaps if you would just have a word with him to clarify the situation? No, Prime Minister, it may seem that he is behaving like a jumped up little Hitler as you put it, but I think he is genuine enough. He is quite highly spoken of in this part of the woods. He is only being careful. Good, Prime Minister, I'll pass you over to him now."

Greene handed Mr Harding the phone, whispering, "address him as Sir," and sat back. I'd never seen Mr Harding nervous before. He seemed to be shaking a little as he took the phone. It was quite a few seconds before he said anything.

"Of course I understand the situation Si... Yes, they did show me their identification but I have my responsibilities and one can't be too careful these days. Of course, Sir, now that I have spoken to you the situation is completely different. I beg your pardon, Sir, did you really say… the Honours List…a knighthood… services to education…of course I would accept, Sir, it would be an honour, Sir. Yes… Yes, Sir… Yes, I'll hand you back now. Thank you, Sir."

Mr Harding handed the phone to Mr Greene and sat back in his chair. Then he opened his drawer, took out some tissues and wiped his forehead. Mr Greene nodded towards Perkins and pointed to the door. Perkins left the room clutching a different set of papers.

The next few minutes were a bit strange. Mr Greene drank his coffee, pausing every so often to make comments about the weather or this and that, while Mr Harding and I said nothing at all. In Mr Harding's case it was probably because he wasn't used to talking to prime ministers and in mine because I was just too confused by the whole situation. After a while, Perkins came back in and said that my mother had signed the release papers.

"Come along then, Vince," said Mr Greene, getting up. They both looked at me and waited, so I got up to follow them out of the room. I didn't know what else to do. There was no sign of my mother outside. Their car wasn't what you would have expected. James Bond wouldn't have been seen dead in it. Perkins got into the driver's seat and Mr Greene and I sat behind. Perkins drove quickly down the side street where the school was, out onto the ring road and then to the motorway. I asked Mr Greene where we were going.

"London, Vince. We already told you we are MI5."

Chapter 5

Once we were on the motorway Perkins pulled over into the middle lane and stayed there.

"It's not much of a car," I said, "I thought spies drove fast sports cars."

"Oh, we're not spies Vince. Not everybody who works for MI5 is a spy. It's not all fast cars and beautiful women. Our jobs are quite ordinary. We often work with the police."

It came back to me immediately. The journey back from the police station. That ugly, fat, pig of a policeman.

'You're a prime candidate, Vince. We've had you in mind for ages. I'd watch out if I were you. You never know when it might happen. Couple of strangers, no uniform, tap on the head, one dead Vince, one less problem for society. Job done.'

My mind started to race just as Perkins started to laugh. "Never fails," he said, turning his head round briefly towards Mr Greene beside me. "I could hardly keep a straight face, and all that stuff about a knighthood. How could anyone seriously believe that we could just pick up the phone to the PM like that?"

"What," I asked, "you mean it wasn't the Prime Minister Mr Harding was talking to?"

"Oh don't say that you were taken in too, Vince. Of course it wasn't the Prime Minister. Do you really think that the Prime Minister of the United Kingdom of Great Britain and Northern Ireland would leave a Cabinet meeting to speak to one of us? Well, maybe if I was the President of the United States, or the Queen."

He didn't seem to realise that his words might alarm me.

"No, it was just one of our colleagues in the office who has a talent for impressions. We've used him several times. He was so good at Tony Blair that he even fooled Cherie on one occasion."

I tried to keep calm and think carefully but I suppose I was already panicking. I could see Perkins' eyes in the rear-view mirror, looking at me, just like the policeman had done. All that stuff about MI5, it had to be made-up. It was just crazy to believe that MI5 needed me to help them. It must all be lies; lies to trick me, lies to trick Mr Harding and lies to trick my mum. Why else would she have given me up to them? They had to be the police and I really was on their list to be culled. Or maybe they were paedophiles. There were plenty of them about. The news was always on about them.

I told myself that the police don't go round murdering kids and that paedophiles don't walk into schools and ask the headmaster if they can borrow one of the pupils. Things like that don't happen in real life. But then, neither would MI5 need a school kid like me to help them save the world. One way or the other, it was all completely stupid. Stupid, yes, but I was in the middle of it, and it wasn't a very nice place to be. I decided then and there that I wasn't going to hang about. It wouldn't do to find out the hard way that I was in for a 'tap on the head'. I needed to escape.

"Can we stop please? I need to go to the toilet."

"Can't it wait, Vince," said Mr Greene. "We'll be in London in an hour."

"An hour?" I said, hoping to sound desperate. "I can't hold on for an hour. I'll wet myself, I'm dying to go. I mean it."

Mr Greene told Perkins to take the next exit.

A few miles further on we turned onto the slip road of a motorway services. I'd got an idea. Once before, a mate's brother had driven us to a motorway services for a bite to eat but instead of getting there on the motorway, he'd taken a back entrance that the staff and delivery lorries used. You couldn't get onto the back entrance from the motorway itself, just from an ordinary road. I supposed it must be the same for all the services. If I could get round the back, I might be able to get away from them that way.

"Perkins will go with you, Vince. We wouldn't want you getting lost now, would we?"

That seemed to have put the kibosh on it. I had no idea how I'd get away from Perkins. He was tall and thin and looked as though he could run a lot faster than me. I'd have to play it by ear. I needn't have been concerned. Once we got inside the doors, he pointed towards the shop.

"I'll get some mints while you're in the loo. Meet you back here at the door in a couple of minutes."

I waited a few seconds until he was out of sight then slipped back outside and made a dash for it along the front of the building, round the side, over a low wall and into the service yard. I came to a barrier, ducked under it and found myself at a junction. I turned left into what I thought would be the direction of home. I kept looking back as I was running but there was no sign of Perkins. He was probably still waiting for me at the door, not realising I'd done a runner. I thought I might still have a minute or two before it occurred to him that something was up.

I figured we'd probably driven about twenty miles down the motorway so I'd have to hitch a lift to get back again. But that would mean staying on the road and that was dangerous. Besides, it was a country road and there was almost no traffic. After about ten minutes hard running I came to a footpath sign that pointed away from the road and across the fields. I climbed over the stile and made for the shelter of some trees I could see in the distance. At least I would be able to get my breath back and think about what to do next.

Coming up with a plan wasn't easy. If they were the police then they'd soon have their mates looking for me and they'd be listening in to my phone and watching my mum as well. Besides, she'd only taken a minute to agree to let them have me, so even if I did manage to get to her, she might just hand me back over again. My dad was out of the question too because he was in prison and I didn't even know which one because he kept getting moved about. In any case he'd probably just turn me in too; after all, he'd already agreed to let them have me in return for a get out of jail free card. I supposed I could try one of my mates, Nath or Digby maybe, to see if they'd hide me but I knew they'd just think it was all a laugh and not take it seriously. Then there was Miss Williams. To tell you the truth it was thinking about her that depressed me the most. I thought I could trust her but she must have told them all about me. Perhaps she'd been in on it with them too, right from the start, just leading me on. Even if she wasn't, if they'd tricked her, they'd probably be watching her as well, just in case. And I didn't even know where she lived or have her mobile number.

I'd left my bag in the car. I wondered if I'd ever see the notebook again. It wasn't important. I went through my pockets. I had my mobile but the battery was low and there was only a bit of credit, £3.47 in cash and the lighter I always carried, even though I didn't smoke. That was all. There was nothing else of use. It was mid-afternoon and it was a cool March day. At least it was dry. There was no one I could go to so I'd have to fend for myself. I needed food and somewhere to spend the night. I was in the middle of the countryside, not a building in sight. I could go back to the road or head out across the fields. I chose the fields.

This time I walked, checking all around occasionally just in case they were after me. I walked steadily, following the footpath, always choosing the direction I thought home was, whenever the path branched. I avoided villages, skirting around if the path went straight through, picking it up again on the other side. After a couple of hours the sun had set and it was getting chillier. The track came out onto a narrow country lane that led to a row of cottages. Outside one of them, on the verge, was a table with stuff for sale. There were eggs, a few vegetables and some cakes. There was a sign which said 'Farm Produce – take what you want. Leave payment in Honesty Box' and by it was a shoebox with a few coins in. I was amazed really that someone could be so trusting and not even write down any prices. There wasn't much choice but I was guessing that I'd have to rough it for the night and I was already hungry, so I took the biggest cake. Then I remembered about the lighter in my pocket and that I might be able to get a fire going, so I took three eggs as well. It was tempting not to leave any money but I thought better of it and put a pound in the box. I could say that was the start of the new, honest me but really I was just being careful. I thought I saw a curtain moving in the next cottage and felt that there were eyes watching me. I didn't want anyone phoning the police to notify them of a young thief.

Half an hour further on and back in the fields, the light was fading. Away from the track and in the distance I saw some sort of building, too remote and too small to be a house. As I got nearer I could tell it was derelict. The window was broken and the door was just a piece of corrugated iron, propped up and jammed shut by a strong branch. There was no lock. Inside it was darker but not completely dark because half the roof had fallen in. I suppose it must been used as a barn or shed in the past. There was rubbish lying about and lots of cobwebs but it didn't smell bad like it would have done if it had been used as a toilet. Anyway, it was out of the wind and I didn't have any other options, so it would have to do for the night. At least there was nobody about, no prying eyes to wonder about me and report my presence.

Whilst there was still a bit of light I went back outside to gather stuff for a fire. There was a little wood a bit further away, with plenty of fallen branches lying about, so I made two trips until I figured I had enough, then I remembered that you always needed more firewood than you thought, so I went and got some more. I made the fire right underneath the hole in the roof so it would act as a chimney and used the dry rubbish inside the hut as kindling to get it going. I was afraid the branches might be too wet to burn but after some sorting I'd got enough dry stuff to start the fire and pretty soon the place had warmed up. I didn't really know how I was going to cook the eggs, so I put one in a corner of the fire and covered it with embers and ash and another on a stone right next to the flames. I kept the third back just in case the first two got ruined. While the eggs were cooking I used a stick that was alight to burn all the cobwebs away. I never did like spiders.

The first two eggs were overcooked and hard in the middle but I ate them anyway. I managed to get the third just right with the yolk runny, as I like it. After eating the cake as well my mouth was dry and I felt really thirsty. There was nothing I could do about it. I tried to look on the bright side. It wasn't a bad situation, a bit of an adventure, like camping. Not really though, the floor was concrete and felt damp, there wasn't anything to use as a mattress or as blankets and I had absolutely nothing to do. I couldn't even play one of the games on my mobile in case I used up the battery. As I sat there by the fire for warmth, I realised that I'd have to go back, that I couldn't rough it like this forever. Then I suddenly had this crazy idea that the only person left that I could turn to or trust was Mr Harding. After all they'd had to trick him too and he was the last person they would expect me to go to. I considered it for a bit and then told myself I was going mad.

Thinking I was going mad was actually quite useful because it made me think everything over again, carefully. It was true that I couldn't go back to Mum, not because she would want me to get culled but because they would be watching her and she wouldn't have a clue what to do. And it was stupid to think that Miss Williams was part of the police plot against me because they wouldn't have needed to have her or anyone else involved. She might have shown them my notebook but that didn't prove anything. Besides, how could she have shown them the notebook when I always had it with me? Maybe she hadn't, maybe they'd found out some other way. That Perkins bloke, he'd been in the library too. He'd have had lots of opportunities to look at the notebook during our breaks. They'd said that she thought that I was one of the cleverest boys in the school but she'd written that in the notebook, so Perkins could have read it. If that was the case, then Miss Williams might not have even spoken to them and if she hadn't betrayed me then I could trust her, and she was clever so she'd be able to think of what to do. They would probably be watching her too but I couldn't see any other alternative, I'd have to try to find a way to get to Miss Williams the next day.

I couldn't sleep properly sitting up and it was too uncomfortable to try to sleep lying down on the concrete so I just dozed, my back resting against the wall and rousing myself every now and then to put another log on the fire. It was the first time I'd been in the countryside at night and I was struck by how quiet it was. At home there was always the sound of the telly downstairs and the rumble of the traffic on the ring road twenty-four hours a day or the noisy neighbour who spent hours each evening practising his guitar. Out there in that barn there was nothing at all, except the occasional crackle from the fire. It was eerie, but it didn't last.

The sounds started with a single screech, rasping and rough, from way off in the distance. I couldn't tell if it was bird or an animal but its call was striking against the silence. Something, its mate maybe, answered calling three times. That seemed to start them all off, all these voices calling out in the darkness, whooping, screeching, chirping, barking, and yapping. It went on and on, until finally there was this almighty rumpus with loads of things calling out together and some desperate screeching, like the awful screams of a terrified, cornered victim. Well I don't mind telling you, my imagination just went into overdrive. I began to believe that there really were werewolves and vampires, demons and monsters, and all of them out to get me. Or maybe there were villains, murderers or mad people out there in the fields. I have to admit that I was scared stiff. Greene and Perkins didn't seem so scary at that moment. Even having to face that fat git of a policeman would have been better than being stuck out there. I got up and peeked outside to check if I could see anything but there was no moon and no light to see by, so I pulled the door back, as closed shut as possible and built up the fire so that it lit up the room. Eventually, I don't know how long it took, I dozed off again. At one point I seemed to be aware of voices outside, a woman saying they should come away because someone with a fire was inside and a man saying it was probably some old tramp and they could easily get rid of him. She told him to come away as she didn't feel like it any more. I may have been dreaming. Eventually, when I next opened my eyes there was light streaming in and the fire had died down.

I got back on the road as quickly as possible and thumbed down a car. The lady said she recognised the school uniform and wondered why anyone would be wearing it out there, so far away. When we got to the outskirts of town I got her to drop me at a big supermarket and went into the toilet to use the loo, wash my face and tidy myself up. I looked a sight in the mirror, hair all over the place, clothes all dusty and smelling of wood smoke. It's a wonder the lady hadn't said anything. Inside I went to the café, told them I only had two pounds on me and that I hadn't had anything to eat or drink for ages. The waitress took pity on me and gave me a plate of sausages, egg and beans and a cup of tea and only charged me for the tea.

It was still quite early and school hadn't long started, so I hung around the shop for a bit and then walked slowly towards the town centre, keeping to the back roads for safety and to use up the time. The only way I could get in touch with Miss Williams was through the school so about mid-morning I found somewhere quiet and called up the reception lady on my mobile. I'd already worked out exactly what to say, so when she answered I asked her if she could give a message to Miss Williams, the English teacher. She said that she was away that day but that she could phone her home number for me.

"Could you please tell her that there is an extra lesson in the library today, usual time?" Then I hung up before she could ask me my name. It worried me that Miss Williams wasn't at school. Perhaps she was ill and wouldn't be able to meet me or maybe she was away on a course, like once before when she was off school for a whole week. I could only wait and see.

I had the rest of the day to kill, as she never came to the library before five o'clock. It started to rain as I was passing the General Hospital, so I went inside and wandered about until I found a waiting room with lots of people in, where I could sit down. I must have stayed for hours and been through every magazine they had but nobody paid me any attention. I think I might have nodded off for a bit too. It struck me I'd found an ideal place to hide in and I made a mental note that it might come in useful again sometime.

While I was there I began to have doubts about the library. They knew all about it and Perkins had used it to spy on us. They might suspect that I'd try to meet her there and be watching the place. They might already be inside. I wondered what else I could do but then it came to me that Duke Street was a one-way street and she'd have to use it to get to the library. I knew what sort of car she drove so I could wait for her somewhere along the road and not in the library. She might not see me but it was worth a try. I knew that there were lots of CCTV cameras on the roads around the town centre but I had to take a chance. Once I got into Duke Street I got into a queue at a bus stop and waited.

It was quite a dark afternoon and some of the cars already had their headlights on which made it difficult to tell what sort they were but I recognised hers as soon as it came round the corner. There was nothing else for it so I dashed out into the road, waving my hands for her to stop. I heard some woman in the queue scream. She must have thought I was going to get run over but Miss Williams slammed on her brakes and the car stopped with a judder. I ran round the side, opened the passenger door and dived in.

"Don't go to the library, Miss, go straight past. I'm in trouble, Miss, you've got to help me. Go somewhere where we can talk in private. Please, Miss, I can explain."

I suppose it must have sounded a bit garbled. I expect she thought I'd committed some terrible crime or there was a gang of thugs after me, especially when I ducked down as low as I could to be out of sight. She didn't say anything at all. I kept my head down. After a few minutes the car came to a halt and she pulled on the handbrake. I looked up and saw that we were in a supermarket car park, at the far, deserted end and facing a wall.

"Well, Vince," she said, her voice full of emotion and slightly trembling. "I need a very good explanation for this. I'm already in enough trouble."

Her words alarmed me, she looked upset and worried. Even in the gloom I could see that her eyes were red and that she'd been crying.

"Trouble Miss? Are they after you too?"

"I don't know who you mean by 'they' Vince. All I know is that I've been suspended. I am not allowed to go back into the school until there has been an enquiry. They are calling it professional misconduct."

"I didn't know that teachers could get suspended too, Miss. What did you do?"

Her eyes filled with tears as she told me that Mr Harding

had sent for her the previous afternoon and accused her of going behind his back by giving me private lessons.

"It seems that I should have asked his permission. He said that for me to have been having secret meetings with a pupil, especially with a boy, was against all the rules. There will have to be an enquiry. I could lose my job and never be allowed to teach again."

"That's out of order, Miss," I shouted. "They can't do that. There was nothing wrong with it, Miss. It wasn't in secret, it was in the library. Anyone could have seen. They can't do you for just helping one of your kids."

For a few moments I was so incensed that I forgot my own worries. I wanted to comfort her and tell her that everything would be all right.

"Apparently they can, Vince. I wasn't even allowed to finish the day. Just told to get my personal things and leave immediately. I shouldn't be here now Vince. It will make things far worse for me if anyone sees us but the Head said that you had been taken into care, and I was worried when I got your message that you might have run away. What's happened Vince? Why are you in trouble?"

My thoughts returned to my own predicament. As best as I could, given that it was all so bewildering, I tried to tell her everything that had happened. She interrupted before I got to the end.

"This is ridiculous Vince. You can't expect me to believe this, it's just not possible. I'm getting angry now. I'm in danger of being fired because of you and you come out with this cock and bull story about spies."

"But it is the truth Miss. You have to believe me. I wouldn't lie to you Miss, you know that. Mr Harding was there like I said. He knows it's true."

"What, you want me to phone Mr Harding now, do you?"

I'd never heard her so angry before. I had no idea what I could say to convince her.

"No, Miss. I don't know what else to say. I'm sorry, Miss. It's all my fault. I'm sorry if I've got you in trouble. It's always my fault. I'll get out now, Miss, I won't cause you any more problems."

"Stay where you are and don't say a word," she yelled at me as she reached into her handbag, took out her phone and selected one of the contacts.

"Don't interrupt this, Vince. Maybe it's not such a bad idea." With that she started to speak.

"Oh hello, it's Miss Williams here. I need to talk to the Head. Is he still in school by any chance? Yes, I'll hold."

I was startled and very alarmed. What was she doing? Mr Harding would surely just hand me over. Was she involved after all? In my terror I reached for the door handle to try to escape, but she grabbed my sleeve, pulled it hard towards her and shouted at me.

"No you don't. Keep still and don't interrupt. If you want me to help you I need to know. Stay there, keep quiet and don't move."

We were both quiet for a few seconds before she spoke again.

"Sorry to trouble you Mr Harding," she said, trying to sound natural but with her voice still quivering, "no it's not about the suspension, I realise it wouldn't be appropriate to call about that. It's just that I've had a strange phone call from somebody calling himself Mr Greene, who says that he is from MI5. At first I thought that it was just someone having me on but then he said that he had been in your office yesterday afternoon and you could confirm who he was. He said it was a matter of national security. Is this true Mr Harding? Did he see you yesterday? Is he really from MI5?"

There was a long pause before she spoke again.

"Thank you Headmaster…no I can't say any more. I'll be in touch." With that she put the phone back in her bag, paused to take a deep breath and then smiled at me.

"I'm sorry for doubting you Vince. This is all totally crazy. I want you to tell me the whole story all over again. Take your time and try not to leave anything out. Everything, Vince. Tell me everything that was said and done."

So I went through the whole tale again, right from the point when the two policemen had driven me home. Miss Williams listened intently, her expression serious except when I got to the part about Mr Harding speaking to the Prime Minister.

"What's funny, Miss? What's a knighthood?" I asked.

"It's when somebody gets knighted by the Queen and has a Sir put in front of their name. No wonder Mr Harding was pleased. I'd have liked to have seen his face."

"I'm scared, Miss. Who could they really be? Why are they after me? Do you think it could be the police trying to get their own back for all the trouble I've caused? I'm afraid they want to kill me. I know it's stupid, Miss, but I can't think of anything else. They want to punish me for being bad. I'm for the cull, like he said. I don't know where I can go, or what I'm going to do tonight."

"We'll think of something Vince. I'm sure it's not them. They wouldn't do anything like that. You might have upset a few of them in the past but this isn't a police state, they don't go around murdering people, least of all kids. I think we might have to go to them Vince. That's what they're there for. They will know what to do. They'll make sure that you are safe."

I wasn't convinced. Going to the police was the last thing I wanted to do. There was only one thing I could think of.

"Couldn't I go home with you, Miss?" I think my voice must have been almost pleading.

"We can't do that, Vince. It would be the end of my career if Mr Harding found out. I'm sorry, Vince, and besides, if what you think is true then they would be sure to look for you at my place. Maybe we can think of something else. We could drive to another city and go to the police there or maybe we could go to a newspaper and tell them about it all. Hey, that's not a bad idea, Vince. A national newspaper would be able to investigate. Maybe they could put you up somewhere safe while they did it. What do you think?"

It sounded a very good idea to me. A newspaper would be able to find out the truth. That's what reporters did; investigate to get to the bottom of things. They never got the chance. At that moment all hell let loose. The car doors opened and arms reached in, grabbing us, pulling the keys out of the ignition, pushing us down. I heard Miss Williams screaming, saw her arms thrashing about, then a hand, fingers outstretched, smothered my face and blocked my mouth. It happened so quickly, I don't really know what was going on but I do remember that the face of the fat git policeman and what he had said came vividly to mind. By the time I realised that further struggling was useless, I was vaguely aware that someone was getting into the back seat. I really thought they were going to kill me.

Chapter 6

"Try to compose yourself, Miss Williams. We mean you no harm."

The voice from the back seat was calm and familiar.

"It's all right; you can let them go now."

The hand that smothered my face was immediately removed and I looked up to see Perkins.

"Sorry about that, Vince," he said, smiling. "I do hope I didn't hurt you. You're very precious to us, you know."

"You've got a very funny way of showing it, attacking us like that."

Miss Williams was smoothing down her clothes as she spoke. She looked red and flustered and she was definitely not smiling.

"You frightened us both to death and who the hell are you anyway?"

"Quite so, Miss Williams, we really are very sorry but we couldn't risk Vince getting away again. Allow me to introduce myself. I'm Perkins and this is Mr Greene."

Miss Williams and I both turned round.

"Please call me Felix," said Mr Greene, "we don't need to be formal. I shall call you Karen if that is okay. Hello again, Vince, we've been quite worried about you. What a song and dance you've led us on; it does rather confirm that we were right in choosing you in the first place. I can quite understand why you were so keen to get away from us after what you said about that policeman. Believe me, Vince, the police do not go about culling difficult teenagers and we are not about to harm you in any way. Once all this is over I shall see to it personally that your policeman friend is severely disciplined for trying to frighten you like that. Apart from anything else it has cost us a whole day and we really don't have much time. Now why don't we all go into the café here and I will explain things over a hot drink. You could have something to eat as well Vince, you're probably rather hungry."

As we all got out I noticed a shiny black limousine that had pulled up right behind our car.

"A bit better than the last one, eh Vince?" said Perkins, rather proudly. Then he told the uniformed driver, he was the one who'd held Miss Williams down in her seat, to park it properly and wait for us.

In the café Perkins queued up for the drinks while Mr Greene, Miss Williams and I sat down. I was still bewildered but the panic I had felt in the car had gone. It didn't seem like they were going to harm me. Someone who is going to murder you wouldn't capture you like that and then take you into a supermarket for a hot drink before doing you in.

"How did you know all that, about the policeman and what he said to Vince?" asked Miss Williams.

I was wondering about that too.

"Listening device I'm afraid, in your car and a homing signal as well. Perkins installed them last night after Vince had absconded. There were some in his bag as well only he left that in the car with us. We've had our people located in all the places that you might have gone to Vince but you seemed the most likely, Karen. You really are very clever, Vince: Perkins and I have been in that library for nearly an hour. We might have known you'd have intercepted her outside.

Now, I do need to get down to the serious business. We really are from MI5 and that means that we are responsible for tracking down spies and terrorists and anyone else who intends to harm this country. We are not the police and despite your earlier fears we have not come to punish you for any of your past misdemeanours. Something has happened, something very serious, which could affect Britain and the rest of the world. We have tried to deal with it but we have failed. You may be our last hope, Vince. Our intention is to take you to London tonight. We can do that because we are legally responsible for you at the moment. In London we have a number of safe houses. They are houses where we can keep people in secret, people who might otherwise be in danger. Don't worry Vince, you are not in any sort of danger, it will just be somewhere to stay. Tomorrow we will take you to headquarters and explain everything to you. We will show you what the threat is, why we think that you might be the person to help us overcome it and what we want you to do to that end. You do not have to help us, Vince. After it has all been explained it will be up to you. If you decide against it then Perkins will drive you home immediately. If you agree to help us then it will take a week or so. That's about all the time we have."

Perkins arrived with the drinks and a burger as well, for me. I felt just as confused as I had in Mr Harding's office and didn't know what to say.

"You aren't giving him a lot to go on," said Miss Williams, as if she'd read my mind. "Can't you explain in more detail? What's it all about, why is Vince so important and what exactly do you want him to do?"

"I'm sorry Karen but it's all covered by the Official Secrets Act. I can't say any more to Vince at the moment, let alone to you. Tomorrow it will be different. Vince can sign the Act and then we can tell him everything. He, indeed both of you, will just have to trust me at the moment. Actually, Karen, you might be able to help as well. I'm sorry that you've been suspended from your post but the timing may well work in everyone's favour. Try not to worry about your job; I'm sure they won't sack you. I don't think there's any tribunal on earth that would dare to have you dismissed, whether you had the Head's permission or not. It would make them look like complete imbeciles to sack a teacher who was giving up her own time to help a pupil as you were. I may be able to help too. We have been monitoring your meetings in the library and will be able to verify what went on. I could have a letter drafted. The thing is that it will probably take them at least a week to set up their enquiry or tribunal or whatever and in the meantime you would be stuck at home worrying. At the same time it would be much easier for Vince, in coming to London with us and preparing for his assignment, if he had a friend with him, someone he could trust and share his thoughts with. What I'm proposing Karen is that you could be that trusted companion. You could come with us to London and stay with Vince in the safe house. You could come along tomorrow too when it's all explained and help Vince decide whether he wants to help us or not. I'm sorry to spring it on you like this. You must be completely bewildered by today's events. It's a lot to think about. Perkins and I will let you talk it over. Take your time, think it through carefully. We'll be waiting in the limousine. Come out and find us when you're ready."

With that he drained the last of his coffee and stood up to leave.

"Oh, and Vince," he said with a smile, "please don't run away again. I had enough difficulty explaining yesterday away to my boss. If it happens again I think I'll be washing dishes for the rest of my career."

If I'd been bewildered before Mr Greene had started to speak I was completely clear about what I wanted to do by the time he'd finished. After all, what boy of my age would not have been impressed with the idea of staying in an MI5 safe house and being the one person who could help them overcome this terrible problem, whatever it was? Add in the prospect of having someone like Miss Williams stay with you and being able to impress her with your heroism. Well, my imagination was already in overdrive. I was just concerned that she'd simply dismiss it all and tell them there was no way.

"What do you think, Miss?" It was all I dared say.

"What I think, Vince, is that this situation is ridiculous and I don't know what to think. Nothing like this has ever happened to me before. They trap us and capture us like that and then bring us in here for coffee and talk to us like friends. I'm just confused, Vince, totally confused. I don't know what to say or do for the best. What do you think?"

"I dunno, Miss. It sounds exciting. Part of me wants to go with them but it's frightening too." I paused before the next bit, hoping it would be the right thing to say. "It would be easier if you came. I'll go if you come too."

It seemed ages before she answered.

"All right, Vince, I'm game. I couldn't just let you be taken away alone by strangers, whoever they are. I'd never be able to forgive myself if anything happened to you. I'll come, Vince. I'll try to help. If he's telling the truth we can make a final decision tomorrow anyway, and he'll bring us back if we decide against it."

I felt very relieved.

"Thank you, Miss, thank you. Let's tell them now. Let's get on with it, whatever it is."

"You might as well eat your burger first. It'd be a shame to waste it. We don't know when we'll next eat."

I took the green stuff out of the roll, squeezed two sachets of ketchup and one of mustard into it, added the salt and pepper and ate it as fast as I could.

Miss Williams watched with an increasing frown on her face.

"Here," she said, handing me a serviette to wipe the sauce off my chin and hands, "at least we'll have a few days to teach you some table manners."

I thought that was a bit uncalled for.

Miss Williams knocked on the window of the limousine to attract Mr Green's attention. He seemed delighted at what she had to say.

"I'm really pleased, Karen, it will make things so much easier for Vince. Now we'll need to get your car back to your house and you will need to pack a small suitcase. We are fully prepared for Vince but didn't realise he'd have a lady friend with him. You go first and we'll follow. Vince, you can come with us."

Miss Williams shook her head.

"I think it's better if Vince stays with me. We have to be able to trust each other, don't you think?"

"Clever girl," said Mr Greene. "That's fine. Let's make a move. No time to lose."

"What was that about Miss?" I asked, as we pulled off.

"To test his reaction. If he'd got angry and threatening we would have known it was all an act. I feel better now. He does seem trustworthy. He wouldn't be letting us go off on our own if he had evil intentions. One more thing, Vince…" She glanced momentarily in my direction.

"Yes, Miss?"

"…Will you please stop calling me 'Miss'? If we are going to go through this together you might as well call me Karen. It's not actually very nice to be called 'Miss' every few seconds."

"Sorry, Miss."

"Vince!" she reprimanded.

"Sorry, Miss. I don't think I can, Miss. It wouldn't seem right."

Miss Williams laughed. She had a lovely laugh.

By the time we'd got to Miss Williams' place and she was ready it was completely dark. Nothing much happened on the journey, except that Miss Williams had to put her fingers on this scanner thing to have her fingerprints taken and then sent through to the safe house so it would let her in. Apparently they already had mine. Mr Greene sat in the front and told the driver to turn on Radio 3. It was a really boring station that played sad music with no adverts. Mr Greene spent most of the time moving his hands about like our music teacher did when she was trying to get us to sing. Miss Williams whispered to me that he was pretending to conduct the orchestra, so I figured it was an old people's type of air guitar. Miss Williams gave me her MP3 player, saying that I'd probably like that more. I was beginning to like Mr Greene. He was quite small, very thin and had silvery hair. You could tell he was getting on a bit because he had hairy eyebrows like old people do but he didn't have hairs coming out of his ears or nose which was good because I always thought that was revolting. He had a nice voice too and he spoke properly, like the people on the telly when they're reading the news. I thought Perkins was a bit of an idiot. He was thin too but tall and gangly with it. He had the sort of voice that comedians use when they're taking off the people who read the news on the telly. And he seemed to smile and laugh too much, like he was trying too hard to be friendly. He certainly tried hard to be friendly to Miss Williams because he spent most of the journey trying to talk to her and making dull jokes that only he laughed at. I couldn't get that image of him with the messed up hair out of my head and, let's face it, only some sort of idiot would go the trouble of all those disguises and then turn up each time with the same old briefcase. It struck me that he might be on work experience or something like that. The best thing about the journey was sitting next to Miss Williams for so long. Because I had the MP3 on loud so I didn't have to hear the stuff on the radio, she squeezed my arm a few times to get my attention. I really liked that and wondered about squeezing hers too but I didn't have the nerve.

It was mid-evening by the time the limo got into London. Then we spent ages going down little side roads until the driver pulled up outside a big house, all on its own, the sort you had to be very rich to live in. Mr Greene turned round to talk to us.

"This is the safe house. You are the only guests tonight and the only ones who can get in or out. Outside the front door you will find a touch screen. Place your fingers on it and leave them there until a green light comes on. This means that your fingerprints have been recognised and you can go in. There are similar screens beside each door. Only certain doors have been programmed to let you in. Some of the house is out of bounds. All the windows are locked. That door is the only entrance. You will find a kitchen on the first floor where there is food for tonight. It's only basic I'm afraid. I hope one of you can use a microwave. On the second floor are your bedrooms. We've bought some fresh clothes for you Vince I hope you find them acceptable. You have your own of course, Karen. An alarm is set to go off at 7.45 tomorrow morning and you should be ready to be picked up at 9 o'clock sharp. You will then be taken to your first briefing. I will be there and everything will be explained. You will then have to make your decision. Is that all clear? I'm sorry I can't take you in to get you settled but the security on the house will only allow you two to enter. Even the Queen couldn't get in tonight. You will be perfectly safe and I will see you in the morning. Any questions?"

It was all quite exciting. I pressed my fingers on the screen, a light came on and there was a click. After a few seconds the front door opened automatically. We went inside and it closed behind us, by itself. Inside, on the ground floor it didn't seem like a home, more like offices, with plastic signs on each of the doors. I put my hand on all the screens but none of the doors opened. Up one flight of stairs we found that we could only go into three rooms. One was a toilet, one the kitchen and one a sort of living room, with some comfy chairs, a telly and a stereo. On the next floor only two doors opened, my room and Miss Williams'. Each room had a door in it that led to our own bathrooms, with a toilet as well. Miss Williams said they were called 'en suites'. I told her I knew but I didn't really because none of the flats where I lived had things like that. The rooms were nice and clean and I had a double bed, which was a bit different. I opened the wardrobe and found a whole load of brand new clothes and all in my size. The jeans were really cool, not a supermarket own brand. Back down in the living room there was a cabinet under the telly, with a PlayStation and some games, although they were all a bit tame.

Miss Williams said we should have something to eat as it was getting late. In the kitchen there were some ready meals in the fridge. Miss Williams said she had expected something better than junk food but I was quite pleased because there was quite a few to choose from, and one of them was a spag bol which was my favourite. There was also some fruit juice, some cans of Coke and a bottle of white wine. I tried to impress Miss Williams by asking for orange juice with the food, instead of the Coke. I did drink three cans later on though. She had the wine.

I thought Miss Williams was rather quiet all this time but I supposed she was tired and it had been a lot to take in. I was pretty tired too, but I felt a bit miffed when she said it must be past my bedtime. It made me feel like a little kid. I did perk up though when she said she'd look in to see how I was when she turned in. Normally I just sleep in my boxers, but when I pulled back the duvet on the bed there was a pair of pyjamas, stripy ones. I'd never had any pyjamas before but I thought it might be a rule to wear them so I put them on. I thought they made me look really stupid but I didn't take them off. I still had my boxers on underneath anyway. Normally I fall asleep as soon as my head hits the pillow but whether it was everything that had happened or because the bed felt so big compared to what I was used to I don't know, but I lay awake for ages. Actually, it may have been because I was waiting for Miss Williams. At some point I went to the loo and when I was in there I heard her come upstairs and then the noise of the shower. The bathrooms must have been next to each other because the sound was quite loud. It was a bit exciting to think that she was there, with no clothes on, just the other side of the wall. I looked round to see if there were any cracks or holes I could look through but there weren't. Bit disappointing. After the shower stopped and it went quiet I got back into bed. Eventually there was a knock on the door and the click as it opened. Miss Williams stood in the doorway. She was wearing a pure white dressing gown and her hair was still damp and tied back in a ponytail, so you could see more of her face. She hadn't got any make-up on at all.

"Goodnight, Vince. It's been a strange old day. Sleep well. I'll get you up in good time in the morning."

I thought she looked really beautiful.

"Goodnight Miss," I replied. It took me quite a long time to get to sleep afterwards.

Chapter 7

The face of a man flashed up on the big screen on the wall in front of us. He looked middle aged, with slightly chubby cheeks and the start of a double chin. His forehead looked a bit too wide because his hair had started to go and what hair he had was a sort of mousey colour and curly. He was wearing glasses but nothing trendy. He looked completely ordinary and reminded me of a friend's dad. We were in a small room inside the headquarters of MI5; Miss Williams, Mr Greene and me. Perkins had picked us up from the safe house earlier that morning but had been sent off to fetch something.

"Look at the face carefully; Vince," Mr Greene told me, "he is what all this is about. His name is Peter Grant and he is a university professor of microbiology. In fact, to be precise, he is a professor of virology. I'm not sure I understand it all myself but I'll try to make this as simple and straightforward as I can. Grant is an expert in plant viruses. He is particularly interested in how these viruses mutate or change. It isn't the most glamorous side of virology; most of the attention has been on viruses that attack humans or animals; bird flu, AIDS, that sort of thing. Grant has worked away quietly on his own for years and nobody has paid him much attention. Several months ago he walked into the offices of the Ministry of Agriculture in London with a large, sealed box and told the people there that its contents could wipe out humanity if they were let loose but would be perfectly harmless if quarantined in a sealed laboratory where they could be studied. He then left them with the box and told them that he expected they would want to get in touch when they had worked out what it was inside.

Given his background they had to take it seriously, so they put the box in a secure room and opened it. Inside were three trays of plants growing in compost. A note told them to grow them on over the next few weeks and monitor what happened. The plants were wheat, oats and barley. For a few days the plants continued to grow strongly but in the following week they all withered and died. Dissection and analysis showed that they had been attacked by a virus, but the particular one in question was completely new to all of them there and, in fact, to everyone who was given access to it."

Mr Greene paused to ask if we had followed it so far. Miss Williams nodded and looked at me. I nodded too, though I was afraid that it would be beyond me if it got any more technical.

"Of course, plants are attacked by many types of virus. Usually they weaken the plant or disfigure its appearance, sometimes they are lethal. The big problem here was that this one was completely new. No one knew where it had come from, whether it was out there in the wild so to speak or just in the Professor's lab. Nor did anybody know what vector or vectors it could use to spread – I'm sorry, Vince: a vector is just that, the thing that allows the virus to spread. Often with plants the vector is an insect that carries the virus from plant to plant but lots of things can do it."

Well, I'll tell you, the panic bells began to ring in London. Grant was not exaggerating. If this virus got out into the open before the scientists had found a way to kill or control it then harvests would be devastated everywhere. Can you imagine what the effect would be if harvests of cereal crops failed all over the world? There would be mass starvation, death on a colossal scale. It really could be the end of…"

"But couldn't people just have other things for breakfast instead of cereal?" I interrupted and then wished I hadn't.

"You misunderstand, Vince. We aren't just talking of breakfast cereal. Bread is made from flour which comes from wheat. So is pasta. Wheat is a cereal, so is rice. Cereals are the basis of much of the world's food consumption. It's not just that Vince, almost all the meat we eat is from animals fed on cereals. No cereals, no meat and no dairy products either. And the scientists weren't sure if this virus only attacked cereals or whether it could affect other kinds of food crops. They set about investigating it at once, knowing that it was going to be a race against time but the virus proved to be very complicated. The early estimates were that it could take as many as three years to properly understand its characteristics and at least two more to develop some sort of protection against it.

Of course, they were hammering on the Professor's door as soon as they realized what they were dealing with, and he was very helpful. He showed them all his development notes, explained how he had come upon the virus and how it could be spread. He apologised for the rather dramatic way in which he'd brought it to their attention. He said that he had been trying to develop an anti-virus but without much progress. All in all Professor Grant could not have been more cooperative and nobody had the slightest suspicion about him."

Mr Greene paused again and took a sip from the glass of water on the desk. This time it was Miss Williams who spoke.

"It does sound very serious Mr Greene but what in heaven has it got to do with us? Why do you need Vince? I'm very confused."

"I'm coming to that Karen. You need the whole story. Please be patient. Have you heard of the Holocaust, Vince?"

I certainly had. We'd done it in history the previous term. It was really good. I don't mean good in that way, but in the sense that it was interesting. The teacher had showed us a video of a bulldozer moving piles of dead bodies. They were all starved, just skin and bones. I actually felt sick, the way the bodies moved as though they were still alive. I explained to Mr Greene that it was when Hitler had all those millions of Jews put to death, just because they were Jews."

"And have you heard of the Holocaust deniers, Vince? Do you know about them?"

I shook my head.

"They are a group of people who deny that any of that took place or that if it did, it was only on a very small scale."

"But that's stupid. My teacher said it was the worst crime in history. They killed people from all over Europe just because they were Jewish, and what about all the pictures of it? They wouldn't teach us it in school if it never happened."

"It may seem stupid to you, and it does to me too, Vince, but these people do exist and there are rather a lot of them. Some of them are anti-Semitists, they are people who don't like Jews and some are Nazis as well, people who admire Hitler. Some of them genuinely believe what they say and some know it's a lie but have their own reasons for denying the Holocaust. The most famous example is probably David Irving, a British historian, who was sent to prison in Austria for saying it."

That threw me.

"What, do you mean that you can get sent to prison just for saying that the Holocaust didn't happen?" I asked.

"In some countries you can. Austria was part of Germany during the Second World War and people there find that part of their history very disturbing."

"Look, this is all very interesting," it was Miss Williams who interrupted again. She seemed impatient and anxious to get to the bottom of things, "but what has it got to do with this Professor and what has it got to do with us?"

"I told you, Karen, you need to know the whole story. It turns out that Professor Grant's first teaching job was in Cairo. He was there for years and fell in love with the country and the culture. In that environment he must have been only too aware of the Arab – Israeli conflict, of the situation in Gaza and the plight of the Palestinians. He returned to the UK eventually, got married and worked in several universities until he got his present post. We don't think he was dangerous at this stage but his experiences in the Middle East obviously stayed in his mind and made him receptive to radical ideas. A few years ago he started to become actively engaged in Middle Eastern issues. He went on pro-Palestinian demonstrations in London, attended rallies and meetings. Some of these meetings were about Holocaust denial. One or two were even addressed by Mr Irving. Our Professor is a Holocaust denier, Vince, and we think that may be crucial."

Felix clicked the computer mouse and the following message appeared on the screen.

YOU HAVE SIX MONTHS TO TRANSFER ALL THE JEWS IN ISRAEL TO AMERICA.

IN THE PLACE OF ISRAEL THE STATE OF PALESTINE IS TO BE ESTABLISHED.

It would be such a shame if Professor Grant's virus got out.

"Letters containing this message have been received by Downing Street and the American and Israeli embassies. You will, I think, appreciate the significance of the last sentence."

There was quite a long silence. At first I didn't twig but then I realised that it was like a blackmail note using the virus as the threat.

Miss Williams reacted first and she sounded shocked.

"My God," she said, "this is terrible. Who sent the message? What are you doing about it?"

"The answer to your first question is that we don't know. We don't know who wrote it. It was sent via Royal Mail to all three addresses and the letters were posted in London. Really, that is all we know. We have received other letters since, all restating this message and reminding us that time is running out, but we don't know who is sending them or if they are serious. Obviously the demand to dismantle Israel is a non-starter now, but nothing would be ruled out if cereal crops started to fail. We would be like putty in their hands."

"How long is left, of the six months, I mean? You must have been trying to do something, surely you would..." Miss Williams was speaking again but Felix interrupted.

"The six months are almost up. Of course we have been doing everything in our power to investigate. MI5 is involved; the American, Israeli, the French, even the Russian security forces are working on it, but the letters are all we have to go on and they don't yield any clues. Of course, one of the first things we did was to take a closer look at Professor Grant and that was when we became aware of his time in Egypt and his views on the Holocaust. That made us really worried. We had him taken in under the Prevention of

Terrorism Act and subjected to the most intense interrogation allowed under the law. Of course, he denied any knowledge of the letters or any involvement in any terrorist conspiracy. He said that no one knew about the virus, except him and us and that if anyone else had found out about it or got hold of it then it must be the fault of the Ministry people he'd given it to. He even offered to intensify his efforts to find an anti-virus and to share all his existing expertise with any other scientists we chose to select. When we confronted him with our knowledge of his attendance at Holocaust Denial meetings, he just shrugged and said it was a free country and that attending a few meetings did not make him a criminal.

While he was in custody we searched his house and his university office and lab, but we didn't find anything to connect him with any group or individual that might be of interest. There was, however, one thing that was suspicious, but it wasn't much to go on. Just before the first letter was received Grant changed the hard drives on his home computer and on the one in his office. He said it was just a coincidence that both of them had failed at this time but when your office computer breaks down, unless it's something very simple, you call in the IT people from work to deal with it, not try to fix it yourself and at your own expense. Grant just said that it was the quickest way of getting it done but, of course, all the information on the hard drives was lost to us and that might have been information to connect the Professor to terrorists and to a conspiracy."

Felix turned towards me, smiled and spoke in an apologetic tone.

"I'm sorry, Vince. I've been forgetting about you. Have you been able to follow all this? Do you understand what's going on?"

I thought for a few seconds and then answered.

"I think I understand it. There's this Professor who's invented a virus that could cause everybody to starve to death and someone is threatening to let it out unless everyone in Israel moves to America. You think it's the Professor who's doing the threatening but you can't prove it. Is that it?"

"In a nutshell," answered Felix.

I felt really pleased with myself.

"But what I don't understand is what it's got to do with the Holocaust and Holocaust deniers, and why they want people in Israel to move away. I just don't understand how all that fits in. Sorry if I'm being thick."

"You aren't being thick, Vince, you just don't know all the history of it. I think I can explain." It was Miss Williams speaking this time.

"Correct me if I'm wrong Mr Greene but before the Second World War there was no country called Israel. It was called Palestine and most of the people there were Arabs or Muslims. During the War, as you know Vince, the Nazis put to death millions of Jews from all over Europe and when all the details came out people were horrified. There was a lot of sympathy towards the Jews left alive. The general feeling was that the Jews would only be really safe if they had their own country and the decision was made to turn Palestine, which was then ruled by Britain, into a Jewish country called Israel. The only thing was that nobody asked the Palestinians what they thought of the idea and it's caused terrible problems ever since, including wars and terrorism, because the Palestinians want their country back. The deniers claim that the Holocaust was a con trick thought up by Jews to make people feel guilty, so that they would be allowed to have their own country. I think that's it. Felix is saying that if Professor Grant is a Holocaust denier then he would want Israel to be given back to the Palestinians, and that is what this threat is all about. Even though there isn't any proof that he has got anything to do with the letters, it seems logical that he must be involved."

"Excellent, Karen," Mr Greene seemed impressed, "you've got it completely. Do you follow now, Vince?"

I nodded, although really I was still trying to take in what she'd said and I was completely at a loss as to what the hell this had to do with me.

"There's a bit more that should tie-up all the loose ends."

Felix clicked the mouse again and a woman's face appeared, middle -aged and suntanned.

"The former Mrs Grant. They had been married for about ten years, and had a young son when she suddenly deserted both of them and ran off with another man. They live in Tel Aviv now. That's in Israel, Vince. Apparently the Professor took it very badly. His colleagues in the university say that he became depressed and withdrawn. We think that this was when his obsession with the Holocaust began. We've spoken to her, not let her in on the details of course, but asked her about him. She says that he was always a bit weird in his ideas, but only about things like UFO's and crop circles, never about anything political. He didn't even vote in elections. She'd never even heard him mention anything about the Holocaust.

I said they had a son. He was called David. After Mrs Grant left the Professor devoted his life to him. They did everything together. Grant even had a lab built at home so that he could work from there during the school holidays, and they could be together. David was killed in a car accident a couple of years ago. He would have been sixteen now. You can imagine how his father took it. It was a genuine accident, not the driver's fault, but Grant was completely devastated. We think it was the final straw that pushed him over the edge. You see, the driver was Jewish. We know it's not rational to want revenge on a whole country for what one person did, but we believe that, in his mental condition, Grant was far from rational at that time. It was from then on that he became really obsessed with the Holocaust and started to attend Denial meetings. Some of the people he met at those meetings were themselves under suspicion of terrorism and under surveillance; although Grant simply maintains that he knew nothing about them.

So, we think it all fits together. His love of the Middle East, the people he blames for ruining his life and for taking that of his son, his knowledge of virology and his discovery of the virus. We think that this is enough to connect Grant to the letters, even if we don't have the physical proof. If that were it, if it was just one madman acting on his own, then our job would be simple. But that is very far from it. When the most recent letters were received, Grant was under observation. We know that he did not post them, so someone else must have. This confirms that Grant is not alone: he is part of a conspiracy. What is even more worrying is that whoever else is involved must have their own store of virus, because the only traces of it we found in his labs were dead. There must be a batch of living virus somewhere else. We have been watching and following his every move for months now and Grant has not visited any other labs or any other place where the virus could be. The logical conclusion is that the others, the people Grant is working with, are in possession of the virus.

We have discussed all this with our allies. The Americans were in favour of shipping Grant off to Guantanamo Bay and the Israelis wanted to let Mossad loose on him, but finally we agreed that it would be best just to keep Grant under the closest surveillance. If he had disappeared then it might have provoked his fellow conspirators into early action, and if they have got access to the virus then that could be disastrous. So we have been watching him. His house is under observation twenty-four hours a day. His telephone calls are recorded, his internet use is monitored. He is followed every time he sets foot outside. I'm afraid it hasn't been enough. He has not led us to the others, and time is running out. The six months are almost up. We've got the best virologists in the world working on the virus. We are trawling through millions of e-mails to see if we can connect Professor Grant to any specific terrorist group or with any particular individual who might be in on the conspiracy. We are monitoring grain shipments and purchases to try to detect unusual patterns, to see if anyone or any country is stockpiling. It isn't enough. We are very afraid that we won't achieve a breakthrough in time. It all boils down to this. We need a way of getting through the Professor's defences. There has to be a vulnerable spot, some chink in his armour, a way to get him to give us the information before it is too late. We think we may have found it. You are the key, Vince. There is one final slide for you to look at. You will recognise the face and you will be surprised but you will finally understand why you are here. This is the last photograph of Professor Grant's son David, taken a few days before his death."

Felix pressed the mouse button one last time, and the image of a boy of about fourteen flashed on the screen. Nobody spoke for what seemed an eternity. Miss Williams kept turning her face to look at the photo and then at me. I knew why and it made me feel very uncomfortable. The resemblance was uncanny. The face on the screen that smiled towards us was not only that of David Grant, it was my face too.

"This is getting creepy," I said. "Why does he look so much like me? Are we related? Is he like my cousin or something?"

"Absolutely not, Vince," answered Mr Greene, "it's just a coincidence but a coincidence that we may be able to use to our advantage. Vince..."

He paused at that moment, as if trying to find the right words.

"Vince, we want you to break into the Professor's house and deliberately let him catch you."

I can't remember whether I was shocked or frightened at what he said. For a few seconds I don't think I thought anything at all but then it came to me that I might have guessed it would be another bloody catching. First the fat git policeman said he was going to catch me, then Greene and Perkins had actually caught us in the car and now they were going to let me go again, just so this mad Professor geezer would be able to catch me. I was beginning to wish I hadn't been so keen to impress Miss Williams with my bravery. I looked at her but she was still staring at the picture with the amazed look on her face.

Mr Greene waited for a bit before continuing. I think he was giving us time to take it all in.

"Vince, he would recognise his own son in you immediately. It would be a shock for him. It would be disconcerting. It would put him off his guard. He might have been expecting us to send someone to befriend him and get the information out of him that way but not a child. You might just be able to persuade him to let you stay. You could say that you have run away, tell him about your violent father, plead with him not to turn you in. He might just do it. Gradually you might be able to find things out, get information out of him. I'm not saying that he'd tell you directly but he might let things slip, snippets of information that we could use."

He paused to take another drink, this time draining the glass.

"We don't think you would be in any danger. He has no history of violence. We could fix it so that he already knew about a local runaway. And we've devised a clever way of listening to everything that he says to you. Perkins will be here with it shortly. I want to be honest with you Vince, if you were to agree to do this thing there would be no reward, no payment, no public praise or glory. It would be an act of altruism for the benefit of mankind. It must be your decision though. There's nothing much else to tell. There would be a few days of instruction first, more information about the Holocaust, about denial. And we'd have to teach you about the layout of the house, how to break in, that sort of thing. Just a few days mind you. We don't have much time. We need to move as soon as possible.

You need to think it through. Talk it over with Karen, hear what she has to say. Weigh it up in your mind. Take as long as you like. Don't feel under any pressure to accept. If you don't think you can go through with it that will be fine and we'll take you home. It's a lot to ask, I know. I'll be waiting next door. Tell me your decision whenever you're ready."

Mr Greene went out leaving Miss Williams and me alone. This time I wasn't so sure.

"What's an act of altruism for the benefit of mankind?" I asked.

She told me. I thought about it. I'd never really ever done anything before that was simply for someone else with nothing in it for me.

"You have to be a special kind of person to do something altruistic," she continued, "but it's not completely true that people don't obtain anything by doing it. It gives a very positive feeling to do something for others without any expectation of gain for oneself."

I thought about it. That would be something new, to be able to feel positive about myself, to feel proud. I couldn't remember ever having done anything to be proud of. Maybe it would be a good thing to do, not just for everyone else but for me as well.

"I suppose you want us to say no," I said.

"Of course I want us to say no," said Miss Williams, quite sternly I thought, but then her tone changed and her voice became gentler.

"Of course I want us to say no, but I don't know whether we should. If everything that Felix has told us is true then everybody in the world is in danger. It looks as though you might be their only hope. I know you've already been through a lot. I can see that it would be a really frightening thing to do. I'd certainly be scared out of my wits if it was me who had to break into some madman's house and let myself get caught, but I just don't see that there is any alternative. Felix says you are their last hope. Maybe we should put our fears aside. Millions of people could starve. Maybe you should say yes. No, I don't know what to say. How can I tell you to put yourself in danger? No, I can't tell you. It has to be your decision, Vince."

I could see she was torn. She was frightened for what might happen to me if I said yes and frightened for what might happen to me and everyone else if I didn't. I didn't think about it. I looked at her and saw how worried she was and I found the words just coming out.

"I'll do it for you," I said. "I know it will be dangerous. He must be a weirdo to threaten everyone like this but I'll do it for you."

Miss Williams didn't say anything. She just looked at me and smiled. Then she put her arms around me and gave me a long, hard hug, her face against mine. I thought it was definitely the best moment of my life so far and that altruism had a lot going for it.

A few seconds later the door opened and Perkins walked in, followed by Mr Greene, who apologised for the intrusion but said that Perkins thought I might like to see 'it' before finally making up my mind. Perkins was opening a small package as Mr Greene spoke and placed the contents in front of me.

"Well, what do you think?" he asked.

I didn't know what to think, not having been warned about it or knowing what the thing was. In fact, the first thoughts that came into my mind, as I looked at it, were of a well-known television presenter of nature programmes who could make fire without matches and eat almost anything at all if the need arose. I had a mental picture of him in Australia digging under the roots of some bush and eating the large, whitish grubs that he found there, for the thing on the table really did look rather like a large grub. It was white, between one and two centimetres long, half as wide, slightly rounded at one end and going in at the other.

"I'm not eating that no matter what you say," I said sharply.

Perkins looked perplexed.

"Why should we want you to eat it?" he asked.

"Isn't it one of them grub things?"

There was a couple of seconds of silence before Perkins and Mr Greene both smiled and Perkins laughed his silly laugh.

"I see what you mean," said Mr Greene. "It does look like some grub or slug, but it really isn't, Vince. It isn't alive. Here, feel it. It's a transmitter. It can receive and transmit messages. If you decide to accept our proposal then you'll be able to wear it when you are inside Grant's house and we will be able to listen in. Where's the rest of it Perkins?"

Perkins took a second package from his pocket then opened it. He held up half a rubber finger for me to see.

"This is the covering for the transmitter, Vince, a new finger for you, in place of the one that's missing."

I was fascinated. I looked at it and then held up my left hand and looked at the little stump of a finger. It would be good to have it made whole again and even better if it was a transmitter as well. I'd be bionic. Nathan and Digby would be well impressed. Perkins took the transmitter back, pushed it into the finger sleeve and handed it to me.

"Try it on," he said, "but don't be too concerned about its appearance. This isn't the finished product. If you were going to go ahead with this we would make a sleeve that matched your skin colour perfectly."

I pushed the stump of my missing finger into the sleeve. It was a tight fit and I had to twist it round so that the nail part of it was in the right place, but even though it wasn't the final product I could see, by holding my hands in front of me, that it was exactly the right length. As I clenched my hand, the finger still bent at the knuckle.

I was disappointed at Miss William's reaction. She didn't seem impressed at all.

"Surely you've got his house bugged anyway, with listening devices I mean. What would you need something like this for?"

"Actually no, Karen," answered Perkins. "The phone is tapped but when we went over the house and installed the outside cameras we were already aware that he never has any visitors, so listening devices wouldn't really have been any use. He must be a rather lonely man. Besides, the thing about Vince's finger is that it's two-way. We can talk to him as well as listen."

"But you'll never be able to make it look completely natural. Grant is sure to notice it. What will he think?"

"That's the beauty of using Vince, my dear," said Mr Greene. "Vince can just tell the truth, only not all of it. He can tell the Professor about the accident with the door, about his parents' reaction, about the operation in the hospital and then go on to say that this prosthesis was made for him. All of it true, just nothing about the transmitter. It's one of the things that make Vince so well-suited to this job. He'll be able to tell the truth about lots of situations and that's important because when you tell the truth you're less likely to make mistakes. It's when people start telling lies that they can come unstuck, trap themselves in inconsistencies, forget what they have invented before." Felix paused for a second before adding, as if as an afterthought, "And by the way Vince, have you decided whether you are willing to help us?"

"Yep, we'll help," I said, trying to sound cool, "but how

does this finger work?"

Perkins gently took my hand to show me.

"If you squeeze it on both sides, just here," he demonstrated, "it turns on the transmitter. It will send out anything it hears within a few yards. So we'll be able to listen in to all your conversations with the Professor. If you squeeze it here it turns the receiver on instead. There is a very small speaker built in. Basically you just put the end of the finger into your ear and you'll be able to hear any messages we send you. Only you will be able to hear them but it would be advisable not to keep sticking your finger into your ear in front of Grant. It would be best to do it when you are alone, in the loo, that sort of thing. If we want you to turn it to receive mode we can make the finger vibrate slightly. You will feel it and know that we have something to say. We might want to give you an instruction, tell you what questions to ask him, push you in the right direction and, of course, we could tell you if you needed to get out in a hurry. Don't forget to switch it back to transmit mode after and don't worry about it falling off," Perkins smiled, "we'll stick it on with super-glue."

So it was set. I, Vince Viggors, was going to do my bit to help save mankind from the threat of a madman armed with a deadly virus. I had no idea how I was going to do it or what was in store for me. It was exciting and frightening at the same time. One other thing that was decided was that Miss Williams would be my link with the outside world, on the other end of my finger so to speak. She asked if she could and the other two agreed immediately, although Mr Greene did wonder, mischievously I think, what Mr Harding would say about Miss Williams whispering in my ear. We all had a good laugh at that.

Chapter 8

I was crawling along the branch of a tree. The tree was by the side of Professor Grant's house and the branch was high up, almost as high as the top of the roof. As it got farther from the main trunk the branch became thinner and I had to lie along it and try to pull myself forward. I made the mistake of looking down and the drop made me feel giddy. I had to wait at least a minute to regain my composure before moving on, this time keeping my eyes firmly fixed on the sloping roof that came slowly towards me. As it became narrower the branch also became less rigid and I could feel it begin to move and bend under me. It was very scary. I wanted to quit. Eventually, when I was almost directly above the guttering, where the roof met the wall, the branch was so narrow and swayed so much that I felt sure it would crack or break under me. And that was the easy bit.

I knew what I had to do next but I wasn't sure I could manage it. At one point I considered giving in and moving back along the branch to safety. I don't know why I didn't. First I had to move my hand to my back pocket and pull out the length of rope that was stuffed in it. Then I had to loop the middle of the rope round the branch a couple of times and let the two ends fall down. It was really difficult because I basically had to keep my balance by trying to grip the branch with my knees and elbows. It was at this point that Perkins called up from below.

"Careful now Vince, this is the dangerous part."

I jumped in surprise, lost my balance, flipped over and fell. The feeling of panic was overwhelming.

I felt the harness take my weight almost immediately and then I was dangling in the air. As my head cleared my temper took over.

"Why the sodding hell did you do that?" I shouted angrily. "You stupid fool, you made me fall off."

"Sorry, Vince," said Perkins, "it was a bit brainless. Let's get you down and give it another go."

"Typical of modern youth," I heard Miss Williams comment, "always just hanging around."

I was going to shout at her too, until I realised it was a joke.

"Very funny, ha ha," I replied, trying to sound sarcastic.

We were in a large warehouse that Perkins called the 'movie set'. A mock-up of Grant's house had been built for me to practise the break-in until I could do it perfectly. When she'd first seen the height of the branch and the distance below to the open window, Miss Williams had wanted to call the whole thing off. But Perkins insisted that it was the only way in. Grant would suspect that both outside doors and all the lower windows would be watched, so the break-in couldn't be downstairs. Besides, that small window was always open.

"It looks out of the lab he has up there. It must be something to do with fumes and ventilation or whatever but it's always open, so Grant must be confident that no one could use it to get in. I expect it hasn't crossed his mind that someone could come down from the branch."

"It's much too dangerous for a child to do," insisted Miss Williams.

"It has to be done by a child," said Perkins, "the branch couldn't take the weight of an adult."

Miss Williams didn't seem convinced.

"You told us that Grant's house was under constant surveillance. Is he aware of this?"

"Yes and no," answered Perkins, rather confusingly, "there is a car parked outside in the road all the time. It has darkened windows but Grant knows that there are men inside watching."

I think he was going to continue to explain the 'no' bit but Miss Williams cut in to make her point.

"So won't Grant get suspicious if he thinks that your people have watched a boy break into the house and then not done anything about it when he doesn't come out again? Won't he suspect that the watchers and the boy must be connected and acting together?"

"It's a good point, Karen," answered Perkins, "but that's why we've got the car positioned where it is. This window can't be seen from the car. As long as Vince can persuade Grant that he got into the garden at the rear and not at the front, then Grant should think that no-one else knows he's in there. We've tried to anticipate every possibility, Karen. Nothing's completely foolproof but we have to take a chance, the stakes are so high. Before Grant was released from custody we placed disguised cameras all around the outside of the property and we're pretty sure that he's not aware of them. We do have the whole place constantly monitored. The men and the car are really only a diversion. The idea is to make Grant think he's in control of the situation when really we are."

After getting me down and giving me a break, they made me try again. If anything, the second attempt was even more nerve-wracking than the first, given that I'd already failed once. This time, after I'd fixed the rope into position, I had to wriggle round so that my tummy was lying across the branch, with the rope hanging down between my legs. Then when I felt confident enough I was supposed to move my body down until it was only my chest on the branch. Then I had to manoeuvre one arm to grab hold of the two strands of the rope and then let go of the branch altogether, hang on tight to the rope with the one hand and grab at it with the other. It might have been a simple thing to do a few feet off the ground, but up there I was terrified. I don't know how I managed it, just that when the time came it only took a second or two and then I was under the branch, both hands firmly clutching the rope and trying to get it between my legs to hold on with them too. I think the word is elated; any way, it felt good.

The next bit should have been easier. I had to let myself down the rope until my feet were on the window ledge and then reach in through the smaller top window to open the larger one below. Then I was to climb inside. Unfortunately I'd not put the rope as far along the branch as I should have, so that when I'd let myself down I couldn't quite reach the ledge. I had to try to swing myself towards it but did it too hard and my feet went straight through the big window. It could have been very dangerous because Miss Williams and Perkins were right underneath looking up but fortunately most of the glass broke inwards. I was a bit gutted to have got so far and then messed it up but Perkins wasn't upset or annoyed and said that so far I'd done much better than he'd expected, given how difficult the whole thing was. I don't know if he felt the same when I messed up the next two tries but finally, at the fifth attempt I managed to do it all perfectly and get the big window open.

"That's as far as you go Vince," called up Perkins urgently, "we only built the wall, not the room. It's just a drop on the other side."

He made me do it at least a dozen more times before he was satisfied and even then he wouldn't allow it without the harness.

"We can't risk you breaking your neck at this stage of the proceedings."

In the afternoon they showed me a map of the town where the Professor lived and told me about it. There was also a video that showed the town centre. They said that I had to be able to talk knowledgeably about the place if Grant was to believe that I'd run away from home there. I was also told about the school I was supposed to go to and the name of the Headmaster and that sort of thing. It was all written down too so that I could take it away with me and learn it. It was boring stuff but I could see it was important.

Later that same day, our second in London, my new finger was ready. I was excited about trying it on and pleased with its appearance. You could hardly see the join. Perkins had only been joking about the super-glue; they used the same stuff to stick it on that people with false teeth use.

"It will feel strange at first," said Mr Greene, "so we want you to wear it all the time to get used to it."

It did feel strange. I felt clumsy when using that hand and I often found myself feeling the finger and looking at it.

"Try not to, Vince," said Mr Greene. "The Professor might become suspicious if you draw attention to it in that way. We don't want him to think that it's brand new."

They showed me a second time how it worked, where to press it to make it receive and how to make it transmit. Then we had a practice. Perkins was in a room where there was another transmitter. I put my finger in my ear and his voice came through as clear as anything.

"How many is six times eight Vince?"

"Dunno," I replied.

I did know really and anyway I'd forgotten to turn it back into transmit mode. It took some getting used to.

"How do I turn it off?" I asked.

"You can't, it transmits all the time, unless it's receiving."

I thought about it and became rather worried.

"You mean that you'll be able to hear me all the time, even in the toilet?"

"Afraid so, Vince. And we'll get to know if you sing in the bath, although try not to get it too wet. We aren't too sure how well it will stay on if it gets really soaked."

Later that evening, while we were alone and finishing our meal, I asked Miss Williams if she could explain about Jews.

"I know it's a religion as well but I don't really understand who the Jews are and why some people hate them so much."

"How do you mean, who they are?"

"Well, I've seen pictures of Jews in Israel in front of some wall and they looked really weird, all wearing black clothes and with dark beards and long strands of hair, a bit like dreadlocks. They say there are Jews here too but I've never seen anyone who looks like that. And if there are some here, are they Brits or Israelis or are they just on their own? How come they were all over Europe when Hitler was around?"

"I studied it a bit at university," she answered. "I did History as well as English. Let me see if I can explain it to you."

Miss Williams paused to finish her last bit of food, and took a sip of white wine before continuing.

"Thousands of years ago in what is now called the Holy Land, or Israel, or the Middle East, the Jews were one of the tribes of people who lived there. Gradually they became more important and powerful than most of the other tribes. Their land was rich compared to most other places in the region so it kept being invaded and conquered. Each time it happened some Jews were captured and sent away, sometimes because they rebelled against their new rulers and sometimes because some of them were clever and had skills or knowledge that were needed by the conquerors. Some people think that this started when the Jews rebelled against the Roman Empire a few years after Jesus but it had already been going on for many centuries. It just happened on a larger scale under the Romans."

I was already confused.

"A tribe, what does that mean exactly? It's one of the words that teachers sometimes use without properly explaining. I've heard of tribes of Red Indians in America when they had the cowboys."

"And they're still there, Vince. A tribe is a group of people who all speak the same language and have the same religion and their own ways of doing things, their own culture. They may just be from one village or from lots. Before anyone had thought of countries, that's how most people lived; in tribes."

"So Jews are like Red Indians?"

"Not really, Vince. There are tribal groups in countries all over the world and each one is different. Anyway, the Jews that had been sent out of the Holy Land, they're often referred to as the Diaspora. These Jews found themselves living in places where they were in a small minority and minorities tend to get picked on, especially when times get difficult. Other people blame them for living in houses they think they should be living in, or for having jobs they think they should be doing. Sometimes minorities only exist for a generation or two and then they seem to disappear. It's called assimilation. To begin with, they talk and dress differently from the majority of people there but gradually they take on more of the ways of that place, they inter-marry and so on. Their children identify more with that place and not from where their parents or grandparents came."

"And that didn't happen with the Jews?"

"No. Not with most of them. There were lots of reasons. Many of them were very resentful at having been forced out of their homeland and were determined to return, maybe not themselves or their children or even their children's children, but eventually anyway. Their leaders knew that wouldn't happen if they integrated and became assimilated, so they made sure that their traditional ways were maintained, their religion continued to be practised and so on. They discouraged intermarriage. It wasn't just a one-way thing either; Jews were often badly treated in the countries they lived in. In some places it was forbidden to marry Jews and they were made to pay extra taxes and wear special clothes and hats to show who they were. Sometimes they were only allowed to live in certain parts of towns called ghettos and sometimes it went much further than that. Hitler wasn't the first person to kill Jews, Vince. It's happened throughout history, even in England. In York in the twelfth century, a number of Jews barricaded themselves into a castle called Clifford's Tower because the local people were attacking them and burning their houses. It happened in quite a lot of places in England at the same time. Anyway, the English set up camp around the Tower and lay siege to it. In the end the Jews knew that they would either starve to death inside the Tower or be murdered if they tried to leave it, so they decided to kill themselves instead. The fathers killed their children and wives and then they killed themselves. Only a few were still alive when the Tower was finally stormed but they were butchered anyway."

"Bloody hell Miss, sorry Miss, that's a bit out of order. What had they done to make people hate them so much?"

"Well in some ways it was just because they were different but, then again, Jews always suffered more than other minority groups because there were some special factors. For a start, they were blamed for Jesus' death. They were known as 'Christ Killers'. When Jesus was put on trial the Romans offered to let him go but the Jewish religious leaders said no. They were frightened of him because he was a challenge to their authority, so they wanted him to be executed. That story was told and retold every Easter all through the ages. Religion isn't such a big thing to many people nowadays but back then, in the Middle Ages, it was everything. The Catholic Church was more important than kings and governments. Almost everyone had to be a Catholic and go to church, so if you didn't, like the Jews, you stood out and were hated.

That wasn't all. There was something known as the 'Blood Libel', the belief that Jews used to kidnap and kill Christian children and then use their blood in ceremonies. Of course, it wasn't true, but then people will often believe rumours whether they are true or not. So if a child went missing the first thing people thought was that Jews were responsible. You can imagine how awful it must have been for the Jews who were innocent and for the people who feared what had happened to their children.

One other factor was quite important. In those days the Catholic Church did not allow money to be lent for profit, you know, when you take out a loan and have to pay interest on it so that, in the end, you have paid back more than the original loan. Anyway, Christians were not allowed to do this but people still needed to borrow money sometimes so they borrowed it off Jews. Even kings and other important people borrowed money to pay for palaces and armies and so on, and some Jews became very rich. People despised them for this. Sometimes stirring up hatred against Jews or even killing them was just a way of making sure you didn't have to pay back a loan."

Miss Williams paused to refill her glass, while I went to get another can of Coke from the fridge. Then I asked her about Jews today, if there were still some left in Europe after the Holocaust, and if there were any Jews in England too and if people treated them badly.

"Yes, Vince. There are even some Jewish pupils in the school, but most Jews in England don't wear the sort of dark clothes or have the long hair you talked about before. You wouldn't know it unless they told you. Some Jews moved to Israel after the war because they wanted to live in a Jewish state or because they were afraid to go back to their original homes, but many chose not to go. They think of themselves as English or French or whatever, only they have a different religion and some different ways, just like other minorities here."

That got me thinking about the people in our town.

"Like Pakis, you mean?"

"Well yes, Vince," answered Miss Williams although she said it rather sharply and abruptly, "but that's not a nice word to use."

"Why, what's wrong with 'Pakis'?"

"Well, what do you mean by it Vince?"

"Pakis, you know, people who come from India. They wear strange clothes and the girls are allowed to wear scarves and things in school, when English girls aren't and they smell of curry. There are fights sometimes. My mum says they should be sent back where they come from but I don't know because some of them come from here, like they were born here."

"You have to be careful about suggesting things like that, Vince. That's the sort of thing people said about Jews and you know what that led to."

"Yes, Miss, but that was different. That was Hitler and he was a nutter and he was the ruler as well so he could force people to do what he wanted."

"And Clifford's Tower? That wasn't the ruler, it was just ordinary people. Besides, Vince, what you said about India isn't the case. Paki is short for Pakistani, a person who comes from Pakistan, not from India. People from India are Indians. Bengalis come from Bangladesh and India. When people use that word they mean people from all these places, even though most of them are not Pakistanis. Even people from Nepal and Iran get called 'Paki'. It's not a nice word. It's a form of racism. In the 1970's, skinheads in Britain used to brag about 'Paki-bashing', beating up anyone they thought came from any of those countries. It's the same as with the Jews, Vince, picking on people who are in a minority and different in some way. It's important not to let yourself get lulled into using racist language or behaviour."

"So you shouldn't call someone a 'Paki' unless they come from Pakistan?"

"You shouldn't call them anything Vince. Why would you need to unless you were being horrible to them?"

I suppose I went quiet for a bit and I wondered if I was

going red. I'd called kids that on quite a few occasions and it was always in an insulting way because they were a different colour.

"Don't they teach you anything about this in your Citizenship lesson, Vince? That's what it's supposed to be for."

"Oh everyone just mucks about in that, Miss. The teacher is boring and everyone knows it's not important, and you can't do a GCSE in it. Mostly we just get shown videos. They ought to have you teaching it Miss. You make it really interesting."

Miss Williams smiled but I didn't like to ask if it was because of what I'd said about her or because she knew the teacher really was boring.

"I told you to stop calling me 'Miss', Vince."

"Yes, Miss," I answered, also smiling.

That night I found it difficult to sleep. Mostly it was just due to the excitement of the tree climbing and because I was worried about what might happen to me in the Professor's house, but it was also because I kept thinking of what Miss Williams had said about the Jews. I wondered what it must be like to be a Jew today, whether you would want to keep quiet about it or if you'd be proud of the way your people had survived all the terrible things that had happened in the past. I remembered the man who'd come to talk to the year group when we were doing the Holocaust in History. He was very old but he'd been a kid when it happened and he'd actually been in one of the camps and most of his family had been killed. Someone asked him if he hated Germans and he said only bad ones. One of the other kids said that if he was him, he'd want to kill anyone who was a German out of revenge. The man thought for a bit and then he said that the Germans he didn't manage to kill would want their own revenge and so it would go on and on. Better to forgive and remember. I especially remembered that phrase 'forgive and remember', because it wasn't what you'd expect, but it was also very clever, when you thought about it.

After that I got onto thinking about how angry Miss had been when I'd said that word. The thing was I'd known it wasn't nice to actually call someone a Paki to their face, but me and all my mates said it lots of times between ourselves, in ordinary talking and even made jokes using it and none of us ever thought anything of it. It made me realise how I was always doing bad things without even really thinking about it or meaning to. And that got me thinking about all the times I deliberately did bad things, little things usually, just for the hell of it, like dropping litter or doing graffiti; but sometimes much worse. It came to me then, and it wasn't a nice feeling to have, that if I was always doing bad things, whether I did them deliberately or not, it was because I was just a bad person. That was my problem, I was just bad, plain bad, through and through. Doing bad things came naturally because I was born that way. Maybe the policeman had been right. Like father, like son, he'd said. Well, my father was bad. Hurting people, getting into trouble, being put away, they all came naturally to him. So that was my future then, to be like my father, in and out of prison, beating up my wife and kids, having people cross over to the other side of the road when they saw me coming.

I lay there thinking about it for ages. It went round and round in my head that I was just bad. In the end I was so worked up about it all that I got up and went down to the kitchen to get a drink of water. I must have disturbed Miss Williams because I heard her moving about and come downstairs. She had on that white dressing gown that made her look really lovely. She asked if I was okay and I just lied and said I couldn't sleep because I was worried about Professor Grant. She asked what I did at home if I couldn't sleep, and I said without thinking that I went into Mum's room and got into bed with her. I used to do that when I was younger but not when Dad was there because he didn't like it. As soon as I said it I got really flustered and worried that Miss Williams might think that I was suggesting doing something rude with her.

"Sorry Miss, I didn't mean...me and you. I wasn't..."

"It's okay Vince. I didn't take it that way."

After that I hurried on back to bed and hardly got a wink of sleep all night.

The next morning I was still thinking about being a bad person. Miss Williams must have noticed I was a bit quiet and asked if I was worried about what I'd said in the kitchen in the night.

"It's not that Miss. It's about what we were talking about yesterday. I didn't know I was saying anything wrong when I said that word. I think it's just the way I am, I do bad things without even trying, like I was born that way. The thing is, Miss, I don't want people to think of me like that. I don't want to end up like my dad, in prison. I'd like to be different, for people to see me as good and kind, like you are, to have respect for me. I just don't know how to do it, how to make myself different. It's too difficult, Miss."

She was quiet for a few seconds as if thinking and then she said, very softly, "if you don't know a thing is bad then you can't be criticised for doing it or saying it. But once you know that something is wrong you have a choice about whether to do it or not. You can help yourself, Vince. You can choose to do the right thing and not the wrong. Everyone has that choice. Sometimes it's difficult; bad things can be tempting, but you have to overcome the temptation. It's up to you, Vince. It may be difficult but it's in your hands. In school Vince, there are children that we're just glad to see the back of at the end of Year 11. They've caused trouble all the way through, made it difficult for the staff and for the children that have to be with them in lessons. But there are others we'll miss, kids who have been a pleasure to teach. Kids who we know will go on to make something of their lives. It's up to you Vince, which sort you want to be at the end of Year 11. Until we started the lessons I only saw you as one of the first group, the ones we'll be glad to be rid of, but now, well now I know what your potential is. I've seen it but I don't think you've shown it to any of the other teachers. Have a think about it, Vince."

"Have you ever done anything bad Miss? I can't think that you could ever do anything really bad."

She was quiet again and this time it seemed like for ages. Then she looked at me.

"When I was at school there was a girl my age. We

were just young teenagers, friends, but not special friends. To begin with she just had ordinary glasses for reading but then her eyesight got worse very quickly and she had to have glasses with really thick lenses. People started to make comments and bully her. It got worse. She got picked on all the time and not just about the glasses, and the more upset she got, the more they did it. The thing is Vince, I knew it was wrong, but I didn't try to stop them or help her. I was worried they'd pick on me too. In the end I did it as well. I bullied her too."

Miss Williams had gone quite pale as she spoke. I could sense how upset she was.

"What happened, Miss?"

"She went home one day after school and killed herself."

There was a long pause.

"I'm sorry, Miss." I couldn't think of anything else to say. I'd like to think that was the moment I decided to change but maybe things like that don't happen in a single second. I could see then why she was so upset at the word I'd used. Singling out people and calling them names could lead to what Hitler had done in the Holocaust but it could also lead to what happened to that young girl. I knew it wasn't just Miss' fault, but if she'd been strong and done the right thing, well maybe things might have turned out differently. She'd had a choice, just like she said I had. She hadn't taken it and I knew she'd regret it forever. I thought perhaps I'd better start making the right choices while I still had the chance.

After a break to let breakfast go down, it was back to the movie set to show Mr Greene my break-in skills. He'd not seen me do it before and must have been suitably impressed but when I asked if I could do it without the harness he said the same as Perkins had and I had to argue with him. I told him that I needed to get over the nerves of not having the harness before I did the break-in; otherwise the nerves might just make me slip up (or down as the case would be). He could see I was right so they unbuckled me from the harness and let me have a go. It felt strange because the harness had been quite heavy and bulky, but it was easier to do because of that. I was able to move much more freely and managed the whole thing in no time. Everyone clapped, except Miss Williams who said she'd been so scared for me she thought she'd have kittens. I never did understand that saying.

Later on Mr Greene took me back to his office. He told me that I needed to know more about what Holocaust deniers said and why they were wrong. He said that in the end I might just have to argue it out with Grant and that, in any case, if Grant could see I knew something about the subject, it might encourage him to talk about it and that way he might let things slip.

"They say that the number of those killed is too high, that it would have been impossible to kill six million people in that time but the point about the Holocaust is that the Nazi's made an industry of it. Everything was highly organised, from the rounding up of Jews, to the deportations to the camps and to the actual killings. It was killing on an industrial scale. The camps were factories of killing. Factories are specifically designed to get things made quickly and efficiently, only this wasn't mass production, it was mass execution. And it went on for several years. The camps operated twenty-four hours a day, seven days a week. It would have been far more than six million, if the Allies hadn't won the war when they did.

Killing people is quite easy, Vince, if you are determined to do it. In 1994 in Rwanda, an African country, one tribe of people, the Hutu, deliberately tried to kill as many people from another tribe, the Tutsi, as they could. It was entirely indiscriminate, male and female, old and young, even babies. It lasted for about a hundred days and they reckon that between eight hundred thousand and a million Tutsis were slaughtered, mostly hacked to death with machetes. Machetes are big knives, a bit like heavy swords. Not nice, Vince, but the point is that if that number could be killed in a hundred days then it would be easy to exterminate six million in the several years after the death squads started in 1941.

Killing people is easy, Vince, but getting rid of the bodies is not. We have the evidence of the mass graves used before they built the gas ovens in the camps to burn the corpses. Deniers say there were no gas ovens at Auschwitz and that photographs taken by allied planes flying over the camps prove this because they don't show the tall chimneys that would have been necessary. But most of the photos that do exist were taken from too high up to show chimneys clearly and they were taken at the end of the war when we had command of the skies and it was safe for daylight flights but also when the Nazis had already tried to destroy the evidence in the camps, including the chimneys. Against what the deniers say we have many thousands of photographs, from many different camps, of the conditions, of the piles of dead bodies, of the state of those still left alive. They even took movies of the death squads at work before the camps were constructed, forcing Jews into mass graves and then shooting them. You yourself saw the film of the bulldozer moving piles of emaciated corpses. This is what cannot be denied.

Another thing they say is how come so few civilians in Germany and Poland were aware of what was going on in the camps? But they were prison camps, Vince, not holiday camps. You couldn't just go up and look inside and in any case they were run by the SS and they used Jews to do the dirty work before they too were killed in their turn. In fact, lots of German civilians have testified about what went on. So too, of course, have the many people who actually survived the camps and not all of them were Jews because other groups were imprisoned too. What is striking is that all of these people have said more or less the same thing about what went on. Think about that Vince, thousands of people from many different countries, speaking lots of different languages, all coming up with the same stories about the camps. How could that be faked? How could you persuade all those thousands of different people to tell the same lies? It's simply ridiculous, Vince.

There is one other point, Vince, well in fact there are lots of other points but perhaps we have said enough for now. What happened to them, Vince, if the Holocaust did not happen, as the deniers claim? They were meticulous, Vince, the Nazis, in keeping records of those who were rounded up and sent off in trains. So what happened to them if they weren't murdered? Did six million just vanish without trace?

Impossible. Just impossible.

You must know all this, Vince, and remember it so that you are prepared. Some of these deniers can make their stories sound very plausible and you need to be aware of the real truth so you don't get sucked in, so Professor Grant doesn't sway your mind too. In the end, Vince, if he really is intending to go through with his monstrous plan, it might be up to you to convince him that his ideas are simply wrong."

There were three of these sessions that day about the Holocaust. In the third one Mr Greene pretended to be Professor Grant and put forward denier arguments. I had to give the counter argument each time to show that the Professor was wrong. Mr Greene complimented me on how well I answered and I asked him when the talking would be over.

"When do I break into the Professor's? I'm fed up of all this waiting."

He looked at me and smiled.

"I think you're ready now. We go tomorrow."

I felt excited and rather scared. I had another bad night, with almost no sleep.

Chapter 9

Next morning they let me have a long lie-in so it was past eleven before we got to HQ. They sat me down and introduced me to a lady hairdresser who had to cut my hair to make it look more like David Grant's. After that, Mr Greene spent ages going through all that he'd taught me and testing me again, and then he and Perkins watched as I climbed up the tree without the harness one more time and got as far as the window. We all had a very late lunch together but it was only sandwiches, and after that it was time for the journey to the town where Grant lived. This time there was no Radio 3 and not much talking either. I think we were all just thinking about what was to come. I had the finger on and Miss Williams nudged me every time I touched it or looked at it. I remembered how nice it had been on the way down to London, sitting next to her for so long. This time it just felt ordinary because my mind was on other things.

It was a shorter journey this time. The Professor lived quite close to London. Even so, the light was fading by the time we arrived. I think they fixed it that way so there wouldn't be too much time waiting around and getting anxious. We actually passed Grant's house and they pointed it out, quite a big building but a bit lopsided in shape, as though it wasn't all there. I couldn't see much really, in the gloom. The place we were going was just round the corner, just a few doors away in fact. It was comforting to know Miss Williams and the others would be so near. They'd rented the house a few weeks before and done it up as the control centre. One of the rooms inside had been fitted out with the receivers and transmitters that would relay the information to and from my finger and with monitors that showed pictures from the cameras hidden around Grant's house. It was linked up to the MI5 headquarters in London, where a group of British, American and Israeli experts would also be watching everything that happened and hear everything I said or that was said to me. That made me even more nervous. They tested out the equipment by making me go out into the back garden and speak into the finger. It was a long garden and I had to keep speaking into it until I got to the end. Then I had to check that the vibration was working and listen to Miss Williams speaking. She said that we'd all be working together to make the mission a success and it sounded rather strange, as if she was embarrassed at having to speak to me like that with all those people listening.

After that they took me upstairs to get changed. My school bag was on the bed and next to it was a pile of scruffy old clothes, not my own, but not new either.

"I'm sorry but you'll find them a bit dirty and smelly," said Perkins. "It has to seem as though you've had them on for several days. We selected them carefully. They're the type of thing that Grant's son used to wear. I have to rub some of this oily stuff in your hair too, to make it look unkempt. Everything has to be in keeping."

The clothes smelled like they were damp. It was unpleasant just to put them on. I looked at myself in the mirror and I didn't look like me at all. My hair was different and the clothes were strange. Perkins had gone out of the room, so I was on my own and it just sort of came to me that this was it, this was the real beginning. It was as if everything in the last few days had all been a big game, scary sometimes but mostly enjoyable and not serious at all. But now it was different, I really was going to be on my own, breaking into a strange house with an even stranger person inside. What would he be like, how would he react to me? Would he get violent? Mr Greene and Perkins said it would be all right, 'he has no history of violence', but they didn't know really, they couldn't have known what he might do when he found a burglar in his house. It was only then, in front of that mirror, that I realised the responsibility I was taking on. How I had to overcome my fear and let this man catch me in order to stop him letting loose the virus and if I didn't do it right then millions of people could starve to death. I felt very small and lonely and for the first time since it all began, I wanted to go home.

When I went back downstairs, I noticed the shocked look that came over Miss Williams' face when she saw me and the way she backed away a bit when she caught a whiff of me. It hurt my feelings, I'd hoped for a hug. Downstairs there was also a copy of that afternoon's edition of the local newspaper. They told me to turn to page 5 and there I found a picture of myself smiling and another of my parents looking stressed out. The headline read:

Parents Plead for Son's Return

And the text explained how I had run away from home three days before, taking only a few possessions in my school bag. My parents were worried and the police were looking for me. The public were asked to be alert and report any sightings. Perkins explained that Grant went out every afternoon and bought the paper, so he was almost certain to have seen the pictures and read the story.

"He'll just turn me in when he catches me," I said after reading it.

"It's your job to persuade him not to," said Perkins.

The picture was strange because it had been taken before I'd had my hair cut but I had David's hair style in it. Perkins explained that they'd forgotten about the hair and had to retouch the picture before sending it off. Apparently Mr Greene had been quite angry.

As it turned out there was quite a lot of time just waiting around. It was only later, when it was getting towards midnight, that the time came. I put on my coat, looked at Miss Williams and asked her to wish me luck. She smiled, put her arms around me and gave me a big hug. The moment was over too soon. Within seconds Perkins and I were on our way.

"Grant usually turns in around eleven thirty, so we're hoping that he will still be awake, reading or dozing and still be likely to hear you. We've put some fluorescent markings on the tree to show you which branches to use to get up to the top. There are three dots on the branch you should use to climb along and three more to show you when you've gone far enough and where to hang the rope. I'll be watching from the garden to make sure you get in safely. After that I'm afraid you're on your own."

It only took a minute or two to reach the house. Perkins pointed to the car outside.

"That's ours," he said, as we continued to walk on for a few yards more until we reached the side road that ran adjacent to the garden. He looked round to make sure that no one was about, and motioned to me to climb over the low fence. A few yards more and we were at the tree. I walked round it and was able to make out the open window, clearly visible in the moonlight.

"I'll give you a push up to the first branch," Perkins whispered, "and for God's sake be careful. We've all grown fond of you Vince. You might be going in by an upstairs window but if you find yourself in any sort of danger just get out by the front door as quickly as you can and run to the car. They'll know what to do."

"See ya!" I said, trying to sound positive, as Perkins gave me a bunk-up to a lower branch.

Getting up the tree in the dark was something that I'd worried about but there was plenty of moonlight and the markings were easy to make out. Very soon I was high up and came to the branch with the three glowing dots. I got onto it and pulled myself along it, aware of the roof that came into view and grateful for all the practising they'd made me do. I was also relieved that this branch seemed a bit thicker and stronger than the one they'd made me use on the set. It didn't seem to shake so much under my weight. I crawled along it until I came to the markings, then stopped and felt in the bag on my back for the rope. I wound it round the branch twice and let the ends fall down. A minute later and I was lowering myself towards the slanting, open window and a few seconds after that my feet were on the ledge. I took the open window off its latch and pulled it up so that it was open as wide as possible. Then I reached in and opened the main window. I remember that I paused at that point and looked down at the ground, hoping to see Perkin's face, looking up. There was nothing. I really was on my own.

I climbed through the window and jumped down onto the floor. I could feel my heart beating and my mind was racing with excitement and trepidation. I stayed still for at least a minute to try to calm down and breathe normally. I told myself that this wasn't the first time that I'd entered someone else's house uninvited. It didn't help. I'd not had to let a madman catch me before. I started to feel my way to the door in the dark, then remembered the rope and had to go back and reach through the window to retrieve it. As I pulled the door open it gave off a loud creak that scared me half to death. I was sure that the Professor must have heard it. On the landing I listened for any sounds from his room but there was nothing. I carried on feeling my way along the landing wall, trying to picture the plan of the layout of the house they'd made me study. I came to the stairs and went down slowly, becoming even more frightened with every squeak and creak that I was sure would alert the Professor to the intruder in his house. Finally I found the kitchen and made for the fridge. I opened it and was grateful for the light that streamed out. If Grant had not already appeared by then they'd told me to start banging about, drop a dish or make some noise to wake him up. There wasn't any need. I heard noises above, the sound of someone moving about, coming down the stairs, sounds that made my skin tingle with excitement and fear. A voice, stuttering and nervous, called out fearfully.

"Who's there? I know someone's in there. I'm armed. I'll get you. You'll be sorry."

Finally, after several more seconds that seemed to last an eternity, there came the click of a switch and light that filled the room. There by the door, in striped pyjamas and brandishing a poker, was Professor Grant. I don't know which one of us was the more frightened.

He was smaller than I had expected and chubbier too, his hair or what little he had, sticking up out of place. He looked at me and the expression on his face changed to one of surprise.

"David?" he said falteringly. "David…it can't."

Then almost immediately the expression changed again to one that was angry and threatening.

"Who are you," he shouted, "and what do you think you're doing in my house? I'm calling the police."

Even before I could reply with the answer we had rehearsed so carefully, the look on Professor Grant's face changed again to one of recognition.

"Why, you're that boy in the paper, the runaway, aren't you? What are you doing here? What do you think you're doing in my house?"

"Please, Mister," I said in a voice that must have expressed the genuine terror I was feeling, "don't hurt me, don't hit me. I'm hungry. I'm starving. I haven't eaten nothing all day. I was only after food, that's all. Please, Mister, just give me some food and I'll go away. Just a bit of food to eat."

"Don't you know that people are worried sick about you? What do you think you're playing at?"

"I told you, Mister, I just want some food. I'm starving. Please don't hit me. Please put that stick thing down."

Professor Grant lowered the poker but did not put it down.

"Calm down. I'm not about to hurt you. I didn't know it was a child down here. Not eaten all day eh? That'll teach you not to run away. Who knows what might have happened to you. There are some bad people out there. All right then, sit down at the table. I'll get you some food but then we need to let people know that you're okay."

"What do you mean, the boy in the paper? How do you know I've run away? Just some crisps or some bread would be fine and something to drink too, I'm thirsty. I'll soon be on my way. Please don't turn me in. Please don't hurt me."

I was relieved and pleased, my fear was subsiding. It was going okay. It was like I was in my element. I remembered the finger and wondered if Miss Williams had heard.

"Calm down," said the Professor, in a more gentle tone, "I'm not going to hurt you. Sit down there. Let's deal with the food first. I don't have crisps. They're not good for you. Too much salt. I'll make you a sandwich. Ham or cheese?"

"Whatever, anything will do," I answered. "What did you mean about the paper?"

"See for yourself. It's over there. One of the inside pages, a picture of you and your mum and dad."

I leaned over to reach for the newspaper. I was careful

not to go straight to the page but pretended to search for the article, then spent a few seconds as if I was reading it.

"That's a joke," I said harshly, "someone must have paid 'em to say that. They hates me. I'm never going back."

Professor Grant was starting to butter some slices of bread but stopped and looked up.

"That's a pretty awful thing to say about your parents. Why would they have gone to the police and the paper, if they hate you?"

"I dunno about that but they does hate me and I hates them. I'm never going back."

"Why do you think they hate you? Parents usually love their children."

"So they say, but not mine. Listen, don't turn me in, I'll just run away again. I told you, I'm never going back. Just give me the food and let me leave. I won't bother you again."

"How did you get in?" asked Grant. "I heard noises on the stairs."

"Though the window up there. The one what was open," I answered.

"You mean the one upstairs in the lab? That's impossible. It's too far up. How on earth did you manage that?"

Professor Grant had stopped making the sandwich and waited for the answer, as if he didn't believe me and suspected something.

"Not up," I explained, "down. Down from the tree. I climbed up the tree and got down to the window."

The Professor said nothing. He didn't look convinced. I pulled my bag round and took out the rope.

"With this, see. I always has a rope. It often comes in handy. You can get into most places with a bit of rope."

"So this isn't the first time you have broken into a house then?"

"I'm saying nothing," I grinned.

Professor Grant handed me the sandwich and a glass of water. I bolted down the food and asked for more. The Professor made another sandwich.

"Where have you been, since you ran away I mean?"

"Here and there, I've been trying to keep off the

streets, too many cameras around these days. I spent the last two nights in a shed. Lots of people don't lock their sheds. I've been watching your house from the shed. I've seen you come and go. I saw the window and thought I might be able to get in that way. I thought that maybe you might not turn me in even if you did catch me."

"Why not? Why wouldn't I turn a burglar in?"

"Because the police are watching you. I seen them. There's a car outside. You should have a look, there's two men in there. Every so often one of them gets out to have a ciggy and whenever you leave the house one of them follows you. So I figures you might not want to tell the police about me if they're after you too."

Grant looked concerned.

"Do you think they saw you get in, the men in the car?"

"Don't think so. I came round the back, through the garden. They can't see the window from the car. Criminal are you? Robber or something like that?"

"Certainly not," said Grant, "I'm a professor."

"What's one of them?" I asked.

"I work in a university," explained the Professor.

"Clever are you?"

"Finish your sandwich," instructed the Professor, smiling for the first time.

There was a short gap when nothing was said. Grant cleared away and washed and dried the things he'd used.

"Tell me about your parents," he asked, eventually. "Why did you run away and why don't you want to go back to them?"

I thought about it carefully. The answer had to be convincing. We'd rehearsed the question several times.

"It's like I said," I replied, "I hates them. They don't really love me, like you should love your own kid. My dad's just out of prison. I ain't ever seen much of him, always in and out, but when he's out he's drunk and when he's drunk he gets angry and starts throwing his fists about. It's out of order. I'm not putting up with it any longer. My mum, she's on the game when he's not around, so I have to get lost a lot of the time. The only thing she cares about is that I'm around when Social Services turn up once a week to check I'm okay."

"On the game?" asked Grant, unknowingly.

"You born yesterday? Surely you know what 'the game' is. You know, when…"

Grant interrupted, comprehension dawning on him. He looked shocked.

"Oh yes, I understand but I'm sure they must care for you. Why would they have reported you missing if they weren't worried about you?"

"How should I know? I wasn't there, was I? I expect they felt they had to. I told you Social Services come round every week. How would they have explained it to them if I'd gone missing and they hadn't reported it? Listen, Mister, please don't turn me in, just let me leave. Thanks for the food. I promise I won't come back. You won't see me again. You won't tell anyone I've been here, will you?"

Grant thought about it for a few moments.

"Are you sure they weren't able to see you getting in… the men in the car outside?"

"Like I told you, I came through the back garden. The window can't be seen from the car."

"All right then but I can't just turn you out onto the street in the middle of the night. It's not safe for someone of your age to be out there alone at this time. You might have broken into my house but you're still only a boy. On the other hand I don't want to start making phone calls and have the police snooping about in here. In fact I know all about the men outside in the car. They've been watching me for weeks. I know they follow me everywhere. Don't worry, I'm not a common criminal, I'm not violent or anything like that. They're hoping that I will lead them to some other people, that's all. So if I can't turn you in and I can't turn you out, then the only alternative seems to be for you to stay here for the night instead. There's a spare room. You can sleep there and leave in the morning. You'll be perfectly safe. Would that be okay?"

I nodded in agreement and at the same time I felt the slight tingling in my finger that told me they wanted to speak to me. I needed an excuse.

"Thanks Mister, it'll be nice to have a proper bed. Can I use your toilet? I need to go."

"Out there in the hall," said Grant pointing. "I'll go and get the room ready."

In the toilet I turned the finger to receive mode and put the end to my ear. Within a few seconds Miss Williams was speaking.

"Well done, Vince. We're all very impressed. You should take up acting as a career! Felix says that that's enough for tonight. Don't ask him any more questions; just leave everything else until the morning. The important thing is that you're inside and he's letting you stay. Well done Vince. Try to get a good night's sleep."

I waited until I had used the toilet and flushed it before turning the finger back into transmit mode. There were some things I didn't want Miss Williams to hear.

Grant was waiting for me on the stairs. He led the way up. With the landing light on, I could see David's room at the top, football posters on the wall.

"In there is it?" I asked, trying to sound innocent.

"No," said the Professor, abruptly. Then he paused before continuing.

"That…that's my son's room. The spare is along here."

I thought about it then decided not to say anything. On the landing he opened up the airing cupboard but then waited a few seconds before reaching in and taking out some pyjamas. He handed them to me.

"My son's," he said quietly, "you might as well use them. Please have a shower before getting into bed. There should still be enough hot water. You'll feel better for it after roughing it all this time and a shed can't have been the cleanest of places to have slept in. If you look inside the bathroom cabinet you'll find a spare toothbrush you can use. I'll get you a towel and a dressing gown. If you leave your things outside the bathroom I'll put them in the wash. You might as well have clean clothes for tomorrow. That's the door to your room. I've had a quick tidy and I keep the bed made-up. It's all ready for you. I'll say goodnight. I get up early in the mornings. Come down tomorrow whenever you're up and running."

I was glad of the shower. It made me feel fresh. Afterwards, out on the landing there was no sign of the Professor and no light showed at the gap underneath his door. A little later I lay in bed, thinking of the evening's events. Grant seemed to be a gentle, even slightly sad person. Not the type to be threatening the world. I wondered if they'd got it all wrong. I thought of his son too and it dawned on me that I was wearing pyjamas he'd worn before he was killed. I hoped it wouldn't bring bad luck. Later still, my thoughts turned to my parents. I wondered if my mum was missing me and if they'd let Dad out of prison yet. I felt a twinge of guilt about what I'd said about them to Grant downstairs. It was only a twinge though, most of it had been true.

A knock at the door woke me. I'd slept like a log, as if I didn't have a care in the world. It was a moment or two before I remembered where I was. Then I opened my eyes and saw the strange room. There was another knock and a voice asked if it was all right to come in. I muttered something and the door opened. Professor Grant was there, fully dressed, hair still damp and flattened. He was smiling.

"I've brought you a cup of tea. I put sugar in. Most children like it with sugar. Is that okay?"

I nodded.

"I hope you slept well. It's quite a firm mattress. I didn't know whether to wake you or not but it's getting quite late. Your clothes are in the bathroom. I've ironed them. Breakfast is downstairs. Please don't go near any window. There are net curtains but I don't want to run the risk of the men outside seeing you. Come down when you're ready. Have some breakfast before you go."

I listened to the sound of the Professor's footsteps as he went down the stairs and then spoke quietly into the finger.

"Are you there Miss Williams? Can you hear? I think I should try to get him to let me stay by saying that the men might spot me in the daylight. What do you think?"

I waited for an answer, then realised I hadn't changed

the mode.

"I'm here, Vince. You could try that. Felix says that you should try to get him to talk about his son. He must still be amazed at your resemblance. It might make him hesitate before letting you leave. Remember you don't know anything about David, especially that he's no longer alive. Be careful, Vince. Grant might seem kind but he really is a very strange person. Remember we're very close by if you need to get out. Over."

Downstairs I found the Professor in the kitchen making toast.

"There isn't much," he said, "I live alone. Toast and cereal too, if you want it."

"Toast is okay. And maybe some coffee, too."

I didn't like the toast. I hadn't really liked the sandwiches last night either but hadn't liked to say so then.

"Haven't you got any proper bread?"

"I'm sorry," replied the Professor, "I only have wholemeal, it's better for you than white. White bread has all the goodness taken out."

"We done it in History," I said. "In the olden days rich people ate white bread because it looked better and poor people had to make do with all the brown stuff. Now it's the other way round."

"Do you like History?"

"It's my favourite subject," I paused for a moment, remembering that Miss Williams was listening, "History and English are the ones I like best."

"Are you good at school?"

"How do you mean?"

"Do you get good results?"

"Yes and no. I could get high marks all the time but my mates would take the mickey, so I pretend to be a bit thick. Not in everything though, not in English."

"Why not in English?"

"It's the teacher," I continued, "she's good. I wouldn't want to let her down."

As I spoke I remembered what they'd said about always trying to tell the truth. It was working. I was telling the truth and it made it easy.

"Where will you go?" asked Grant. "When you leave here, where will you go? Do you have any plans? Is there anyone you can go to?"

I thought about it carefully. There was no truth to tell this time but I'd practised this answer with Mr Greene.

"I was thinking of trying to get to London. It's a big place, easy to get lost in. I thought I'd try to get a job on a market. There's lots of markets in London. Just casual work, shifting crates, loading stalls, that sort of thing. Fiver here, tenner there, no questions asked. I'd have to rough it for a bit but I've looked up about squats on the Internet. There's lots of squats in London. I might be able to find one that would take me in or I might start one myself. Lots of empty places in London, has to be in a big city like that."

"London would be a very dangerous place for someone of your age, alone."

"I can handle it. I'm used to looking after myself."

"How will you get there?"

"That's the bit that's bothering me. I thought that if I kept hidden for a few days after I ran away, if people was looking for me they'd give up and I'd be able to get on a bus or hitch a lift down to London, no prob. But having my story in the paper like that could've sort of messed things up. Somebody might recognise me from the picture. I think I might have to stay hidden for another few days or so until people have forgotten about it and then give it a go. Suppose I'll be looking for another shed."

It was supposed to be a prompt for the Professor to offer to let me stay. It would be better if it came from him, rather than me asking, but he didn't take the bait. When Grant spoke again it was only to ask if I wanted more coffee. I said yes immediately, knowing it would give me a little more time.

Mr Greene had wanted me to get Grant to talk about his son.

"Who's David?" I asked. In an instant the expression on the Professor's face changed.

"How do you know about David?" he demanded. "I

never used his name."

I thought I might have messed up big but then it came to me.

"Last night," I answered, trying to sound calm although I could feel the rush of blood, "last night, when you first saw me, when you turned on the light, you called me David. You said it twice and you looked as though you recognised me."

"Oh," Grant's voice was calmer, "I do remember. It was a bit of a shock."

"Is he your son? Is your son David? Is that his room upstairs?"

The Professor sat down, slowly, wearily.

"Yes."

"Do I look like him then? Is that why you called me by his name? It must be weird to have someone break into your house who looks like your own son."

I didn't wait for an answer. Seeing the Professor lower his face and stretch his hand over his forehead so that his eyes were hidden, I went on.

"Said you lived alone. Lives with his mother does he? Divorced are you? She got custody. See him at weekends or in the holidays, do you?"

The Professor said nothing. I was afraid I might have gone too far. I didn't want him to get angry. Eventually he spoke.

"You do look like him, very much so in fact. It was a shock, 'a bit weird', as you say. It was a shock seeing you in the paper as well. I'd rather not talk about it anymore, if you don't mind. It's only your appearance. In every other way you are totally different. You can stay, if you'd like. You can stay until you think it's safe to head off to London. I could do with a bit of company. I've a lot on my mind, at the moment. What do you think? It must be better than a shed."

"Thanks, Mister, that'd be cool. I was hoping you'd ask. I promise to behave myself and not let those coppers outside see me."

For the rest of the morning I was left alone while Grant worked upstairs in his lab. The instructions from Miss Williams were clear, to stay out of the Professor's way and not to ask anything else for the time being.

"If you ask too many difficult questions too soon he might become suspicious. Wait till a natural opportunity arises. Just do as he wants for now."

Doing, 'as he wants', meant finding a book to read. One whole wall of the living room was taken up with shelves full of books but I couldn't find anything vaguely interesting. Most of it seemed to be boring scientific stuff. With nothing else to do I was soon at a loss and turned on the television to watch that. He didn't have any satellite channels though, and the few channels he did have were useless. After about half an hour I turned it off and thought I might have a little rootle about to see if I could find out anything useful about the virus that I could tell Mr Greene. I went around quietly opening drawers, looking in cupboards, in vases and ornaments. I went through the mail and papers in his bureau. I even looked behind things in case there were secret compartments or other hiding places. When I didn't find anything in the living room I went into the kitchen and did the same there, all the time listening in case the Professor came back down the stairs. Eventually I'd gone through all the downstairs rooms, except the cellar and discovered absolutely nothing. It struck me afterwards that I hadn't really known what I was looking for anyway. I might have already found something important and not realised it. By the time Professor Grant came down I was back in front of the telly again. He pulled a face but then apologised, saying that he should have realised that his books were unsuitable.

Lunch was more sandwiches with more wholemeal bread. I tried to make it seem I was enjoying it. While we were eating he asked me what my favourite meal was. When I told him it was spag bol his face lit up.

"Ah, Italian, good choice. How does your mother prepare it, does she have a special recipe?"

"She doesn't make it," I said, "I does."

"Very impressive, Vince. Being able to cook is a useful skill. Tell me how you make it."

"Takes it out of the cardboard, puts a few holes in the top, five minutes in the microwave and Bob's your uncle."

He looked shocked, I didn't understand why.

"Something wrong?" I asked.

"Is that how you usually eat, a ready-made meal from the supermarket?"

"Mostly, yes, unless we get a takeaway."

"I'm sorry Vince, I didn't mean to frown. But don't they teach you at school about junk food? The sort of food you're talking about, ready-cooked meals and takeaways, they're full of salt and saturated fat and chemicals. It's why so many people are overweight and unhealthy nowadays. Doesn't your family have any proper home cooked food?"

"I told you, I cook spag bol at home and sometimes I have chicken tikka or a Chinese at home too. We do cooking at school sometimes. It takes hours and hours and it doesn't taste as good as shop bought anyway. What's the point of going to all the bother if you can just pop out to the supermarket and get it?"

I didn't like to argue with him but I was feeling a bit bewildered. Here was this man who was deliberately going to let a killer virus loose that would make everybody starve to death and here he was lecturing me about what sort of food to eat. It struck me that he really was a nutter and he didn't let it end there.

"Tell you what," he said, smiling as though he would really enjoy it, "why don't we have proper spaghetti Bolognese for dinner tonight? We could make it together. I could show you how. From scratch mind you, nothing pre-prepared, except the pasta, I really don't have time to make pasta today. What do you say? I'm sure you'll find it a hundred times better than ready-made and it will be good fun. It's a long time since I cooked a decent meal. We could have a go at something else tomorrow."

I thought Miss Williams and the others must be having a good laugh and I nearly did too but made myself control it. I tried to sound enthusiastic when I said it was a good idea. At least he was talking as though I'd be staying a while.

He went back to his work for a couple of hours after lunch and I was left alone again with nothing to do but watch telly. When he finally came down he was looking tense and he spoke in a different way. He told me that he was going shopping, would be out for about an hour and that there was no money or anything valuable lying about. It was a few seconds before I sussed what he meant and I reacted without thinking.

"You saying I'm a thief? That I'd go through the house and steal things while you're away? That's right out of order. Think I'll be on my way if that's what you think."

"But that's what you were going to do when you broke in last night, wasn't it? You were going to steal from me."

"That was different. I was starving. Everyone's entitled to eat. It wasn't like proper stealing. I wouldn't steal from someone who had been nice to me like you have."

"So you would steal from someone who had been horrible to you?"

All of a sudden what had seemed easy had become difficult. I was struggling for what to say next.

"I didn't mean that. You're twisting my words. I mean you can trust me. You could've turned me in or sent me away and you didn't. I thought you were okay with me."

I waited for a reply, making eye contact, standing my ground. Eventually he looked away, the tension left his face and the nice Professor Grant returned.

"I'm sorry. It was a mean thing to say. I do trust you. Please stay. I'll go and get the shopping. Is there anything I can get you, something to help pass the time perhaps?"

"That's all right. It must be difficult to trust a stranger even if I am a kid. No thanks, I don't need anything, well, maybe a mag or a comic. Something more my age than the stuff in your books."

"Right you are then," smiled the Professor, "I'll see what I can find. I am sorry."

He paused for a second before continuing in a gentle voice,

"You could have a look round in David's room if you like. He was about your age. There's sure to be something there you'd find interesting, only… please don't disturb anything. I like to keep it the way it is."

As soon as he was gone I talked to Miss Williams.

"Did you hear that? It's like he's two people. One minute he's getting excited about cooking a meal together and the next he gets really nasty. I don't know that I like it here, it's as if he could do anything."

"We heard it, Vince. Felix says it's quite common with people who are disturbed. There's a medical condition. You did very well. Felix says to have a good look around upstairs while he's away. Go into David's room, as he suggested. Find out what kind of things he was interested in, music, football and so on. It could come in useful later, a way into a conversation. Go into the Professor's bedroom and the lab too. You're looking for anything that could be connected to the letters or a conspiracy. Make sure you don't disturb anything though, leave it all exactly as you find it. Try not to be frightened, Vince, we can hear everything. The car is right outside and we're only a few yards away. We'll give you a warning buzz a couple of minutes before Grant gets back. You're doing really well. Mr Harding would be impressed."

I slowly opened the door to the lab, wondering if a trap had been set. The computer was on but locked and I had no idea of the password. I found nothing of interest either in any of the Professor's papers or files. Most of it was double Dutch to me anyway, but none of it seemed to be about Israel or the threat of wiping out human beings. His bedroom was quite large and there were pictures of David on the wall. There were several photos loose in a pile on the bedside table as well, all with David in and some with the Professor too. Some of them weren't whole though, one side torn away. On a couple of these an arm from the torn side was around David's shoulder. I knew who it belonged to. Professor Grant must have felt very bitter towards her to do that. I didn't like being in there. It really felt as though I was interfering in someone else's private place.

David's room was much more interesting. There were Manchester United posters on the wall, Giggsy and Wayne Rooney and a big pile of football magazines. The bed was a proper one, not just a couple of mattresses piled on the floor like I had at home. There was a big wardrobe full of nice clothes, neatly folded or hanging up. The desk was like new with a stereo and a stack of CDs. In the drawers were school books, files, pencils, colours, paints, all sorts of gadgets and schoolboy things. And propped up on a stand there was a guitar, an acoustic one, but with an electric pick-up and a big speaker next to it. I picked it up, strummed at the strings and wondered if David had been able to play it properly.

I was pretty well entranced by that room. You would probably just see it as an ordinary bedroom but to me it was like the best bedroom I could have ever wished for. I thought of my own room back home, with the torn, dirty carpet, the wallpaper stained with damp and peeling off, the broken furniture and the heaps of tatty clothes, almost all from charity shops. I could see my mum and dad shouting at me, swearing at me, ordering me to 'get this bloody mess cleared up' and being ignored. All of a sudden this feeling of sadness came over me and I almost started to cry. It was obvious that this was the bedroom of a much-loved son, and I wondered what mine said about me.

I got back downstairs in good time and when Grant returned I was sitting at the kitchen table reading one of the footie magazines from upstairs.

"You found them did you? I've got you the latest one."

"You said it would be okay," I answered. "Supports Man U does he? I'm a Gunners man myself. Did you get the stuff for the spag bol? When are we going to do it? How long does it take? What's that long stuff sticking up?"

He explained that the long stuff was a packet of proper Italian spaghetti, the sort you have to wind round a fork to eat.

"How do you cook it," I asked, never having seen it before, "have you got a special long pan?"

The Professor smiled and laughed. In fact he laughed so much that he went quite red.

"What's funny? What did I say?" I asked, smiling too. Actually I hate it when adults do that, laugh at you for not knowing something. They were kids themselves one time. Kids can't know everything. It stands to reason.

"I'll show you how we cook it later on. I treated myself to a bottle of Chianti to go with it and I've bought you some cola, though much against my better judgement. I decided to go the whole hog, so I've got us some Italian starters and some tiramisu for dessert. Dinner will be at eight o'clock prompt. We have work to do."

It took about three quarters of an hour to make the meat sauce. I was tempted to say that it proved the point I'd made earlier but decided against it. Peeling and cutting up the onions made my eyes sting and water and the garlic made my hands smell. Then he made me unwrap the mince and put it into the pan.

"You always need to check underneath, often there's a sheet of paper," said Grant. "You'll have to pick it off."

I'd never handled mince before and I didn't like it.

"It's dead cow, innit?" I said.

"It's beef, yes," replied the Professor. "But not the same as that which goes into your burgers and fast food. This is free range, organic beef, Vince. Do you know what that means?"

I told him I didn't, which was true.

"There's an awful lot you don't know, Vince. I'll explain."

He told me all about factory farming and battery hens. How animals and chickens were kept in crates they couldn't even turn round in, and how they never got to see the outdoors. Most people, he said, didn't know about it or if they did they didn't care. All they were interested in was cheap food.

"This meat was more expensive Vince but that's because the animal was well treated. It lived outside in the fresh air as animals should, and it was slaughtered humanely. You shouldn't buy cheap meat Vince. Most likely the animal it came from was treated horribly."

Once again I was puzzled. Could it really be true that this man, who was threatening to do something which could kill millions of people, was worried about how pigs and chickens were treated? He must really be a nutcase.

When we'd made the meat sauce and it was simmering away, I plucked up the courage to bring up the subject of his son again.

"What did you mean when you said that your son was about my age? Did you mean when he lived here? Is he a lot older now?"

The Professor sighed.

"It's a long story Vince. I don't really want to talk about it."

I shut up and turned to one of the football mags. I wondered what it would take to get through to the Professor.

The vibration told me they wanted to say something. I made some excuse, went upstairs to my bedroom and closed the door. It was Mr Greene, not Miss Williams, the first time he'd spoken to me directly.

"Hello, Vince. I'm really proud of you. Things have taken a more serious turn at our end, Vince. We've received another letter. It was taped to a package but unfortunately they got delayed in the post. It was mailed over a week ago. The letter said that we were obviously not taking them, it used the word 'us', Vince, which is revealing in itself. Anyway, it said we were obviously not taking them seriously since the six months they gave us were almost up and nobody from Israel had been resettled in America. It gave us a week to issue a public statement of intent to move Jews out of Israel and establish a Palestinian state. If the statement is not made then a large quantity of Professor Grant's virus will be released into the open air. This is very serious, Vince, because the package attached to the letter contained traces of the virus to show us that they have it. We have not had this proof till now. As before, the package was posted in London on a day when we had Grant under surveillance and when he did not leave the house except for a few minutes. It's more evidence of a conspiracy. We've just about run out of options Vince. You've got a day, perhaps two at most and if you haven't managed to get anything more out of him by then we'll have to bring you out and have him arrested. The Americans are keener than ever to get their hands on him. At dinner tonight try to get him to drink as much of that bottle of wine as possible and find a way to get him onto the subject of the Holocaust and Israel. Perhaps you could use your History lessons at school as a way in. Maybe the alcohol will get him to open up. Do your best, Vince, we're running out of time."

Chapter 10

A while later the Professor said he was going out to buy the local evening newspaper. He'd be gone about half an hour. I was pleased to get rid of him for a bit because I hadn't had a look down in the cellar yet, and it seemed best to do that while he was really out of the way and not just working upstairs. The door to it was in the hall. I opened it and peered inside. The stairs were steep, it was dark and I had to feel about for a light switch. I flicked it on but it wasn't much help. Down below it was distinctly cooler and there was a smell of damp. I didn't like it at all. I imagined there might be rats lurking about, waiting to bite me and maybe bats too. He didn't seem to use it as a proper room. Mostly it just contained old junk and everything was very dusty. All except one of the walls were just bare bricks but the far one had been whitewashed or something and I wondered why. There were two quite large bookcases pushed up against it and high up was what I suppose you would call a trophy cupboard, just a little one with one shelf. I stood up on tiptoe to try to get a look in and saw a few small cups like you get on sports days. It struck me that David might have won them but then I realised that if he had ever won anything like that then his father would never have kept them down there. The bookcases were more promising. There were only a few old books in each but I was more fascinated by what might be behind, rather than in them. I figured that one of them might be concealing an entrance into a secret passageway or something like that and by discovering it, I would have solved the mystery. I pulled each of them away from the wall in turn and looked carefully behind but there was nothing, just wall. I even knocked on the wall in a few places but it didn't sound at all hollow. It was quite disappointing. I pushed the bookcases back again.

I suppose I was only down there for five minutes max before I'd had enough. I got an awful shock on the way out. Grant was there at the top of the stairs, waiting by the doorway and he didn't look happy.

"What were you doing down there?" he asked, in a quiet but insistent voice.

My mind was racing again, trying to think of an answer. "Just exploring. Don't mind do you? I saw the door and wondered where it led. It's a bit spooky down there. Sort of place to find creepy crawlies or dead bodies. You should do it up. Put some lino down, splash of white paint on the walls, some proper lights. When are we going to finish making the spag bol?"

Professor Grant said nothing. He stood aside to let me through, then shut the door and locked it. He put the key in his pocket.

"Perhaps that's why the men in the car outside are watching me," he said, almost whispering. "Perhaps they think there really are dead bodies in my cellar and they're waiting to catch me with another victim."

He had a wild look on his face and I was really scared.

"Cut it out will you? That's not funny. You trying to scare the living daylights out of me? Well you're bleeding well succeeding."

The look vanished and he smiled. "I'm sorry, Vince. It was a bit of fun. I didn't think you'd take it seriously. I decided not to bother with the paper today after all. I've already had a good walk to get the food. You don't really think I'm a maniac, do you?"

I saw a chance, it was an opening.

"But that's the problem. I don't know what to make of you. Those coppers in the car outside, watching you, they've been there for days. The police don't spend days watching someone's house unless they think it's really serious. You could be a serial killer for all I know. What are they doing there? What did you do? What do they think you did?"

I'd tried to speak as earnestly as possible, to make him think I was really worried. Grant looked at me and smiled.

"I told you, Vince, they think that if they wait long enough I will lead them to some other people they're looking for."

"Then those people must be really dodgy if the police want to find them so badly. If you know them why don't you just tell the police where they are? Doesn't it make you an acc..."

"An accomplice, Vince?"

"Yes that's the word, an accomplice. You must all be up to something for the police to be staking you out for so long."

"Really, Vince, I have nothing to hide. I'm just a scientist. I study viruses, that's all."

"That can't be all, can it, for them to be outside like they are? I don't know that I believe you."

"I discovered a new one."

"A new what?"

"A new virus, Vince. Something completely new to science."

"What, like swine flu? That was a virus, wasn't it?"

"A bit like that Vince, but different. This virus kills plants, not animals or people."

I interrupted again, trying to sound interested but innocent.

"So not dangerous then, if it only kills plants. Couldn't cause a, what do they call it, a pan…?"

"Pandemic. Yes it could, a pandemic among certain types of plants, the ones that we use for food, like wheat and barley. This virus kills cereal crops and if it was to take hold it could cause mass starvation. Millions of people would die."

"So it is dangerous. But why would that make the police watch you?"

"Someone is threatening to let the virus loose unless certain things happen. The police are watching me to find out if I've got anything to do with it."

I waited a few seconds, wondering if I should ask him outright. I decided I would.

"And have you?"

"Have I what?"

"Got anything to do with it?"

"I discovered the virus, Vince, so I am involved."

"That's not answering the question," I continued. "I asked if you had anything to do with the people who've threatened to let it loose. Have you?"

I was trying not to show my excitement but I was thinking that this was it, the big moment when he would admit to being part of the conspiracy. I nearly sighed in frustration when he spoke.

"I think we should finish preparing the meal Vince, these matters are too difficult for someone of your age to understand. Let's just say that you are perfectly safe with me. There are no dead bodies in my basement."

I didn't know whether to press the point or leave it but the vibration in my finger told me that they probably knew what to do. I made an excuse about having to use the bathroom.

"Felix says good work. You were almost there, Vince. Perhaps he'll say more after a few glasses of wine. Now that he's told you about the threat and our fears about him, you have lots of openings for questions without him becoming suspicious. It's looking good, Vince. Go and do the cooking now. Long pan indeed. Had us laughing as well."

I was pleased, if slightly confused and embarrassed about the long pan thing, which I still didn't understand. I soon did. Back in the kitchen the Professor had filled a large saucepan with water and put it on to boil. When it was bubbling he told me how to hold the long strands of spaghetti and push them gradually into the water as they softened. I realised my mistake but I made another when I got the cheese out of the fridge and started to grate it, like he asked.

"You've been done," I said, "it's gone stale."

He gave another of those understanding smiles.

"It's Parmesan Vince. That's how it comes. It's a hard cheese, a very hard cheese in fact. It'll be fine once you've grated it. I'll set the table. We'll do it properly, napkins and all. I haven't entertained in ages. I'm rather enjoying your company Vince. It's good to have a boy in….."

His voice faltered and his eyes began to water. I knew why and kept quiet.

The first course was olives and very thinly sliced ham. I'd never had olives before and I didn't like them but I forced myself to eat a couple just to show willing. The ham was quite different to the usual stuff I had out of packets, but very tasty.

"It's Parma ham, have you had it before?"

I shook my head and Grant went on to explain that it hadn't been cooked in any way, just hung up to cure for a long time. I felt a bit narked that I'd been conned into eating raw meat without being told and wondered how an animal that was dead and cut up into pieces could get better by being hung up for ages. Somehow, however, I guessed that I'd got hold of the wrong end of the stick and that if I asked about it everyone would be laughing again.

"Your finger, it looks strange. Is it all right?"

I felt a shiver of tension.

"It's not real. I had an accident. My finger got crushed in a door. They had to amputate it. This one's a pros…"

"A prosthesis."

"Yeah, that's the one, a prosthesis."

I was feeling more confident. I held up the finger for him to see.

"Cool, innit?"

"It does look very realistic but I'm surprised they make prosthesis for something so…well, so insignificant as a finger."

I thought quickly.

"It's not insignificant to me. They used to make fun of it at school. Called me 'half-fingered Vince' and stuff like that. It got me down so the doctor said he'd do something about it."

The Professor smiled.

"Yes, schoolchildren can be terribly hurtful without even meaning to."

The spaghetti Bolognese turned out fine. Even I could taste how much better it was than the ready cooked stuff. The Professor showed me how to manage it with a fork and spoon, curling it round and round and we both had a laugh as I made a thorough mess of it and got more of it on my chin than in my mouth, at least for the first few attempts. He suggested I use a knife and fork to cut it up and eat it normally but I was determined to get the hang of it and managed quite well in the end. I kept remembering the instruction to try to get him to drink as much as possible but the Professor needed no encouragement. The bottle was soon more than half empty. Just to be sure though, I refilled his glass as his back was turned to fetch the pudding.

I didn't much like the tiramisu, it was too bitter for my taste. Puddings are supposed to be sweet. He finished his quickly and continued to talk.

"You seem to be a clever boy, Vince. I want you to reconsider this idea of going to London. It's not just that you're too young and that London is full of dangers. What about your education, Vince? There would be no school, no learning, no qualifications. You know how important these things are. You'll be able to leave home in a few years anyway. Couldn't you hang on until then? You said you were clever at school but didn't like to show it. What if you did show it? What if you went back, tried hard, and did really well in your GCSEs? You could go on to sixth form college, university, get a good job, earn real money, not peanuts. Have you really thought it all through, Vince?"

"Ain't none of my family ever been to university," I told him. "I don't really know what one is, except it's a place for clever rich kids. Most lads round where I live get chucked out of school or leave as soon as they can. I've wondered about sixth form college though, the teachers talk about it a bit."

I paused to think. I'd had an idea and I wanted to get it right.

"My history teacher says I should do GCSE History because I'm really good at the stuff we're doing now, about Hitler."

He took the bait just like that. He looked up from his second helping of pudding, put his spoon down and turned directly to me.

"And what have they taught you about Hitler?"

This had all been prepared with Mr Greene and I knew exactly what to say.

"He was a rubbish artist and a tramp and he got to be the leader of Germany, even though he wasn't even German. He wanted revenge for the way Germany was treated after the First World War, so he started the second one and he hated Jews, so when everyone's backs was turned because of the War he rounded them up and had them slaughtered. He done it with bullets first but that was too slow, so he had these camps built. They crammed them into huts that were supposed to have showers and killed them by dropping poison pellets though a hole in the roof. Then they burned the bodies in big ovens, like kitchen ovens but much, much bigger, only still using gas. There was millions of them, six million, my teacher said. He said that Hitler used the Jews as a scape…. I forget the proper word, something to put the blame on….scapegoat, that's it, scapegoat. I knew it was about an animal. Anyway he fooled the German people into believing him. My teacher said it was the greatest crime ever done and that if there is a hell, Hitler will be right there at the bottom, along with the Devil."

I paused for breath knowing that I'd said enough. I'd made up the parts about the goat, hell and the Devil just for effect.

Professor Grant had sat still while I was speaking, then he asked calmly.

"Do you believe your teacher, Vince?"

"I dunno about the hell bit, but what do you mean?"

"I mean, do you believe that what you have been told about Hitler is true?"

"We done it in lessons. It was in the textbooks. We saw a video about it with Hitler sticking his hand up, you know, in the Nazi way and ranting on. We saw these piles of bodies being shoved around by bulldozers. Why wouldn't it be true? They wouldn't teach us it if it wasn't true."

Professor Grant pushed his dish to one side, rested his elbows on the table and placed his hands together in front of his face. I wondered if he was about to start praying but instead he began to speak.

"I've no doubt that your teacher is sincere but most teachers have never found out for themselves, they just teach what they were taught or they get it from books written by people who also got it from books. There is very little genuine research. That is what has allowed these misconceptions to be perpetuated. What you have been taught is only partly the truth. It is true that Hitler was an artist but not true that he was a rubbish one, as you put it. Many of his paintings exist. They aren't the work of a genius, true, but they do show some talent. It is also a fact that Hitler went through a difficult period of homelessness after the First World War but then many people find it hard to readjust to ordinary life after the horrors of fighting. Look at the number of British ex-soldiers who have ended up homeless and living rough after their experiences of fighting in Iraq or Afghanistan. Hitler was gassed and decorated for bravery. No doubt he suffered from depression after the war but he picked himself up and turned his life around. It is also true that Hitler was Austrian, but it is not true that he wasn't German. Austria is a German country, Vince, the people speak German. In the past it was the most important of all the German states but when these states were united by Prussia in 1871, the Prussians kept Austria out because they were afraid of Austria's potential to dominate the new Germany.

It is also true that Hitler disliked Jews, but your teacher probably didn't tell you that this dislike had existed in many countries for centuries, and that this had regularly resulted in outbreaks of violence against them. Your teacher probably didn't tell you either that Jews had brought much of this dislike on themselves because of their secretive ways and practices. People were naturally suspicious of these foreigners living among them, with a different language, different religion and different habits; people who kept to themselves and always put their own community before the good of the country.

You have been taught about the so-called 'Holocaust', Vince. There is a basis of truth in it, but what you have been told is also misleading. It is true that Jews from different countries were rounded up and sent away during the war. It is true that some of them were put to death. There is documentary evidence of this. There is corroborated testimony. Some of the firing squad executions were filmed. The films exist. There is no doubt. What is misleading Vince is the claim of six million Jews killed, and mostly by gassing. Of this there is no decisive evidence but there is plenty of proof to the contrary. It has been shown that the controlled use of cyanide gas in buildings so large would have been virtually impossible, would have killed those who went in to retrieve the bodies, or would have required such tall chimneys to safely disperse the gasses as to have been clearly visible for miles around. The same is true of the supposed gas ovens, and the crematoria used to burn the bodies. Yet the reconnaissance photographs, taken by our own RAF, during the War show that such chimneys did not exist. Experts have shown that between two and three hundred thousand Jews were put to death by the Nazis, a figure not dissimilar to the number of gypsies and other groups that were executed, but nowhere near the six million claimed. Six million is an impossibly high figure, it is a fabrication. Nor is it supported by any of the documentary evidence from the time. The Germans were meticulous about keeping records of everything they did and these records exist for the outrages I have spoken of but not for the so-called Holocaust.

Don't get me wrong, Vince, I'm not a supporter of Hitler. I'm not one of those pathetic individuals who decorate their homes with swastikas and make a religion of Nazism. Hitler was responsible for some dreadful things. He caused another terrible war. If anything I think he was a fool. When he became leader in 1933 there were no German armed forces to speak of, yet just six years later he'd built them up to such an extent that he was able to conquer most of Europe and it took the combined efforts of Russia, the USA and Britain to defeat him. Just imagine if he had been more patient, if he had waited another two or three years before unleashing his army. If he hadn't alerted the world with his idiotic demand for Czechoslovakia. The German army would have been so strong by then that Hitler could have done whatever he wanted and no leader of any other country could have lifted a finger to stop him. But Hitler was greedy and impatient, he wanted it all too soon and in so doing he brought ruin and destruction to the very country he loved so much."

Grant paused again and drained his glass.

"I was like you, Vince, I took it for granted that the Holocaust happened just the way most people said. Then I became interested, made enquiries, found out that there were people who disputed the official story, read what they said, started going to meetings. Now I know better."

"I don't understand why they would make up a story like that," I said, knowing that this would lead the Professor on.

"There are a number of reasons," replied Grant. "Firstly, Jews were treated horribly during the war and there was a lot of sympathy towards them. Some of the Jews saw a way to make money out of this sympathy by exaggerating what had happened. Millions of pounds have been paid in compensation and it's still going on. For others it was a question of revenge. Their families in Germany and throughout Europe had been displaced, some of them were dead but Hitler and most of the Nazi leadership were also dead. They couldn't get their revenge on Hitler so they decided to take it out on the German people as a whole, by inventing a crime that was so horrendous and on such a wide scale that, they argued, most Germans must have been aware of it while it was happening. Therefore, those Germans also bore some of the responsibility because they did nothing to stop it. Generations of Germans have grown up with the shame of a crime that never happened.

The final reason is the justification for the creation of the state of Israel itself. Jews had been trying to get hold of Palestine for decades. There were already numbers of Jewish settlers there but they weren't content just to live in harmony with their Palestinian neighbours. They wanted it all. They wanted all the land, all the riches, all the power, all the control. The Holocaust was the perfect excuse. 'Look at what the Nazis have done', they said. 'We will never be safe until we have our own country. You owe it to us because of what we have been through.' And finally they got their own way and the state of Israel was established.

Do you understand how unfair that was, Vince? Jews had suffered and Palestinians were to be punished for that suffering, even though they had nothing to do with what had happened to the Jews during the War. Innocent people were being made to pay for the crimes of others. Imagine, Vince, if someone in another town from you committed a crime against one of their neighbours and the authorities decided that the neighbour could have your house because of what had happened. What would you think of that, Vince?"

"It wouldn't be fair. They ought to punish the person who done it, not us."

"And what if it was later discovered that neighbour had just made the whole story up to get sympathy and there wasn't a crime after all. What would you think of that?"

"It would be right out of order. They ought to do something to put it right. They ought to punish them and give us back our house."

"And what if they didn't bother? What if they ignored the truth and just allowed that person to go on living in your house? What would you do then Vince?"

"I'd have to do something about it, take the law into my own hands if necessary."

I was smiling inside. I felt pleased. I'd taken the Professor right to the very heart of the matter. Miss Williams and the others listening in must be delighted. Now it would have to be a gamble. Grant might react badly, might become suspicious but it was worth the risk. If they were going to take me out tomorrow or the next day then I had to get the information they wanted. I looked directly into the Professor's eyes and asked him.

"Is this what it's all about? You, the virus, somebody threatening to let it loose, the police outside. Is this why the police are watching you? Is it all about Israel and the Palestinians?"

Grant didn't even stop to think.

"Yes, Vince. Things are moving to a head. They were given an ultimatum, six months to clear the Jews out of Israel and give it back to its rightful owners. They've had plenty of time, plenty of time to move them all out. Not just anywhere, mind you, not to some third world backwater, a malarial swamp in Africa or a piece of frozen tundra in Siberia. No, they were to be moved to America. The U.S.A, Vince, just think of it a huge country with masses of open space. They could easily all go and live there, somewhere out in the west. Even the climate there is similar to Israel's. It would be easy for them in America compared with what the Palestinians have had to put up with for all these years. It would be good for America, too, all those well educated people moving in and all that money saved no longer underwriting the Israeli state. It would have been a win-win situation, good for the Israelis, good for the Palestinians and good for America."

Grant was beginning to get agitated and his voice was getting louder. All of a sudden he banged his fist down on the table, hard.

"The fools haven't done it. They know what the virus can do, they know how many will die but they are prepared to risk Armageddon, rather than give justice to the people of Palestine. History will condemn them. A dark time is coming Vince. The virus will cause mayhem. There will be famine, disease, war and all because a few selfish people would not give back what they had stolen."

Grant wiped the sweat from his brow and looked around him as if to check that there was no one else there. There was one more question I needed to ask, the vital question.

"So these people who've threatened to let it loose, you're one of them too. Who are they? Is it al-Qaeda? They want to destroy Israel, don't they? It's obvious you couldn't do it all by yourself, so who are you with?"

For a few moments Grant was silent and still, as if contemplating his answer. Then he looked towards his empty glass and then at the bottle.

"Good gracious, have I drunk that much? I've got work to do Vince and I'll need a clear head for the morning. You can get down from the table. I'll clear up. I need to listen to the weather forecast. I've felt a bit like Duke William these last few days."

"What...who's Duke William? I don't understand what you're saying."

That was an understatement. One moment it looked like I was going to get right to the bottom of it all and the next he was talking gobbledegook.

"Oh don't worry Vince. I'm just talking to myself really. Go on, you get off and watch TV or have a read before bed.

Tomorrow might bring a surprise."

Up in the bathroom I turned on the tap so there was no chance of him hearing my voice and spoke to Miss Williams.

"I was so near. He almost told me. I really thought he was going to tell me who he was with. Who's this Duke William? I thought he was a prince, you know, Prince William. Him and Harry. Is there a difference? Why does he feel like him?"

Miss Williams said they didn't know. They were working on it. She told me I'd done brilliantly. The way I'd led him on had been fantastic. She was really proud of me. She said they'd all been on tenterhooks. Perkins had been on the edge of his seat, as if he was at a football game when his team were about to score.

A few minutes later I felt the finger vibrate again.

"We should have got it immediately. Perkins realised, thank goodness. William, Duke of Normandy, who won the Battle of Hastings and became William the Conqueror, waited all summer long in 1066 for the wind to change so that it would blow his invasion fleet across the Channel to England."

I remembered. We'd done it in History in Year 7.

"That's why he needs to listen to the weather forecast. We've checked with the Met Office. The wind has been blowing from the east for most of this week. That means it has been moving towards the Atlantic Ocean. Tomorrow there is a chance that it will veer round and blow towards the south east, towards the Channel and Europe. Felix says it probably means that the plotters are probably going to use the wind as their means of spreading the virus. We've not known that until now. If it's released when the wind is in a south easterly direction, it'll be blown all across Europe and perhaps into Asia too and maybe even down into Africa. It's good and bad news, Vince. Good because we now have more to go on but bad because it seems that the Professor and whoever he is conspiring with are really intending to go through with it. Felix says he definitely wants you to remain with Grant for the time being. You may be able to get even more out of him. Is that all right, Vince? Are you okay there?"

Of course I was. I knew I'd done well. I was excited. I wanted to see it through to the end. Perhaps it might even be up to me to stop them releasing their horrible virus.

"How will they get it into the air?"

I thought it might sound a stupid question but I didn't know if they could just stand in a field on a windy day and throw handfuls of it into the sky or whether they'd need a rocket or something like that.

"Felix thinks the most probable way would be from a plane or helicopter. That way it would be high enough to be taken up in the airstreams and not drift straight back down again. He's not sure though. They're discussing it right now with London. One or more balloons could be another way or from the top of a high hill, they just aren't sure but they're looking for possible locations within a fifty mile radius of here. Things are starting to move fast now. It's all because of you Vince. Well done."

That night in bed it was particularly difficult to sleep. Sometime very late on I heard floor boards creaking and the sound of footsteps on the landing. They seemed to stop and wait for a minute or two and then they went on down the stairs. I waited for ages for him to come back, wondering what he was up to and thinking that whatever it was had to be something to do with the virus or the conspiracy. In the end I got up and went downstairs as quietly as I could, hoping to be able to spy on him and find out. I could always say I'd gone down for a drink if he saw me. I couldn't find him. I looked in each and every room but he wasn't anywhere. I checked the cellar but the door was still locked. The only explanation I could come up with was that he must have slipped out of the house, so I dashed back upstairs and spoke into the transmitter to ask if they'd seen him leave and if they were tailing him. It was Perkins who answered, Miss Williams was asleep. Grant had definitely not left the house. The cameras would have picked him up and there were motion detectors too. Maybe I'd been asleep and dreamed about it. Maybe I'd heard him go downstairs but been asleep when he came back up or maybe I'd been awake and just not heard him. He told me to get back to bed. I needed to be fresh for the morning.

I did as I was told but only slept in fits and starts. It seemed that I'd hardly slept at all when there was a knock at the door and the Professor came in with tea. He looked tired too, his hair still ruffled from sleep and his face unshaven. I felt certain he must have been up half the night but I had no idea where he might have been. I remember thinking that there must be some room that I and the others hadn't found but that seemed impossible. They were experts. They would have checked out every possibility.

The radio was on when I got downstairs and a weather forecast was just starting. I began to say something but he motioned to me to be quiet. He'd said he needed to listen to a forecast the night before as well, so maybe the direction of the wind was crucial, like Miss Williams had said. I decided to ask.

"Duke William waited all summer long in 1066 for the wind to change direction. Is that what you're waiting for too? Is the wind important for the virus?"

He looked at me but his face was expressionless.

"The Battle of Hastings," I added, in case more explanation was necessary, "we did it in History. I was lying in bed and thinking about what you said and it came back to me. Year 7 had a trip to Normandy to see the Bayeux Tapestry but we couldn't afford it."

He didn't say anything.

He didn't say much all day. I kept trying to badger him with questions but he either ignored me or fobbed me off with useless answers. In the end I thought I'd better shut up in case too many questions made him suspicious. The others were frustrated too. Miss Williams said that after the previous evening they'd hoped he would open up completely but his mind seemed preoccupied to the extent that he didn't want to talk. There was still a possibility though and they wanted to leave me there just a bit longer.

He spent a lot of that day in his lab but came down at least three times to turn the radio on for the forecast. The last was early in the afternoon. I remember the broadcast clearly. It was turning cooler. The wind was veering round to come down from the north-west and was set to stay that way for a few days. It would be windy with a possibility of light showers. Soon after the forecast Grant announced that he was going out to get the paper and to buy food for the evening.

"We'll keep up the Italian theme," he said with a smile on his face, as if his mood had changed completely. "I'll make pizzas. You like pizza, don't you? Everybody likes pizza. It was David's favourite."

I pretended not to notice the 'was'. He'd never talked of his son as if he was dead before. I don't think he noticed either.

Not long after he got back there was a vibration in my finger. In the loo they told me that while he was out he'd made a call from a public telephone box. It was almost certain that it was to someone or about something he didn't want them to find out about because he could have phoned from the house or used his mobile. It happened too quickly for them to put a trace on it. He'd read the number from a scrap of paper he'd taken out of his coat pocket and then put back. They'd debated with London whether to take him in immediately to get the number but decided to use me instead. That way, if it proved to just be something ordinary, then they wouldn't have spoiled their chances. I was to see if I could get it. I mustn't let him see me, of course and I had to put it back afterwards.

It should have been easy. He usually kept his coat in the cupboard under the stairs but instead of putting it back there he hung it on the back of a kitchen chair and said we should make the dough. He measured out the ingredients and explained how the yeast would make the dough rise but that it took time which was why we were doing it so early. Then he told me what to do and sat down to watch while I got on with it. Pretty soon my hands were completely covered with all this sticky, white, dough stuff and it was then that he remembered something and left the room to fetch it. There was no way I could go through the coat pockets with my hands in that state so I tried to wash the dough off as quickly as possible at the sink. I hadn't even dried my hands when I heard him coming back. That was the only chance I got.

As soon as he sat down he went through his coat pockets and took out everything that was inside. He crumpled up several bits of paper that looked like till receipts but one bit he looked at, then folded up and put in his front trouser pocket. I knew that it must be the piece of paper with the number on. Now I've acquired a lot of dodgy skills in my time but picking front trouser pockets isn't one of them. It's much too difficult. As soon as he put it there I knew that was it. I told the others and they said not to worry but I could tell they were disappointed.

The rest of the afternoon dragged by. I had nothing to do and he worked upstairs. Much later on we finished making the pizzas. He'd got some salami to go on mine but he had anchovies and olives, and little green things he called capers, for his. He said kids didn't usually like anchovies on pizzas or anything else and he was right, because he gave me a little bit of his to try later on and it was disgusting. Mine was very tasty though. He had wine to drink but it was only the remains of the bottle from the night before and it wasn't enough to make him vaguely happy. He wasn't grumpy though. His mood had changed when he'd heard the last weather forecast and it stayed changed. Afterwards, while I was watching telly and he was reading, he looked up and told me that I would have to leave the following morning. He had to go away and I couldn't stay there on my own. When I asked him where he was going he thought for a few seconds and then he said, "I'm going to see my son. I'm going to be with David."

Chapter 11

That third night seemed to last the longest. I'd told him I wanted an early night, partly as an excuse to speak to the others but mainly because what he'd said had scared me and I wanted to get away from him. Upstairs in the bathroom, tap running to muffle the sound of my voice, I told them how afraid I was, that the Professor was clearly intent on killing himself and that I was worried he might decide to kill me as well.

"What else could he mean?" I asked anxiously, holding my finger close to my mouth.

"His son is dead, so how else could he be with him? I don't know if I want to stay here anymore."

The reply came through straight away.

"Felix is concerned too. There doesn't seem to be any other possible interpretation. We're consulting about this. We don't think he intends to harm you, Vince. Remember that he said you had to leave in the morning anyway. Tomorrow is clearly going to be the crunch day. Felix will be able to speak to you in a few minutes and tell you exactly what you should do. Try not to worry. You're doing so well. Try to stay calm."

I was quite het up by then and I got cross and told her that it was easy for her to say that when she wasn't the one alone with a madman. As soon as I'd said it I felt bad because I knew she was just trying to help. I called back and said sorry and afterwards it struck me that it might have been one of the first times I'd ever said sorry and really meant it. That and when she'd told me about the girl who'd killed herself. She said it was okay and she knew how I must be feeling.

I finished in the bathroom and went into my bedroom to wait for Mr Greene to call back. I had to wait ages. Eventually I felt the vibration in my finger and switched it into receive mode.

"Good work, my boy. Now listen: you can leave straight away if you want to. Just go down to the front door and let yourself out. I'd rather you stayed though, Vince. You've got so close to the really vital information. He might just tell you more about it in the morning, where he's going, who he'll be meeting, what the plan is, that sort of thing. We'll be following him anyway but if you could manage to find out where he's intending to go we could have men there waiting. He said you have to leave in the morning, so whatever his plans are they don't involve you. What do you think Vince? You can come out right away if you'd rather. It wouldn't ruin the mission. You've already done very well. It's your decision."

I thought about it and eventually said I'd stay. I think that was quite brave because the Professor had really spooked me but Mr Greene clearly wanted me to stay and I didn't like to let anybody down.

"Good lad. We'll be listening all night long and we're moving extra men into position around the house. Try to get some sleep. It'll all be over in the morning."

I didn't sleep well. I kept waking up and listening for any strange noises. In the middle of the night I heard his footsteps on the landing again. They stopped and I was sure he was waiting just outside my room. I was petrified. I wanted to speak into the finger and call for help. It seemed ages before I heard him moving again, going down the stairs. This time he was only gone a few minutes before he came back up. It was a relief when I heard his door shut, but even so, I didn't sleep a wink after that. The morning was a long time coming.

I didn't wait for the usual knock at the door but got up and dressed as soon as I heard him up and about. It was about half past seven when I got downstairs. Professor Grant was standing at the stove, frying bacon and sausages. He seemed relaxed and smiled when he saw me.

"How about a full English this morning? There's a lot to do."

I nodded in agreement. He seemed disappointed.

"Just a nod to say yes to bacon and eggs, with all the trimmings! I thought you'd be jumping at the thought. Didn't you sleep? I had a very good night."

Then he changed the subject.

"Where will you go? Will you still need somewhere nearby to lie low around here or do you think it's safe to head for London now?"

The question came as a surprise but he didn't give me time to answer anyway, just started going on again about how dangerous London was and how much better it would be if I went back to my parents and continued in school.

There was no real conversation during breakfast. The food was good and we both tucked in. I asked for more fried bread and he went back to the cooker to make it. I knew they wanted me to get more out of him but I wondered how to do it. Eventually I plucked up the courage to ask him about seeing his son.

"Is David far away? Will it take long to get there?"

The expression on his face changed instantly and he snapped back at me.

"What do you mean? Why do you keep asking about David?"

"You said.... last night.... that you were going to go to him today and I'd have to leave."

"Oh yes, I'm sorry, Vince, I forgot. No, it won't take long, an hour or two. Nothing for you to be concerned with."

"Is it about the virus too? Is that where it is, at your son's? Is it today when it gets released?"

"So many questions, Vince, but I don't suppose it will matter now. Yes, it is about the virus and today is the day. The wind is in the perfect direction to blow it across southern England and over to the continent. Within a few days it will reach northern Africa and central Asia. After that, nowhere will be safe from it. I told you that things were coming to a head."

"You'll never get away with it. The men outside in the car, watching you, they'll follow you and stop you."

"Not this time, Vince. They won't be able to follow me this time. They don't know the half of it. No, I'll be on my own. Nothing can stop me."

He wasn't worked up or shouting. He spoke calmly as if he really had got it all under control. I was totally confused. How could it be that he wouldn't be followed? How would he get away? And if no one did follow him what was to stop him or whoever he was going to meet, from letting loose the virus?

"You need to get ready to leave now, Vince. Can I make you some sandwiches? I'll give you some money to tide you over for a couple of days. I have to go soon."

I don't know what made me say it. I was thinking that if they couldn't follow him then the only person who might be able to was me, but how would I be able to do that without him seeing?

"I'm coming with you. I want to see how you do it."

He looked at me and smiled.

"Completely out of the question. It's nothing to do with you. You'd only get in the way."

"If everybody was starving it would be to do with me. I'm part of everybody. I'd be starving too."

"I'm sorry Vince. You've been good company these past few days."

"If you don't take me with you I'll just go out and warn the men outside right now, before you have time to leave. Please take me with you. I wouldn't get in the way. I could tell people about you afterwards, explain why you did it, tell them that you weren't just some sort of nutter. You'd have to go into hiding, wouldn't you? You couldn't tell them yourself."

He was quiet for a few seconds.

"I have already made plans so that people will know why I did it, why governments are to blame for not preventing a tragedy and..."

"I promise to behave. What do you think it would be like for me to have you go off and not know whether you done it or not? Please let me come."

He stayed quiet for several more seconds.

"Why not, I don't suppose you could do any harm? It might be sensible for someone else to see and be able to give witness if I'm not able to. All right then, but you must do exactly as I say at all times. Is that clear? Do you promise?"

I promised.

"We'll leave in fifteen minutes prompt, half past the hour. Go and get yourself ready. We'll do it together Vince."

The finger started vibrating at once. Miss Williams said I was not to go, definitely not. She sounded cross. I reminded her about what the Professor had said about not being followed. What if he was right and they couldn't follow him to stop him? I had to go. She said that was exactly why I shouldn't go. How would they be able to protect me if they couldn't follow? It was much too dangerous. I hadn't thought of that, hadn't thought that they might not be able to follow me as well. But I had the finger. I could keep speaking, telling them things. They would be able to follow me because of the finger. She didn't sound convinced when I told her that but she wasn't so sure any more. Mr Greene came on and asked if I was really serious, if I was really prepared to go with the Professor. They hadn't planned for it, not thought out the possibilities. Anything might happen. I might be on my own. Could I handle it?"

"Bloody hell," I thought, "I've really dropped myself in it this time."

I didn't have much to do, just clean my teeth really. There was nothing much to pack, just the few things in my bag. The Professor was on the landing as I came out, standing outside his son's room. The door was open and there were tears in his eyes. When he saw me he quickly pulled it shut and went down the stairs. I gave him a minute before following. Downstairs, Grant was waiting in the hall by the cellar door. His eyes were dry. He already had his coat on and he was turning the key in the lock. Looking back, I know I should have said something, asked him why we were going down into the cellar, something like that to alert the others. I just didn't think to. Once inside he re-locked the door.

"What are we doing down here?" I asked.

He said nothing but went to the side where there were a few tools and bits of junk. He picked up a small wooden ladder and pointed to the far wall.

"That's what we're doing down here Vince."

"What, the wall? I don't get it."

"It might look like a wall and indeed it is but it's also the entrance to my secret world. Let me show you."

Professor Grant walked over and reached up to the door of the trophy cupboard. He tugged at the handle and the door opened outwards. Then he propped the ladder up against the lower edge of the cupboard and climbed up a few steps. He reached in and felt around on one side and I heard a faint click. Then he climbed up another step and pushed against the single shelf. It swung backwards, taking its small collection of cups and the back of the cabinet with it. They disappeared from sight.

The Professor got down from the steps and smiled at me.

"In there, that's my secret world. You go first. It'll be a bit of a squeeze, even for you. Try not to put too much weight on the cupboard itself. It's reinforced but we don't want to try our luck. There's a ledge on the other side. It goes back for a bit and then there are some steps down. Here, take this torch to help."

I climbed up and pointed the torch inside. There wasn't much to see. It was a bit like a cave or tunnel, just about as wide as a doorway, with only a narrow space between the ledge and the top. Not much like a secret world, more like a dungeon. I was panicking a bit at that point, afraid that it was just a trap that he was going to wait till I was inside, then shut me in and leave me to die. He was telling me to go on, asking what I was waiting for. In the end I just forced myself, put my arms in, then my head and pulled myself through as quickly as possible.

The ledge only went a few feet. I leaned over the edge and saw a ladder, tied into place, going down a few feet to some more steps that went further down. I turned myself round to climb down and saw his head coming through from the other side.

When he was onto the ledge he turned round too but then he reached back in, got hold of the ladder and pulled it up and through. He passed it to me. Then he reached back in again, tugged at the cupboard door to close it and then swung the back of the cupboard, with the shelf with the cups on, back into place. They clicked shut.

I was pretty much gobsmacked. It was dead clever. No one would have possibly guessed that a small, narrow cupboard half way up the wall would have led anywhere. He explained that there used to be a proper doorway but he'd bricked it up, leaving only the small opening and then he'd painted the wall to disguise it. He'd even backfilled with earth and rubble on the other side to create the ledge and so that there would be no tell-tale hollow sound if anyone knocked where the door used to be. No wonder Mr Greene's men had missed it.

I was calmer by then. At least he hadn't shut me in. He led the way down the steps to a passageway, narrow but high enough for me to walk in without stooping. It was lined with bricks and dripping wet. I remembered about the others, wondered if they understood where we were. The sound down there echoed and distorted and I wanted to make sure they knew.

"What is this tunnel on the other side of the cellar wall?" I said, as if I was asking him.

As soon as I said it I felt really nervous because it must have sounded so strange but he just said it was a funny way of putting it and then he told me.

"I only found out about it a few years after we moved in. The people before us left the cellar full of junk and I didn't even know about the door because there was a huge bookcase in front of it. When I did eventually decide to have a clear-out I moved the bookcase and found the door. About the same time I came across a diary written by the person who lived here during the war. He didn't only own the house, he had a factory next door that made propeller blades for aeroplanes. When war was imminent people were told to dig bomb shelters in their gardens. This man already had the cellar to use as a shelter but he was worried that the factory would make the whole vicinity a prime target for the German bombers. He was afraid that a direct hit could bring the house down on top of the shelter, so he had a second one constructed several hundred yards away where he thought it would be safer. There were no other streets around here then. It was just the factory, the house and its grounds."

We were walking as he talked, Grant leading the way, picking out the walls of the tunnel in the torchlight, with me following on behind. It was cold down there and very damp.

I was quite edgy. My fear that he was leading me into a trap returned. You start to imagine all sorts of things in a place like that. He just carried on talking.

"According to his diary, after he'd had the shelter built he decided that it might be dangerous to leave the house during an air raid to reach it, so he had this tunnel constructed. Must have cost him a lot of money but then, as a factory owner, I suppose he was well off. It was a very prudent idea as the house did take a direct hit from the Luftwaffe. One side of it was completely demolished, and never rebuilt. The factory closed down and was demolished after the War and he gradually sold off the grounds as building plots to finance his retirement. He never wrote about the air raid shelter again. His last entry was in the mid 1960s. He was about to leave to go to live in Cornwall."

"To begin with I didn't pay it much attention. The door into the tunnel was locked and there was no key. The thought never entered my mind that I should break the lock and have a look at what was on the other side, but I looked through the local council papers from the war years to see if he'd submitted any plans that might tell me where the tunnel led. There was nothing. I don't know if you would have needed planning permission in those days but he certainly didn't have it. In the end curiosity got the better of me and I took a heavy hammer, broke the lock and found the tunnel. That was quite a few years ago. There, we're nearly at the end now."

Ahead of us in the torchlight I could make out another door. As we reached it I noticed a humming noise from the other side. Grant undid the bolts at the top and bottom of the door and opened it. The humming sound was instantly louder. He flicked a switch and bright light flooded out. It was a second or two before my eyes became accustomed to it.

"My other laboratory, Vince: the important one. I hope you're impressed."

The room that had once been the bomb shelter was quite small and narrow but it had been painted a gleaming white and it was full of scientific apparatus. There were computers too and a line of narrow containers from which the humming came. Grant pointed to them.

"These are the incubators Vince, where I grow the virus."

"What, you mean you were serious about the virus?" I asked. "I kind of thought it was just a joke. Are you really going to let it loose?"

"We are Vince, you and I both, today. There's just one more job to do before it's ready. You'd better put these on."

He handed me a surgical mask and goggles.

"You're going to let it out in here?"

"No Vince, not now. This other container over here contains pollen that has to be mixed with the virus. The virus is harmless to humans but the pollen could give you an allergic reaction, a bad dose of hay fever. I'm not affected but you may be."

I put on the mask and the goggles whilst Grant connected one end of a plastic tube to the line of incubators and attached the other end to the container holding the pollen. Then he flicked a switch and the whirr of a motor cut in. He waited for a minute or two and then turned off the motor and disconnected the tube.

"You can take them off now. This is it, Vince, the virus and the pollen that's going to spread it around the world. I've beaten them all, Vince. Every step of the way I fed them the information I wanted and they swallowed it all, hook, line and sinker, just as I intended."

"I'm confused," I blurted out. "I don't understand. What are you on about? You could at least explain it properly."

It was at that moment that I noticed the other door. It dawned on me immediately, how it was true that Mr Greene's men wouldn't be following. He could come and go from this place as he pleased. Then it all fell into place. His own secret lab, the place where he made the virus, his own private entrance. It was just him. He could've done it all on his own. He had done. There wasn't anybody else, no conspiracy, just him alone, Professor Grant on his own. And, as if to show me that my ideas were completely right, he did as I'd asked and calmly explained it all.

"I was forgetting, Vince. There's still a lot you don't

know. When I discovered the virus my first thoughts were to keep it to myself, not to tell anyone, not even my colleagues. I was so worried that it might fall into the wrong hands and become a tool for terrorists or a weapon of blackmail, or that some madman might let it loose just for the hell of it. Then I got to thinking about the wrongs that had been done to the people of Palestine and how the Israelis had resisted all efforts to arrive at a reasonable solution that would benefit both sides. How they had continued to take over Palestinian land and build their illegal settlements on it. How they condemned the inhabitants of Gaza to life in a living hell. And I realised that the only thing that would make them change, the only thing that could bring justice to Palestine, was a threat of real and imminent devastation and that my virus had the power to become that threat. At that point I considered contacting anti-Israeli groups and working through them but the dangers were too great. They could be under surveillance themselves. They might take the virus and use it in ways I had not intended. They might sell it to someone dangerous like Bin Laden or the despot who runs North Korea. It was just too much of a risk."

The Professor was busy as he talked, turning off incubators, logging off the computers.

"So in the end, Vince, I knew I had to do it on my own. But I also knew that doing it on my own would be difficult. They would have to have proof that the virus existed and that proof would inevitably lead them to me. I'm the world's leading expert on plant viruses. My research data at the university, the testimony of my colleagues, everything would lead them to me and once they were aware of me, they would have investigated further and found out about my time in Egypt, my views on the Holocaust and on the Palestinians. And once they had done that they would put two and two together, identify me as the source of the threat, arrest me and effectively prevent me from carrying out the plan. That was my greatest fear and the only solution that I could see was to make them believe that I was not alone, that I was part of a group and that the others would be able to carry on without me. In that case I was certain that they could not detain me for long. They needed me free, on the outside, able to lead them to the other conspirators."

"This place and the tunnel were the keys that would allow that to happen. As long as they didn't know of their existence then I had a way of slipping out of the house without them knowing, with them thinking I was still inside. That's why it was so useful that the man who had the tunnel built never applied for any permission. It isn't mentioned on any plans. As far as anyone else is concerned it doesn't exist and there is nothing else on the other side of that cellar wall. The only gamble was that they might remove the screws that fix the cabinet to the wall to look behind but why should they? Nobody in their right minds would possibly think that there might be some hidden passageway behind a small cupboard two thirds of the way up a wall. I'm quite proud of that cupboard, Vince. I built it myself. The bottom has a wood veneer but under that is a steel frame that provides the necessary strength. Even the dust is glued on to make people think that no one has touched it in ages. I did it all myself. On the other side of this door here, there are some steps that lead to the back garden of a house that's a full two streets away from my own. When I finally got the door open I introduced myself to the owner, an elderly gentleman I'd seen about from time to time. He'd been down a few times but never through the other door into the tunnel. We became friendly. I began to do odd jobs for him, fetching groceries, mending fuses, that sort of thing. I told him how the tunnel led to my own house, how it was a much quicker, easier way of getting between the two. I told him I needed a space like this for my work, asked if I could do it up. Gradually I was able to convert it into the lab I needed, and to come and go whenever I wanted. The last piece of the puzzle was his car. When he began to find it difficult to drive and was going to sell it, I persuaded him to keep it on, to add me as an unnamed driver to his insurance. In return I'd pay the expenses, do his shopping, and take him for rides in the countryside. It made the rest very easy. All the important letters I sent, the threats to unleash the virus, all of them were posted in London. I'd get up in the early hours, come through here, drive down to London and post them and get back in time to leave the house for a morning stroll and all the time them thinking I'd been tucked up safely in bed. And of course, if they thought that I hadn't posted the letters then someone else must have posted them instead, so there had to be others involved in the plot."

I'd almost stopped listening by then. He was just going on and on as if he was so proud of what he'd done, he just had to boast about it to someone, even a kid like me. My mind was already thinking about how the others would be reacting to what he was saying. They were probably cheering away at the other end. Mr Greene and Perkins and all the others at MI5, the Americans, the Israelis, whoever else, they'd spent nearly six months trying to find out if there was a conspiracy, who it involved, where they were and where the virus was produced. I'd found it all out in three days. They must really be ecstatic. They'd probably got men in the tunnel already, coming to get Grant and rescue me. It was all over bar the shouting. I'd won. I'd definitely won. I really was a hero. And suddenly, without ever meaning to, without thinking about it, I found myself holding up my finger and shouting at it.

"Did you hear that, did you hear? It's all you need. I've done it, I've done it. He's on his own. There's no one else involved. There's no conspiracy. There aren't any others, only him on his own. Now get me out. Get me out now. It gives me the creeps. Here, now, please…"

Grant just stood there, rigid, astonished. I don't suppose he had any idea what was going on. Then, after a few seconds, his look of bewilderment turned into one of menace and hate. He lunged at me. I didn't have time to react, to move out of the way or anything. He grabbed my wrist hard and pulled me towards him. Then he yanked my arm round and pushed me to the floor with his knee in my back to pin me down. He was twisting my arm so much and the pain was so bad that I thought it would come off altogether.

"What's happening?" he shouted. "You'd better tell me the truth now. I haven't got time for games."

"My arm," the pain made it a struggle to speak, "you're killing me. Please let it go."

Grant relaxed the pressure slightly and the pain eased.

"I'll tell you," I said. "It doesn't matter now. You're finished. I'm with them, with MI5. They sent me in. You're not so clever now. They know everything, they've heard everything. My finger, it's not just a finger, it's a radio too, a transmitter. They've heard every word you've said. They'll be on their way already. It's all over. Give up. Just give up, please. I know all about it, all about how your wife went off with the bloke from Israel, how the driver that knocked over your boy was Jewish. It turned your mind. You're not really bad, it's just made you go a bit crazy, that's all. Give up now. They'll be here any second. It's all over."

He let go of my arm and took his knee off my back. I rolled over to face him. He looked...well, he looked devastated.

"You know all that?" he said, speaking in little more than a whisper.

"I told you I'm with MI5. They know how much like David I look. They thought you would be taken in by it."

"They sent a boy…? They sent a boy?"

I could only nod. He stumbled over to a chair, sat down and buried his face in his hands. I could hear him whispering the name of his son, over and over.

"I'm sorry," I said and I really meant it too. I thought he was going to cry.

"Let me see it."

Professor Grant had stood up suddenly, with that wild look on his face again.

"What? See what?"

"Your finger, show it to me."

He wasn't whispering any more. I lifted my left arm towards him. He took hold of it roughly with one hand and held the finger with his other. He looked at it for a moment and before I had time to do anything, he gave a sharp, hard tug and the finger came away in his hand. The pain was bad, much worse than when you rip a plaster off. The end of the stump was already bleeding. He didn't say anything, just reached into a drawer and took out a sharp knife. I was terrified for a moment, scared that it was meant for me but he put the finger on the worktop and pressed down hard with the blade to cut through the plastic and split it down the middle. He looked at it with a magnifying glass and used some tweezers to pull out a small fragment.

"Very interesting, Vince. There's certainly some electronic circuitry in here but look at this my boy," he said calmly, pushing the tweezers and what they were holding up to my eyes. "This is the battery. It's so very small and weak. It certainly couldn't send a message through the many tons of rock and earth between here and the surface. Whoever is supposed to be listening, MI5 you said, yes I suppose that is plausible but I doubt very much if they've heard a single word that has been said down here. In fact I doubt if they've heard anything at all since we went into the cellar. Listen, Vince," he paused at that point for several seconds and looked around, "do you hear anyone coming to rescue you? I can't hear anyone. You're on your own. It seems you haven't 'done it', as you put it. In fact it seems that the only thing you've done is to give the game away to me."

I listened as hard as I could, desperately hoping to hear the sound of rescuers. I knew he was right, the only sound was silence.

Whilst he was speaking, Grant had reached into the open drawer again and taken out a roll of sticky tape, not the transparent stuff you use for wrapping presents but the wide, tough stuff for sending parcels. He asked if I wanted him to tie me up by force or the easy way. I didn't really have a choice so I held my hands out together in front of me.

"No, not in front Vince, too easy to undo. Behind would be better, more secure. Turn around."

He didn't just bind my wrists, he wrapped the tape right around my body too, so I couldn't move my arms either and he did the same with my legs and feet. I only tried to struggle when he put it over my mouth. I thought I wouldn't be able to breathe but he stopped before my nose and he left my eyes uncovered too. When he was finished he lifted me off my feet and lay me down on the floor.

"I'm sorry we have to say goodbye like this Vince. In fact I'm rather sorry that I ever set eyes on you. It was a wicked thing to do, impersonating David like that. You very nearly wrecked my plans, but very nearly isn't good enough. You blew it, Vince, right at the very end. When you were so close to winning, you blew it. I don't think that there's anything that can stop me now. Goodbye, Vince, goodbye forever."

With that he picked up a bag that was on the printer and the container with the virus and pollen inside. Then he moved quickly to the door, opened it and went through, flicking the light switch as he did, so that the room was instantly in complete darkness. I heard the grating of the key as he locked the door and the clatter of his feet on the steps outside. Then he was gone.

Chapter 12

I lay there on my side in the darkness. The tape across my mouth was so tight it hurt. I listened, hoping to hear sounds from the tunnel, the sounds of the others coming to rescue me. There was nothing. After a couple of minutes I did hear something very faint, the rumble of a car starting up, then fading away as it drove off. I presumed it was the Professor.

I felt utterly miserable. Grant had got away, he had the virus and he was intending to release it that day. I knew what he'd said was true, that I'd blown it. Just when I thought I'd succeeded, I'd blown it. I should have realised they wouldn't have been able to receive a signal from down there. I should have had the sense to keep quiet until we were outside. Then it would have been okay to shout into the finger or maybe just snatch the container off him and do a runner. Now he was gone and the others were probably still waiting, wondering what was happening. Misery turned to panic as it suddenly occurred to me that if they hadn't heard anything, then they still wouldn't know about the trophy cabinet. They'd think we had slipped out of the house some other way and I'd be left down there, all alone in the darkness, slowly starving to death. I felt like crying.

My ears were tuned to the silence by then. After a bit I made out the whir of another engine but getting nearer this time. It must have been very near when it cut out. My mind was racing again. Could it be them? Was I going to be rescued after all? Someone hurried down the steps, the sound of a key grated in the lock. The door opened, light streamed into the room and there, once again, was Professor Grant.

"Don't struggle or try to make a noise," he instructed. "It probably means I've gone soft but it occurred to me that they might never find you. You would have starved. I shouldn't be worried, should I, especially now I know the truth about you; but it is not in my nature to leave a child to die like that. I'll have to take you with me after all."

With that the Professor bent down and pulled me up by the shoulders to get me on my feet. Then he propped me over his shoulder and carried me outside. As he turned to lock the door my head grazed the wall behind. I could see it coming but there was nothing I could do. It hurt like hell. He didn't even notice. At the top of the steps he stopped for just a second or so, checking, then he made a dash for the car. He bundled me into the back and told me not to struggle, as if I could anyway, trussed up like that. At least I was facing forward and able to see a bit, the back of Grant's seat and his head, sticking up. I watched as he put on a wig and glasses. He'd thought of everything.

As the car started to move he wondered aloud whether to drive past his house to see what was happening.

"Better not, they might be stopping everything that's moving. I expect they'll be getting worried about you by now, Vince. It's some time since you finger was working. A clever idea that. I must say you answered very coolly when I asked you about it the other evening. I would tell you where we're going, except that you just might have some other tricks up your sleeve. You'll just have to wait and see."

He drove on for some time, about twenty minutes I reckon, without saying anything else. I could tell we were out of the town because there were far fewer buildings and more trees. He stopped twice, about ten minutes apart, each time leaving the engine running while he was out of the car for just a few seconds. After the second stop he turned round to explain.

"I've been posting letters Vince. I thought it better to use two post boxes some way apart, less chance of something going wrong. Letters to politicians, newspapers, religious leaders, anyone who can make their voice heard. Fifty letters Vince, explaining that the Israelis had the chance to prevent this disaster but chose not to. Fifty letters saying that the virus has been unleashed, and warning of what will follow. Fifty letters that will tell the world that it is the Israelis' fault. Israel is doomed. No one will lift a finger to help them after this. The people of Palestine will be avenged. The Israelis will lose. They could have had it easy in America, but no Americans will help them when the virus gets to work and they learn the truth. Israel will get the blame."

He drove on. It was an old car and it had sounded a bit

ropey from the start but within a few minutes it was sounding distinctly worse. The engine was coughing and spluttering and I could feel us losing speed. Eventually it stopped altogether. I was quite elated to think that his plans might have been wrecked by an old banger and he must have thought so too. I'd not heard him swear before, let alone use the f-word but he said it then, several times. He got out and I heard him lift the bonnet up. A little later I could make out the growl of another car coming towards us and the sound of its brakes as it stopped. I was excited. All the driver needed was a glimpse of me in the back to know that something was very wrong. It never happened. I heard Professor Grant thanking him for stopping but saying said that he could manage on his own. Then the car drove off. Almost immediately one of the back doors opened and Grant was there, apologising.

"I'm sorry to have to do this to you Vince but I can't take the risk of anyone else stopping, even a police car maybe, with you trussed up like this. It would take bit of explaining, wouldn't it?"

With that he leant in and grabbed hold of my feet. One thing that the whole experience taught me was how many different thoughts can go through your mind in a really short space of time. It was like that then. First I thought he was going to push me off the seat and put me on the floor. Then I was afraid that he'd dump me by the side of the road and drive off but then I figured that it would have to be in a ditch or on the other side of a hedge, so I'd be hidden from view. Then I really started panicking that maybe he was just going to kill me after all. And all that time I was still lying there on the seat, as he waited while another car went by and until there was no traffic noise at all. I was wrong about his intentions. It was none of those things. He put me in the boot instead. It was horrible. I had to have my knees bent to fit in and even so I was really cramped up. There was no carpet, just bare metal, cold against my face. I was lying on tools, too. It wasn't just uncomfortable. They dug into me and hurt. The worse thing was when he pushed the lid down shut and it went completely dark. That was really horrible. I heard him tinkering with the engine for a few more minutes, then came a bang and judder as he closed the bonnet. I felt the car sink down a bit as he got back in and then he tried the ignition a few times and the engine started up. I had this sinking feeling as we set off again.

It was much bumpier in the boot than it had been in the back. My head banged on the bare metal and the tools really hurt me. I knew I'd be bruised. I wouldn't have been surprised if I was bleeding too. I think that was the worst thing I'd been through up till then, being cramped up in the dark and bumped about and still with all that tape around me and over my mouth. I tried to keep calm, telling myself that it couldn't be much farther. The thing that got me worked up the most was that I remembered an item on the local news on the telly; you know, the bit they have after the main one. It was about some dogs that had been put in the boot of an old car and when the driver got to wherever he was going they were dead. It was the fumes from the exhaust that killed them and the reporter said that it should be a warning to everyone never to travel in the boot.

It's difficult to keep track of time in that sort of situation. I tried counting Mississippi's, but kept forgetting how many I'd got to. I think he must have driven on for about another fifteen minutes before he stopped. He got out for about a minute, then he got back in and we started off again, only this time it was very slowly and even more bumpy. I could tell from the sound that we were off the road. We only went a few yards and then he stopped yet again. This time he got out, opened up the boot and looked in, smiling. I felt very relieved but I think it was more the stopping and the light than seeing him smile.

"You get out here, Vince. Don't worry; I'll come back for you later. It may take about twenty minutes or so but I will be back. Don't try to move. You'll be perfectly safe."

With that he reached in and pushed his arms underneath me to scoop me up and lift me out. He ran with me half over his shoulder but only for a few yards before he stopped, already puffing, and put me down on my feet. We were in a grassy field, in it but very near the edge where a hedge formed the boundary. I could see an open gate, with the car just beyond, on the verge. Then he picked me up again and struggled on a few yards further away from the gate, to where the hedge was higher. This time he laid me down on the grass. It was cold and damp. He didn't say anything else, just went back to the car, got in and drove away.

As soon as he was gone I tried to get myself up onto my feet but couldn't manage it. I was able, however, to flip myself over so I was facing the other way, looking into the field rather than at the hedge. I couldn't see much more. The land seemed to slope down towards the hedge, so all I could see was the few yards of grass in front of me. At least there weren't any animals, bulls or things like that. I'm not very good with wild animals, or even pets, come to think. I wasn't sure that he would really come back for me. I pictured myself being out there for hours and hours and wondered how cold it would get in the night. Perhaps I might even freeze or starve to death. I tried to struggle against the tape all around me but I couldn't loosen it at all. Then I wondered how I'd feel if he did return. He'd said he'd be gone for twenty minutes and I figured that was all the time he needed to carry out his plan to release the virus and it was all my fault because I'd lost the plot and messed everything up in the shelter. I was on the verge of tears at that point, feeling so guilty that I'd let everyone down but I really gritted my teeth against it, not out of bravery but for fear that crying would block my nose and I'd suffocate.

It was very quiet out there, not even the sound of birds chirping or leaves rustling. Wrong time of year, I suppose. Every so often my hopes would be raised by the rumble of a distant car coming towards me, only for me to be disappointed when it went straight past without even slowing down. Once I heard this squeaking, faint at first but getting louder and I struggled to think what it could be before I realised it must be a cycle. I tried everything to get the rider's attention, whimpering, clearing my throat, any sound I could make with my mouth closed shut. I lifted my legs and banged them on the grass, rolled over and over to try to get nearer the hedge. All I achieved was to hit my head on a stone in exactly the same spot where the Professor had grazed it. I'd forgotten about that until then, but I couldn't after. It made it hurt like hell again. I suppose the Professor was gone about half an hour although it seemed longer just lying there. Then I heard the sound of another engine but this time coming from inside the field, much louder and rougher than a car usually makes, so that I thought that it might be a motorbike or maybe a tractor. It was a plane, not a big jet but a small plane with a propeller at the front, just one, in the middle. It wasn't flying, just bouncing along on the ground. As it came over the brow of the slope it seemed to be heading straight for me and I was frightened it was going to hit me but it slowed down and then I could see Professor Grant in the cockpit.

It was such a surprise that I didn't think anything at first but then the thoughts came flooding in, like he hadn't gone off to release the virus but to get the plane. He was going to drop the virus out of the plane so it would get into the jet streams, like Mr Greene had thought the previous night. But I hadn't heard any plane flying about, just this one coming towards me, so he hadn't done it yet. He was coming to get me for us to do it together. He'd said we would, me and him. So if he still had the virus and he was coming to get me, there was still a chance that I could stop him.

The plane came to a halt just a few yards away. I saw the cockpit door open and Grant stepped out onto one of the wings, then jumped down to the ground and came towards me. As he did so he took a penknife out of a pocket and pulled out the blade but I knew he wasn't going to stab me. He could have killed me plenty of times already if he'd wanted. Instead he started to cut through the tape around my hands, body and legs and to pull it all away, all except the stuff over my mouth.

"You can come with me or stay here," he said, shouting to make himself heard above the sound of the engine. "There's nothing you can do now to stop me but I'll take you up with me if you like. You said you wanted to see how it happened. Please yourself, but I'm leaving immediately."

Grant climbed back up onto one wing and called out to me to do the same on the other. It wasn't easy. My body, my arms, my legs; nothing was working right after being tied up tight for so long. He could see I was struggling so he jumped down and helped me to clamber up onto the wing and then through the door and into the seat. As I got into the plane I could see the container, down by the side of the other seat. For a few seconds I thought I would be able to grab it as he was going back round the other side to get in but instead of that he just came through the same door as I had and climbed over me to get into his seat. Once we were both strapped in he pushed the container right down by his side, his far one, so I couldn't even see it.

"This is something else your friends don't know about."

He was explaining again.

"I got my private pilot's licence out in Egypt but they spelled my name wrong on the paperwork. It was no problem out there and it seemed too much of a bother to get it put right when we got back here, so it's just been left like that. I always pay in cash and use the University address for correspondence with the flying club. They think I'm Peter Brant. That spot back there, where I picked you up, it can't be seen from the control tower. They'll want to know what I was doing. Call of nature seems a reasonable explanation, don't you think?"

Grant adjusted the microphone on his radio headset and began to speak into it. He was taxiing the plane across the grass and I could see the runway ahead. As he spoke I realised they'd be able to hear me too and I desperately pulled at the tape around my mouth. It was stuck hard and it hurt a lot but I managed to pull it down far enough to start screaming for help. It was no good. He'd already finished speaking and he wasn't even bothered.

"You can scream all you like," he said calmly. "They can't hear you now and even if they could there's nothing they can do to prevent me taking off. I told you Vince, you blew it, back there in the lab. Now be a good boy please, and sit back and be quiet. It's not every day you get the chance of a free flight."

It was a few seconds before either of us said anything more.

"Is this it then?" I asked, eventually. "You fly up in the sky and release the virus up there? What's the pollen for? What did you mean yesterday about going to see your son?"

"Questions, questions, always such a lot of questions. Such an inquisitive boy you are, Vince. Still, I suppose you have the right to know. Pollen, Vince: individual spores are too small to see but the air is full of them, especially at certain times of the year, and pollen can travel thousands of miles in the airstreams. Did you know that people who suffer hay fever early in the year are being affected by tree pollen blown over to us from Scandinavia? The virus needs something to carry it. It can't really exist on its own. That's what the pollen is for. My virus attaches itself to the pollen. Once it has it can live for many days, even weeks before it needs to find a living cereal plant to settle on, infect and reproduce in, before it dies. It doesn't mind the cold, up there in the airstreams. And today they will take the pollen and the virus along with it, across southern England and on into Europe. Eventually it will be blown right round the world. Cells will come down every here and there. They will infect a few plants and in those plants the virus will reproduce and then insects, birds, more pollen, will spread it around, so that soon all the cereal plants in each region will be infected. There is no cure. The plants will die."

He seemed to pause mid-sentence but I knew I needed to get him onto another tack. He could've gone on about the virus for ages.

"And seeing your son? How will you manage that?"

"My work will be done Vince. I'll have nothing left to live for. Once I have released the virus I intend to continue to ascend. Eventually I will be so high there won't be enough air. I will blackout but the plane will continue until it goes into a stall or runs out of fuel. Then it will crash. I will be killed. I will be with David again. It is all I want."

"So that's what's going to happen to me then? I'm going to die as well?"

"No Vince. I wouldn't want that. There is one change to the plan. After we've released the virus I will land the plane one last time. You will get out and I will take off again.

You can tell them everything. By then it won't matter."

We'd reached the end of the runway. I don't really remember what I was thinking. I'd never been in a plane before and this one, a two-seater, was not what I'd imagined for my first flight. I didn't know what to expect, what it would be like. I was trying to concentrate on the virus, on somehow stopping the Professor, but I was also fascinated by the plane and the prospect of flying. I think I must have been a bit hyper at that point. Grant turned the plane round to prepare for take-off. He pulled the throttle back to reach maximum power. The noise was intense. Grant held the plane there for a few more seconds, making the final checks on the controls and then he released the brakes. The plane surged forward. There was a terrific rumbling from the tyres along the runway and the whole thing shook, not just a little but really badly, like it was shaking itself apart. We were really hurtling along. Then, I suppose it was when the wheels left the ground, all the vibration and most of the noise was gone instantly and it was suddenly peaceful. I looked out of the window and saw the ground falling away as we climbed steeply and the sight of it really took my breath away. It was exciting and frightening at the same time, like at a theme park on a roller-coaster when your stomach seems to jump up inside you.

It was a dual control plane, a Cessna, I found out later. Dual control means it had controls in front of each seat so that either person could fly it. As the Professor turned the thing that looked like a steering wheel, the one on my side moved too, the same way. I put my hands on it to see what it felt like and I saw the Professor smile.

"You have control," he said.

"What? What does that mean?"

"You have control," he repeated, only that time he took his hands off the wheel. "The plane is in your hands. Try turning the stick gently and see what happens."

I did as he said, very gingerly and saw the left wing begin to drop as the plane started to turn.

"Bring it level again and then see what happens if you pull or push on the joystick instead of turning it. Do it gently though."

I pulled and saw the nose of the plane rise up and felt the plane begin to climb.

"It's easy isn't it? Push it back again until we're level. This instrument here, it's sometimes called an artificial horizon." Grant pointed to one of the dials in front. "Look at it as you turn one way or the other. It shows you when you're level or turning or ascending or descending. The idea is to bring it back to level after each manoeuvre. The line between the blue and the brown is like the horizon between sky and earth. It's very useful when you're flying through cloud or at night."

I watched the dial and saw it respond to each movement of my hands on the stick.

"This is the throttle. If you press it forward gently you'll feel the power increase and you will go faster. Have a go."

I tried and the engine noise increased abruptly.

"Gently I said Vince, just a little."

It was fascinating, too fascinating. There still was important stuff to do and it struck me that he might have been deliberately trying to take my mind off it. I remembered what Mr Greene had said about the Holocaust.

"*Don't believe what he says. He may sound convincing but all his arguments have basic flaws. You need to know them. It may be that you will have to convince Grant that the Holocaust cannot be denied. It might make him reconsider.*"

It seemed that Mr Greene was right. It was up to me to convince him.

"All that stuff you told me about the Holocaust not happening, you don't seriously believe that do you?" I'd started abruptly; there had been no time to think of a gentle way to bring up the subject.

He took it calmly, didn't seem irritated, annoyed or anything like that.

"I explained it to you earlier. Some of it happened but on a much smaller scale. The whole thing was exaggerated so that the Jews could get hold of Israel. There was no systematic killing by poison and no gas ovens."

"That's rubbish. I've seen pictures of them. It wasn't only the Jews that told people about them. Even German soldiers talked about it. How the Jews inside, when they realised what was happening and saw that some people were choking, falling down and dying, how they tried to climb on top of them to reach the fresh air in the hole in the roof where they dropped the poison pellets from. They climbed on top of each other and it became like a twisted pyramid of bodies, all tangled together, by the time it was over. It was on this video they showed us at school. A German soldier explained how his friend took him to show him how it was done. Why would a German soldier make up things like that? And we saw pictures of the gas ovens where they burned the bodies."

"I told you Vince. There were no gas chambers. If they had used cyanide gas it would have been instant death because it is so lethal. The people sent in to take out the bodies would have all died too. It couldn't be done, without large chimneys or extractor fans and there were none. It would have been impossible."

"You're wrong. Listen, Mr Grant; Zyclon B, the stuff that they used to kill the Jews with, they also used it to get rid of the lice and bugs on the people they weren't going to kill, the ones they were going to put to work. It all depended on how much of it they used and how concentrated it was. You could make it so strong that just one whiff of it could kill you but why would they? The strength they used was enough to kill the Jews slowly, the guard said it took about fifteen minutes for them all to die and then they only had to wait a few minutes longer till it was safe enough to send more Jews in to take the bodies out."

Grant looked across at me. He had retaken control of the plane and it was climbing steadily. The gentle smile had gone.

"I suppose your friends told you that did they, filled you head full of lies to deceive you?"

"They did tell me, but it wasn't lies. The Jews they put to death and the ones that managed to get through alive, came from all over Europe, from places like Russia and Holland and Italy. How could people from so far apart, who didn't even speak the same language, all come up with the same story unless it was true? How come, if it was all a lie, that none of them ever confessed to it later on? Surely some of them would have? It wasn't just Jews that came up with it either. The soldiers fighting the Germans, the Russians, the British and the Americans, they all saw the camps and the rotting bodies lying around. The sort of people who could have let that happen, the Nazis, they could have done anything."

The Professor was starting to react. He kept wiping his forehead. I could see the sweat.

"I told you, some of it happened but not on that scale. We've all seen the pictures of the camps as the Allies found them but disease had broken out, people were starving and not only in the camps. It was bound to be horrible. It doesn't prove that six million died."

"I don't see what difference the number makes. If you agree that they killed thousands of Jews just because they were Jews, then why shouldn't they have gone on and killed millions? If you were a Nazi what difference would it make if you had to kill a thousand or a hundred thousand? In some ways it was easier anyway. They showed us a film in school of Jews being lined up in the freezing cold by the side of a big pit and the German soldiers had to shoot them so they fell in dead. A lady who didn't die said she had to stand there with her daughter and wait for them both to be shot; only when she fell in the pit she wasn't dead and she survived. One of the German leaders went there to watch and he was so near that he got splattered with the brain of one of the people who was shot. He went green like he was going to be sick. If he felt bad what do you think it was like for the soldiers who had to do the shooting? They even had to shoot little children. I bet it was easier for them when the concentration camps had been built. All they had to do was lock them in a hut and then one of them had to open up a little hole in the roof and drop some pellets in. They didn't have to watch them while they died or even have to fetch the bodies out afterwards. They made other Jews do that for them."

"It doesn't matter what you say Vince. The truth is that the number of six million put to death was just made up."

"Well what happened to them then? What happened to the trainloads of Jews that were sent off day after day for years? That's all written down. All the journeys, where they went, how many they stuffed in. What happened to them if they didn't die? They couldn't just have disappeared could they? Why were most of them never seen again, just a few survivors? You tell me, what happened to them if they weren't killed? They would have found them if they had just been taken to another place. You can't just hide that many people."

I knew I'd really got to him then. He suddenly reached out with his hand and tried to hold my mouth shut.

"That's enough. Be quiet, Vince. That's what they want you to believe but it isn't the truth. You must shut up now; they've poisoned your mind."

I wasn't going to stop or let him stop me. I pushed his hand away and undid the harness, so I could move a little farther away, out of his reach.

"My mind poisoned! My mind poisoned!" I was shouting by then, desperate to make him understand.

"You're the one going to let out a virus that's going to kill millions of people all over the world, including the people you're supposed to be helping, and you think my mind is poisoned? It's you that's mad. They told me about your wife and about David. You were normal till then. Don't you see? You're the one with the poisoned mind. It made you go mad. The people who think like you do about the Holocaust, they're all twisted. People who always hated Jews, people who think Hitler was good, the sort of people who hate black people, like those weirdos in America that wear those crazy white sheets and the pointed hats, those sort of people. That's the sort of people who deny the Holocaust. You work in a university. You're supposed to be brainy. Surely you can see that you're wrong."

I paused for breath. It wasn't working. He seemed to be back in control of himself again. His eyes were fixed on the sky ahead, the plane was still climbing. He was still determined to go through with it. I could tell by his face.

He started speaking again, much more calmly than

before.

"It would be simply impossible to kill so many people in that amount of time Vince. Six million! A physical impossibility."

I remembered what Mr Greene had said.

"How many Tutsis were killed in Rwanda then? That only took a hundred days. It was about a million and they had to catch them too. Hacked them to death with machetes. It was about a million wasn't it? If it only took a few weeks to kill a million in Rwanda, why would it be impossible to kill six million Jews in three or four years? It would be easy, not impossible. All your arguments are wrong, Professor."

Grant looked across at me, he didn't seem bothered.

"You may be right about Rwanda, Vince. It was a dreadful thing. We're high enough now. It will all be over soon. I'll have to open my door a little, so do your harness up again. It will be very noisy for a bit but there's no reason to be scared. You'll be back down on the ground again in a few minutes."

He'd pulled up the white canister as he was speaking and started to undo the clasps. I was desperate.

"You'll be famous then, Professor. The worst mass murderer in history, worse than Hitler even."

"Some might see it like that." Grant looked up from the container, one remaining clasp in place. "Others will know that I acted to put right an injustice."

"They'll try and work out why you did it. You know what they'll say don't you?"

"I expect you have some idea Vince."

"They'll say it was because of David. David Grant got killed and it sent his father crazy. David will be famous too, the son of the worst mass murderer in history."

"Stop it Vince. You've no right to bring David into this."

He started to splutter. I could see beads of sweat on his brow. I was getting to him.

"But that's what they'll say, isn't it? David Grant, the son of the worst mass murderer in history. Some of them will go further. You know what they'll say, don't you? If

David Grant hadn't got run over then his father wouldn't have gone mad and come up with his crazy scheme, so really it's David Grant's fault. David Grant caused the worst mass murder in history by getting himself run over. He made his dad go mad. It would be better if he was never born. David Grant should never have been born. David Grant should never have been born, David Grant, David..."

He started to speak but he couldn't. All he could do was sputter out a few words.

"I…I told…I told you n…not."

He sounded like he was choking. He was clutching at his throat with one hand like he couldn't breathe. Then he let go of the controls completely and both his hands were shaking in front of him. You could literally see the colour drain out of him and his skin turning grey.

I was like completely rigid for a few seconds. I didn't understand what was happening. I'd never seen a person having a fit or a heart attack before but there was no time for me to do anything. With no one flying it the plane just carried on for a bit, then it gave a sudden lurch, the nose fell downwards and we were hurtling towards the ground. It took me some seconds to react properly because I really was stunned with fear. But then, and just in time I suppose, I grabbed hold of the stick and pulled back hard on it. I saw the nose come up and felt the plane come out of the dive. One minute I had been plummeting and the next I was going up almost as steeply. The engine couldn't cope. An alarm started buzzing, really loud. It felt like we were about to just sort of drop out of the sky. I realised what I'd done, pulled back too far on the stick. I pushed it down again, much more gently this time. The nose came down but slowly, the buzzer stopped and I got the plane level again and checked by using the artificial horizon.

Grant was still moaning in the seat beside me. His skin was a weird colour and his head was hanging down and there was me, first time in a plane and with no real idea of how to fly it. I certainly had no idea of how to land it or even how to find the airport. I looked out of the side window but all I could see was fields that looked like little square patches and no sign of a long thing like a runway. I tried to speak to him, asked if he could hear me, asked if there was anything I could do and I tried to hold his head up. I think I might have made it worse. As soon as I let go again, he slumped over even more, stopped moaning, and went completely still. First thing I thought was that he could have chosen a better time to go and die, like one when I wasn't alone with him in a plane. Then I felt a bit guilty because it was probably what I'd said that had made him have the attack. Then I realized that the virus was still in the plane and his plan had failed and it was all due to me and that I'd saved the world, just me on my own. Then I remembered that I didn't know how to land the plane so it was definitely going to crash and that meant I'd be dead too, with the virus probably scattered about just like the Professor had intended, only not so high up. You'd have thought I'd have been pretty worried about all that but strangely I was almost perfectly calm. I'd looked at the clock on the instrument panel and it said nearly ten forty-five and it somehow made me think about school. Ten forty-five on Thursday morning. Nath and the others would be sat in another boring RS lesson. I'd always hated RS. We'd had the same useless teacher since the beginning of Year 7. He couldn't control us then and it had got worse since. We used to take it in turns to try to get him going, make him lose his temper. That was the only interesting thing about the lesson. Bloody hell, I thought to myself, this had to be better than RS. Then I thought I must be going mad too.

Chapter 13

I flew along for a time, keeping the plane as steady and level as I could. Even doing that was hard, and took a lot of strength. I knew I'd have to do something else eventually or the plane would just run out of fuel and I'd crash. I tried turning the plane around to go back the way I'd come towards the airport, but turning a plane round wasn't like turning around in a car and going back in the opposite direction. There was no road to tell me what was back or forward. Once I'd started I had no idea of how long to keep turning so I just took a guess. Heavens knows what direction I was flying in afterwards.

While I was going along I noticed the stump of my finger and saw that the end of it was black with dried blood from when Grant pulled the transmitter off. It was the finger that made me think about the radio in the plane. Looking back, I can't understand why I hadn't tried to use it before. I reached forward and brought the mouthpiece towards me. It took me a few tries before I realised that it was like my finger and I had to change the mode from receive to send before I could call. There was a button on the top.

"Hello, hello, can you hear me?"

I said it a few times with the button pressed in then let go of it and waited for a reply.

"Please identify yourself."

"I'm Vince."

"Your call sign please."

"I dunno what a call sign is. I'm in this plane and the pilot is dead. There's nobody else. What do I do?"

It was a few seconds before the response.

"You say the pilot is dead? Can you fly the plane?"

"I've never been in a plane before. I'm fourteen years old. There's no one else, just the two of us."

"All right, Vince is it? This is a bit unusual Vince. Try not to worry. Tell me, do you know the height of the plane and whether it is flying level or descending or going up?"

"It was descending. I've got it back level but it's very difficult to hold it steady."

"That will be the trim Vince. Look down between the

seats and see if you can find a small black wheel with notches in it. Turn it one way. If it makes it more difficult to keep control, turn it the other way. Keep turning until it becomes easier to fly."

I found the wheel and turned it with one hand, still holding the joystick with the other. Quite soon it was easier to hold the plane steady and level. It was almost as if the plane was relaxing.

"That's it," I said "it's much easier now. How do I tell how high I'm flying?"

The man on the radio told me which dial to look at.

"Six thousand feet is a little low Vince. We need to get you up a bit higher just to give you more leeway, should anything go wrong. Do you know where the throttle is?"

"Yes, he showed me before he had the fit and the horizon thing, he showed me that too."

"That's very good Vince. You need to find the airspeed indicator. Can you see the dial that says Knots? Tell me how many knots you are flying at now."

I found the dial. It said eighty.

"I want you to increase it to ninety-five by pressing forward on the throttle. At the same time you should pull back on the joystick a little so that you go up."

I did it.

"When you get to ten thousand feet level out and bring the airspeed back to eighty."

While I was going up I tried to explain things to the man on the radio but I honestly think that he must have thought I was loony. Eventually I remembered a special number that Mr Greene had given me to use in emergencies and told him to call it. A short time later he said he'd spoken to Mr Greene and was sorry if he'd been a bit slow on the uptake before. He said it was all rather exciting and that they were sure to be able to work out a way to get me down safely. Oh and someone called Karen had been worried sick about me and sent her love. Mr Greene wanted to know where the virus was in the plane and if any of it had been released. I was to try to find somewhere secure to put it, so that it didn't get thrown about. I thought that was a bit rich because he obviously meant where it wouldn't get thrown about when I crashed but then I suppose, all things considered, that the safety of the virus just then was more important than what happened to me.

When I'd got the plane to the correct height and back level again the man got me to take the radio headset off the Professor's head and put it on, so I could speak hands free. Professor Grant still looked grey and didn't move at all while I did it. I'd never seen a dead person before and I was tempted to touch him to see if he'd gone cold like they say dead bodies do, but I didn't like to, so I just pulled at the headset without actually touching his skin. When I'd got it on the radio man said he'd spoken to the RAF and needed to hand me over to them. He said that they'd definitely know how to get me down but then, he would say that, wouldn't he? People will tell you anything sometimes. I had to change the radio frequency to get in touch with the RAF. He told me how to do it but I was dead worried that I'd forget the numbers half way through and not be able to speak to anyone. Eventually he told me there was a little pouch somewhere near the instrument panel that should have a pencil and a notepad. I wrote down the number I was on and the one I had to change to. Even so I was nervous about doing it. The radio man wished me luck and told me that he would take me up in his own plane as a special treat once all this was over. I thought that was a bit stupid really, as I was hardly likely to think of another plane ride as a special treat after this one, but I didn't say anything except thank you.

The man from the RAF introduced himself as Squadron Leader Barnes and told me that I'd got myself into a bit of a pickle. He would be directing me to an RAF airfield where I was to try to land. First I had to fly the plane around until it had used up nearly all its fuel. That way there would be less danger of a fireball if I crashed it. I thought he could have been a bit less direct. It wasn't as if I wasn't scared enough already. He told me to stay on my present course and to expect company in fifteen minutes.

"We're sending up one of our fighters to guide you down. Don't worry, he'll find you."

After having been so direct at first, Squadron Leader Barnes tried to take my mind off things by asking all sorts of stupid questions about school and my favourite subjects, and what sports I played and which footie team I supported. I thought he must be having a laugh and I think I was a bit rude because I told him that they were the last things I wanted to think about just then and how he should cut the crap and concentrate on getting me down. It probably hurt his feelings but I bet you would have said the same if you were stuck up there like that. He stopped the talking anyway, which was a good thing.

Most of the time up there I was concentrating so hard on the controls and the artificial horizon that I didn't have time to think about anything else. Certainly I didn't think about Nath or RS again. From time to time I had a quick look away from the controls and out of the side window at the ground below. Once I thought I saw the runway because there was this big long thing but then I realized it was a motorway with cars on. After a bit I could see clouds ahead and that really worried me. I asked the Barnes man if I should try to fly round them or over or below but he said I had to keep to the same course and that they wouldn't last long.

"Don't worry Vince. They don't go on forever. You might feel a bit of turbulence, that's all. Just keep straight on."

I could see them coming towards me and then in an instant I was inside and I couldn't see anything else at all. It was horrible. I was worried that the plane that had been sent up to find me would crash into me. It got bumpy too. The clouds had just seemed like cotton wool while I was outside them but they weren't like that at all inside. You could tell it was moisture because there were streams of water being blown along the side windows. It seemed to last quite a long time too. I tried not to look at the outside and just kept concentrating on keeping the plane level. Eventually the cloud ended and I was out in the open sky again. It made me feel a lot happier. I must have got a little cocky about it because I told Mr Barnes that this flying lark seemed a bit of a doddle and how I might take it up myself later on. I was thinking 'if I don't get killed trying to land' but I didn't say that bit.

I nearly jumped out of my skin with surprise as the fighter plane appeared to my left in the sky. I'd always thought that fighter planes were little but this one was enormous compared to the thing I was in and it seemed much too close. I could see the pilot clearly. He waved at me and then his voice came through on the radio.

"Pleased to meet you, Vince. I'm going to be flying just slightly ahead of you. Do exactly as I say, and try to keep me in the same position, relative to yourself, all the time."

"What does that mean?"

"If I turn, you turn. If I go down, so do you. Got it?"

"Suppose so. I'll try anyway."

"Good lad. Now the pilot beside you, are you really sure that he's dead? Try to feel for his pulse. The best thing would be if we could wake him up and for him to take over."

"He's not sleeping. He started groaning, went grey and then stopped moving. He's dead. Shaking him's not going to bring him back to life."

"All right, Vince, you know best. It must be pretty horrible for you with him in the seat beside you. Do you know where the container with the virus is? I want you to make sure that it's securely anchored down somewhere, so that it doesn't get thrown about if we hit any rough weather."

"Or if I crash."

"Exactly, Vince, you know how important it is. But you won't crash because I'm here and I know what I'm doing. Try not to be scared. I'm Wing Commander Jones. Most of the lads call me Jonesy."

I remembered that the radio man before had already asked me to put the virus somewhere safe but I'd forgotten about it. The container had fallen forward onto the floor of the plane when Professor Grant had the fit. It was quite difficult to reach it and to keep control of the stick but I eventually managed to. I couldn't think where to put it but the Professor was slumped quite far forward and I was able to push it down in between the seat and his back. It didn't

go down very far but to get
to undo his harness and pus
to touch him, so I just left
plane crashed badly enough f
and get broken, I would be de
something I'd have to worry al

It was quite easy to fol
everything slowly and explain
before we came near to the RA
runway below me. We didn't try t
had quite a lot of fuel. He made
a sort of rectangle. He said it wa ... and it was
one of the ways they taught learners to fly. He taught me quite a lot too, some of the other instruments and how to turn properly and stuff like that. It was good because it used up the time quickly as I had to be thinking about what I was doing and not on what might happen if things went wrong. Eventually though, it was time for the difficult bit.

"We're nearly ready for the landing Vince. We are going to do a couple of practice runs first. It will be exactly the same as landing only a bit higher up and instead of actually touching down I'll want you to increase the throttle at the last moment and start ascending. I've got you perfectly lined up for the runway. You won't have to do any turning. You're lucky today Vince, there is no crosswind. It should be easy to hold the line. In a minute I'm going to tell you to throttle down. Move it just a little until you hear the pitch of the engine change. Then I want you to press gently down on the stick so that the nose of the plane drops and you start to descend. Use the trim wheel whenever you feel it becoming difficult to fly. Just try to keep me in exactly the same position to you as I am now. Remember, if I go lower so do you. When we are doing the real landing things will happen very quickly right at the end. You will see the runway coming towards you and just before the wheels touch the ground, I will tell you to flare. This means that you pull back a little on the stick so that the front comes up and the plane become level again in the air. In the practices I will tell you to increase throttle just after you've done the flare. Bring the nose up so quite quickly. Then we'll do another ... Are you all right with this Vince? I'll be ... step of the way. Any questions?"

... think of questions in that sort of situation. ... sick feeling in my stomach again. I was worried ... ouldn't be able to think straight and do what he said, ... told him it was fine and we should get on with it. The ... rst practice went much better than I thought it would. The second was a mess because I didn't increase the throttle soon enough after doing the flare, and he was shouting at me to do it quick because there were some tall trees after the runway. We were much lower down on that second run and that made it much harder. The runway really did seem to come rushing towards me and I could make out much more detail, such as the ambulances, with lights flashing and two fire engines that were spraying stuff onto the runway. After I'd got up high enough to be safe I asked Jonesy, and he said it was anti-fire foam in case I did crash.

"Better to take every precaution Vince. That's why the ambulances are there. If anything does go wrong they can give you the best possible treatment immediately. We are going to go for the real thing now Vince. It will be exactly the same as before except that after I tell you to flare and the nose comes up just slightly you will carry on and land. If you didn't flare the nose and propeller would hit the ground first. By flaring the plane is level and the wheels will touch down first, probably the rear one if you have done things really well. You may find that you bounce once or twice and then you must listen very carefully to me. Bouncing is perfectly normal but if you hit the ground too hard and bounce too high it would be dangerous. In that case I will say 'abort' and you must do exactly as we have done on the practices, in other words increase throttle, get the nose up and ascend to safety. If you haven't bounced or if I think the bounces you have done are okay, I won't say anything at all. As soon as you feel that you are firmly on the ground, pull back the throttle as far as it will go, to the lowest possible power, and push down hard on the brakes underneath your feet. The plane will slow down. Keep pressing on the brakes until it has completely stopped. It's quite a lot to remember. I'm going to go through it all once more and then I want you to take me through it as if you were teaching me."

We did all that as we were finishing off the circuit. After the final turn he told me to throttle down to start the descent and we moved steadily downwards and on for a couple of minutes. As we got lower I could make out more and more detail on the ground below and I could see that the fire engines and ambulances had pulled back a little. When we were at one thousand feet he told me to adjust slightly so that I was flying directly towards the centre line of the runway. I got cold feet at the last moment. There were so many thoughts going through my head, all the things I had to remember to do, that I panicked and was sure I'd mess it up. I didn't say anything; just pulled the nose up and pushed down hard on the throttle to get away from the ground. He didn't shout or get cross or anything, just calmly asked me what happened and said he wasn't surprised, when I'd explained. He went through the whole procedure again as we did another circuit and told me that I could do exactly the same again next time, if I still wasn't confident enough. That really helped because I was worried I was making a fool of myself and everybody would be laughing at how useless I was but he just made it seem normal for learner pilots to think like that.

I started the descent again. At one thousand feet the start of the runway was clearly in view ahead of me and I was steadily losing height. Jonesy made me do one more small adjustment to the throttle to reduce my speed. I was perfectly lined up for the centre. It was the point where I seemed to be hurtling along, waiting for Jonesy's command to flare. He gave it and I gently eased the stick upwards. The nose came up and the runway disappeared as the front of the plane blocked the view. It was going perfectly. Then all of I sudden I could see movement out of the corner of my eye and hear moaning too. An arm was thrashing about and then a hand grabbed hold of the joystick, on top of my own hand and it was pushing down with a huge force. Jonesy was screaming over the radio to abort. He said it again and again but the strength of the hand was too strong, the nose had dipped again and the runway had come back into view. I was heading straight for it.

"It's the Professor. He's come back to life," I was screaming. Grant was writhing about but his hand was gripped onto my own hand and the joystick like a vice and it was jerking this way and that. The wings were juddering up and down. I knew what was coming. There was nothing I could do. Everything went into a sort of slow motion. I felt the tip of the wing touch the runway. There was just a little jolt but then the plane seemed to slew round to one side and as it did it started to turn over. It gathered force so that it was like we were being catapulted around, the earth and the sky spinning, changing places, over and over. As the plane began to break apart around me there was this dreadful sound and I could feel this rush of air on my face. The last few seconds were really weird. It was like everything went. The noise, the air, the spinning, they all stopped and my mind was suddenly peaceful, like all the panic had gone and I was just myself. The only thing I was aware of was colour, like all the colours of the rainbow were jumbled up and in front of me, not rushing towards me or spinning or anything, just there, in front, to the side, all around.

Chapter 14

I opened my eyes and saw Miss Williams. I closed them again. I opened my eyes and saw Perkins. I closed them again. I opened my eyes and saw Mr Greene. I closed them again. I opened my eyes and saw nothing. I blinked and then blinked again, still nothing. Thoughts came, the cockpit of a plane, a dead man by my side, the ground rushing towards me, bouncing along, an enormous noise, twisting, catapulting like something elastic, breaking apart, colour, darkness.

'Bloody hell,' I thought, 'I'm dead.'

I lay there, looking up, seeing nothing. I remembered the virus and wondered if it was still in the white canister or if that had been smashed up in the crash and the virus had escaped into the open.

'Hope not,' I thought, 'perfect weather to blow it across to the continent.'

I lay there thinking that this was what it was like to be dead, not seeing, not moving or feeling your body at all, just thinking. It made me think of Mr Milner. He'd told us a story once about thinking he was dead. It was Christmas Eve, he was a teenager, and he had to go to church with his parents. Midnight Mass, he called it. The church was too warm and he felt drowsy and next thing he knew he was keeling over and out of it completely. When he came round they were carrying him out down the centre aisle. He didn't realise he'd fainted and he hadn't a clue what was going on but he could smell the incense burning and he could hear the vicar, so he knew it was something to do with God, and he figured that meant he must be dead, but he couldn't make his mind up if he was in heaven or hell. It was a good story and he swore it was true. As I thought of it, lying there, I had this bad feeling come over me because I knew where I'd be going. Then I remembered that Miss Williams had sent her love, sent her love to me Vince Viggors. Miss Williams had sent me her love. I knew she didn't mean in that sort of way, still, what a result. Not worth getting killed for though. I was lying there thinking and all of a sudden it came to me that if I really was thinking I couldn't be dead.

I lay there thinking and all of a sudden I could hear footsteps, not very near but getting nearer. There was the sound of a door opening and the flick of a switch. I was completely blinded by the light for what seemed ages and then I was able to make out the shape of a head above me. Gradually it took on more detail, so I could see this face, a woman's face, looking at me and smiling.

"Oh you've come round have you? I'm just checking to make sure you're okay. I'll let the others know. Go back to sleep now; it's the middle of the night."

A few seconds later the light switch clicked and the darkness returned.

'Bloody hell,' I thought, 'I made it.'

I opened my eyes and saw Miss Williams, Mr Greene and Perkins. They all smiled. I smiled too, tried to sit up and wished I hadn't.

"Steady there," said Mr Greene, "don't try to move; you've got all kinds of lines and drips attached. You've kept us waiting my boy. We never gave up hope. Karen here has practically lived in the hospital these past two weeks."

I looked at Miss Williams. She was smiling and there were tears running down her cheeks.

'Bloody hell,' I thought, 'two weeks!'

Then I fell asleep again.

I opened my eyes and saw Miss Williams. She was holding my hand. I could feel it, the one with the missing finger.

"Doctor says you should sit up and try to stay awake for a bit. Here, I'll do it."

Miss Williams got up and went to the control panel and pressed a button. The top part of the bed began to bend upwards and the room came into view.

"You were knocked unconscious in the crash and you suffered internal injuries that led to bleeding inside. They had to operate or you might have died. Doctor says that it's good you've stayed under for so long. Your wounds have had a chance to start healing and you haven't had to feel any pain. Mind you, two weeks has seemed a very long time, Vince. I was afraid you'd never come round."

I tried to say something but my throat was very dry.

"The virus, what happened to the virus?"

"Drink this," answered Miss Williams, reaching for a beaker and holding it to my mouth before saying, "well opening your mouth would help."

I opened my mouth and swallowed. It was only water but it was lovely and cool.

"It's okay Vince. The container survived the impact intact. None of the virus escaped. You saved the world Vince. Just think of that, Vince Viggors, 9X6 for English, saved the world. It would make a good title for a piece of imaginative writing under exam conditions."

I thought about it. Saving the world… had I really done that? Not really, the Professor had a heart attack or some sort of fit. He would have released the virus if he hadn't. I hadn't really done anything. Still if that's what they thought...

"Does that mean I'm famous now, if I saved the world? Will I be on the telly and things like that?"

"Certainly not," answered Miss Williams, rather severely it seemed to me, "Felix has made sure that none of it has come out. The whole thing is being kept secret. They don't want to give anyone else any crazy ideas."

I tried to make the best of it and smiled.

"Don't really want to be famous anyway. People looking at you all the time and stuff like that."

Miss Williams nodded as though she thought it was best that way. Then she went on to tell me the rest. Professor Grant was not dead. It was a heart attack but it hadn't killed him and he was virtually uninjured in the actual crash. An ambulance with cardiac equipment had been waiting at the runway. He'd made excellent progress and even been in to see me on a couple of occasions, although a policeman accompanied him each time, just in case he harboured any thoughts of revenge.

"What will happen to him now," I asked, "will he get locked up in jail?"

Miss Williams shook her head.

"I don't think so. It hasn't been decided yet but Felix says they don't want to put him on trial because they would rather it was all kept secret and they also want him to develop an anti-virus for future protection in case something similar was to occur naturally. It would be different if he was still raving on about the state of Israel but since the crash he seems a changed person. Says it was a good job he had the heart attack because it stopped him doing something dreadful. He seems to have been genuinely worried about you too, that you might not pull through and it would be his fault. When you talk to him now, it's hard to think that this was the person who might have deliberately killed off life on earth."

"I'm glad he's okay," I said. "He taught me how to make proper spag bol. He was kind in some ways and I felt sorry for him because of his son. It was a bit scary, there in his house, but it could have been a lot worse. He's been to see me, has he? Will he be coming again, now that I've woken up? I don't know how I'd feel about it if he was in here with me."

Miss Williams didn't know. It wasn't up to her but she was sure they wouldn't allow it if it would worry me.

While Miss Williams was there the doctor came to examine me. He undid my pyjama top and I could see a huge dressing on my chest, going down towards my stomach. There was a big pad of white gauze and several lines of sticky tape holding it in place.

"I'm going to have a look at how it's healing. Hold your eyes up if you don't want to see."

I held them down. There was a great big gash where they'd cut me open and lots of stitches to hold the edges together. They were dark with the dried blood and scab that had been forming.

"Bloody hell," I said "you made a right mess down there."

"I'm rather proud of it," said the doctor in a slightly offended voice. "Just one incision to do all that work inside you. Ten out of ten, I'd say. You'll need to take the medication for some time to control the pain but it's still going to hurt when you try to get up. We'll start that in a day or so. Time for rest, now."

I was in a room on my own. After Miss Williams had gone and there was no one else to talk to, I drifted in and out of sleep for most of the rest of the day, for most of the next few days in fact. It was during that time that the flashbacks began. Some of the events of the past few weeks started to go through my mind but not in any logical sequence, more like a ghastly nightmare, full of weird and frightening images. The worst one was the Professor next to me in the plane. He was dead and his skin was grey and sunk into his bones so that he was more like a skeleton. Then the skeleton suddenly came to life again, like some sort of Frankenstein figure. He grinned at me and the grin was full of evil. Then he attacked me and started to rip out my insides. Another was of me outside my body and looking down on the smashed up wreckage of the plane, blackened debris scattered all over the runway and my corpse still strapped into the seat that had been thrown clear. My parents were there, walking around, tut-tutting and frowning and when they came across my body in the chair they both screamed at me together, "Get this bloody mess cleared up."

The flashbacks were really frightening. Just before the start of one I would get this cold feeling and know what was coming. To begin with I struggled, tried to clear my mind, think of something else, anything to make it go away. Nothing worked. In the end I knew I just had to let them happen. Afterwards I was never quite sure if I'd been asleep and dreaming or if they'd taken over my mind while I was awake. I suppose I should have told someone, a doctor or Miss Williams, but I didn't like to in case they thought I was going mad. It didn't happen in any regular sort of way. Sometimes it might be two or three times a day, but there could be a gap of several days without one at all. I'd think they were all over and done with, only to have another one come on. Another thing about the flashbacks was that they kept developing. Some of the things that happened after I'd left hospital got taken up in them too, so that I began to wonder if they'd ever stop or just get longer and longer.

I was in hospital for another three weeks after I first woke up. They got me up at the start of the second week and had me walking around for an hour or so. It was difficult because I was so weak and because I still had several tubes attached to me and monitors as well, and that meant that I had to go around with a trolley for all the pouches of liquid and that sort of thing. The trolley was useful though, for leaning on and keeping my balance. The doctor came round twice a day at first and a nurse changed the dressing. After about two weeks, when they had taken out all the drips and I didn't have to have the trolley any more, they took me down to a gym for exercises. Some of the people there seemed a lot worse off than me. One guy was learning to walk again because they'd had to cut off one of his legs after an accident at work. The last few days they put me in a ward with nine other people. Most of them were kids like me, but there was one old man as well. They said they didn't have anywhere else to put him. One of the kids died while I was there. You could tell he was really ill because his face was gaunt and white. I woke up in the middle of the night because there was this commotion going on, and lots of nurses and doctors coming and going and they'd put screens round his bed. Next morning there was just a space where he and his bed had been. I asked and the nurse told me what had happened.

Towards the end of the second week after I woke up I began to feel more positive about things. I was getting used to the flashbacks and I seemed well on the road to recovery. I didn't feel so weak or tired and the doctors told me that there wasn't any permanent damage to my insides. More than that I was feeling good about what I'd done. The Professor and his nasty virus had been stopped and even if I wasn't going to be famous, I knew it was down to me. If I hadn't been around he would have gone through with it. And Miss Williams had become a real friend, the first adult I felt I could really trust. She'd even sent me her love.

My first piece of bad news was about Miss Williams. She wasn't going back to the school. I couldn't understand it.

"Mr Greene said the tribunal would clear you. There wasn't anything dodgy about the meetings, they was in the public library."

"I got legal advice from the Union," she explained.

"They said that they would fight it for me if I insisted but either way, I'd be on to a hiding to nothing. Technically I was in the wrong and should have asked the Head's permission. He could refuse to allow me to return but if they argued the point and he was made to back down then it would make my professional relationship with him very difficult. The Union said they were afraid that he would be looking to find every little fault he could and it would make my life a misery. In the end they came to an agreement that I will officially leave when my contract expires at the end of the school year and that Mr Harding will give me a decent reference. There will be no mention of what happened. In the meantime, I'm supposed to be off sick. I'm sorry Vince, I'll have to start applying for jobs and they could be anywhere. I'll probably be moving away."

It wasn't the sort of news I wanted to hear.

Miss Williams visited me almost every day in hospital, sometimes with Perkins. Mr Greene came a few times, but my parents never did. I began to wonder and asked Miss Williams if she knew why. She looked uncomfortable and made some excuse about it being quite a difficult journey if you didn't have a car. I figured that they just couldn't be bothered. It made me sad. One person who did come was the Professor. It was while I was still in the room by myself. A nurse said that there were two people in the corridor outside. One of them was a policeman. They would like to see me. I felt myself panicking immediately. The memories came flooding back. That time in the police car, the fat one and his cull. It wasn't him. This copper had a kindly face.

"Excuse me, Vince, Professor Grant is outside. He wants to talk to you. I would be present the whole time. What do you think? They've told me that you've done something very brave and important and that we should all be grateful to you. Proper hero, they said. It's a pleasure to meet you, Vince, or maybe I should call you Sir. Will it be all right for him to come in? It's up to you?"

I was in two minds, afraid that seeing him would make the nightmares worse but wanting to hear what he had to say and know if he was really sorry, like they said. I told the policeman it would be okay.

I was quite shocked when I saw him. He walked in slowly with little hobbling steps and he looked older. The colour was still missing from his face. It wasn't exactly grey like on the plane but not a long way off. He seemed to have more lines and less hair. He smiled when he saw me but it was a forced smile, not a natural one and almost immediately his eyes filled with tears and he had to take out a hanky. He pulled up a chair and said hello but after that he just buried his face in his hands.

"I'm sorry Vince, I'm so sorry."

He said it over and over until I almost had to say it was all right, just to get him to stop.

Once he'd gotten control of himself he talked a little.

"I don't know what to say really, seeing you in hospital like this. You nearly died and all because of me. I'm sorry, Vince, I'm sorry about everything. You know, when I realised that you were from MI5 I couldn't get it over that they'd sent a boy to get the better of me, but when it comes down to it, I think it had to be a boy, someone who looked like David, to bring me to my senses. It was what you said about David becoming famous as the son of the worst mass murderer in history that overwhelmed me. I couldn't bear the idea of people thinking of him in that way. I'm sure that's what brought on the heart attack. It took you to do it. You don't know how grateful I am. I remember the pains in my chest and blacking out but not anything else. What happened at the end Vince? They said that you were doing brilliantly and then it all went wrong at the very last moment. They said you called out that I was still alive. I don't remember."

I told him how he had gone grey and stopped moving. How I thought he was dead. How he started moving again, thrashing about just as the plane was landing. How he grabbed the control and made the plane crash. He looked distraught, his voice barely a whisper.

"It wasn't deliberate, I promise. I wasn't aware of anything except the pains in my chest. I didn't know I'd done that."

He paused again.

"They told me about your folks. It must be very difficult for you. I asked if I could adopt you but the authorities said it was out of the question. Still, you could come over and see me sometimes. We could make spaghetti again. I enjoyed that. You could come whenever you want. I do mean it. We could become friends, proper friends."

He'd brought a bag in with him. He handed it to me.

"I nearly forgot. It's for you, Vince, a present. I thought you'd appreciate it."

Inside the bag was a book, wrapped up. I tore off the paper. 'Italian Cooking Made Easy'. I smiled and thanked him but my mind was racing. What did he mean about my parents? Why would it be difficult for me? How could he adopt me when I already had parents? They must be dead, how else would it have occurred to him to adopt me? I felt frantic but I wasn't going to ask him. I didn't want to hear it from him, not from him. I said I was tired. He needed to go. I needed to sleep. The policeman came over as if he knew something had upset me. He told the Professor he'd better leave.

I lay there worrying all afternoon and when Miss Williams came I asked her immediately.

"No Vince, they're not dead. It's difficult, Vince; something has happened. I'm not supposed to say. Your dad is out of prison. They're both at home. I'll ask Felix. I'll tell him you have to know. It's all I can say now. Try not to worry."

How could I not worry? She tried to change the subject. She went on about something for a few minutes, then Mr Greene popped his head round the door, smiling and asking how the 'national hero' was today and she jumped up and pushed him back out of the room as he was coming in. The door banged shut but she shouted at him and I heard every word.

"You have to tell him now. It isn't fair that he doesn't know. He can't understand why they haven't been to see him. He thought they were dead. Grant came to see him today and said he had asked to adopt him. He has to know now, he has a right."

They came back in together, Miss Williams pushing Mr Greene into the chair and glaring at him.

"This is going to be very difficult for you my boy, you are going to have to be brave. They're okay, nothing has happened to them for you to worry about, but they haven't been to see you because they aren't allowed. We found something out, Vince. When we were going through your records before we met you, something strange came up. Your blood group and the blood groups of your parents don't match, they are incompatible. They aren't your real parents, Vince. It means you can't go back there."

I was trying to understand.

"You mean I'm adopted. Why would that mean that I couldn't go back? What difference would it make if I was adopted?"

Miss Williams leaned forward, took my hand and squeezed it.

"Not adopted, Vince. You weren't adopted. Something happened in the hospital where you were born. You got mixed up with another baby."

I thought about it.

"So now I've got to go and live with my proper parents?"

"It wasn't an accident, Vince." Mr Greene was speaking again, "Sandra did it deliberately. She's told us all about it. You have to remember that she was still very young when she gave birth. You were a lovely baby, she said. Her baby cried all the time, was difficult to feed. Your real mum had a difficult time having you. She was sedated and unconscious for much of the time afterwards. Your real dad was away in the Army. A nurse had left some unused name tags lying around. Sandra copied the names onto them, cut the genuine ones off and put the new ones on but swapping them around. No one noticed. When she was sent home the following day, she had you with her."

"She stole me?"

"Well, yes, Vince."

"How do you know?"

"We knew early on that you couldn't be her real son

because of the blood groups. When you were having your lessons in the library with Karen you told her that your mum had once said that you weren't her real son. Do you remember? Perkins was listening. It was important. It meant that she had done it deliberately. How else would she know but never have told anyone? We were able to go back over the hospital records and find out which other baby was in the same room and what the blood group was. We had to get them to allow you to be put into our care. Your father was easy. We just had to agree to let him out early. We were more worried about Sandra, worried that she wouldn't give her consent. It was vital that she did, so when we met you at the school and Perkins went outside to see her, he just confronted her with the truth and told her that you were being taken into care because of it. She was stunned but what could she say? She signed the papers immediately and almost ran away. I'm sorry, Vince, it's not the sort of news you need after what you've been through."

I couldn't think of anything to say. What can you say when you've just had news like that? I must have been relieved that they weren't dead, but I was also wondering how she could have done a thing like that and pretended for all those years? I could feel myself getting angry too that Greene and Perkins knew about it all along and didn't tell me, just used it to get hold of me. There was worse to come.

"The other parents, my real ones, do they know? Am I going to live with them?"

"Your real father was killed in the Iraq War. Your mother has struggled to bring up the family on her own. She's had a hard time battling depression. The other boy, your mum's real son, the one you were swapped with, he's been a difficult child and caused all sorts of problems. We haven't told her, Vince. She's got no idea about any of this. We don't think she should be told. In her mental condition she might not be able to take it."

Questions were coming to me thick and fast. I wanted to know everything.

"What will happen to her, to Sandra, for taking me? Will she get done?"

"It's with the CPS. They're the people who have to decide whether she should be prosecuted or not. In the meantime, she's not allowed any access to you, in case it prejudices the situation. All things being equal though, I don't see much point in it. If there were a prosecution then your real mother would have to be involved. It wouldn't solve anything. Sandra knows that you will not be returning. Even though you may think she doesn't love you, Vince, she thinks of you as her son and she is distressed. She is already being punished in a way."

I was going to ask another question but Miss Williams interrupted. She looked so upset.

"They didn't tell me until two days ago, Vince. I was so angry with them. I would have told you if I had known. I promise I would have told you."

"What will happen to me?" I asked, still shocked and bewildered by everything that had been said.

"You've been placed under a care order. It means going into a residential home for young people," answered Mr Greene. That was another night I didn't sleep.

Chapter 15

On the day I was discharged from hospital, Miss Williams and Perkins arrived together to help me pack. They had a suitcase with a few things from home, photographs and so on. I thought that there might be a letter or note from Mum but there wasn't. It was an official car with a driver in uniform. Perkins said I should arrive in style but I was worried how the other kids in the home might react when they saw it, if they'd pick on me because of it. On the way there I sat in the front, with Miss Williams and Perkins sat in the back. My sun visor had a mirror and I saw them holding hands. I didn't know what to think, except it was a bit disappointing.

It was quite a drive from the hospital to the home, right across town and past my estate. I remember thinking how bleak and rundown it looked. I'd not thought about it in that way before. The home was a bit further out. It was a big, old house, the sort you'd have to be rich to own. Lots of the houses round there were like that, but the area wasn't posh. Mostly the buildings were divided up into flats and bedsits and quite a lot were rented out to students. I'd actually been past the house loads of times before because it was on one of the routes I used to take to school, but I'd never really noticed it, not realised that it was a place for care kids.

I was nervous about going in, but they were quite friendly and introduced me to the staff and to the few kids who were around and not at school. There were quite a few adults and we had to call them by their first names. One of the rules was that we weren't to ask their surnames or where they lived or questions like that. I could guess why. They didn't wear uniforms either, like I'd somehow expected. I had a room to myself. It was small, but the furniture was quite new and modern. The bed was soft and had a proper duvet, not scratchy blankets like I'd had before. There was even a small telly which was good because if there had only been one big one somewhere there would have been arguments or fights. It all felt incredibly strange. There were quite a lot of rules, only they called them routines. Everyone had to keep their own room tidy and help clean the common rooms and we had to take turns at setting the table and washing-up. If you came in from outside you had to take your shoes off at the door and put slippers on. You had to be up for breakfast by a certain time, although it was later at weekends and holidays and everyone was supposed to have the evening meal together, not watching TV, which was strange. There was homework time, and everyone was expected to do theirs quietly. The kids who didn't go to school because they'd been expelled or something got set homework by the tutors, who came in most days. Even so, some of them could hardly read or write.

Miss Williams and Perkins didn't stay long. The staff said it would be better if I was left to settle in on my own. Miss Williams said they'd see me again soon and take me out for the day somewhere nice. As she smiled and walked away though, I got the feeling that a special part of my life was coming to an end. She seemed to have been paying more attention to Perkins than anything else as we were shown round. I told myself it had all been a stupid dream that had been bound to end badly anyway, just like everything else in my crummy life. That night, after I'd gone to bed, I held the pillow over my head so that no one would hear and cried my eyes out. I cried so much it made my wound hurt really badly.

In the early hours there was a commotion. Some of the rooms were kept for emergency admissions, kids who had just been taken into care and needed somewhere right away, maybe for the night or a few days, while their case was reviewed. There was an emergency admission that night. I heard screaming and opened my door slightly. It was a girl, about my age. She was swearing and fighting and they had to use quite a lot of strength to hold on to her. The screaming continued until a doctor came and gave her something to quieten her down. It was upsetting. I couldn't get back to sleep afterwards and tried to think of things to do. I opened up my school bag and found the notebook and fountain pen. I read a few things I'd written but it all seemed just a bit stupid, all that business of going to the library, doing the work in secret, so Nath and the others wouldn't make fun of me. I knew that I wouldn't be writing in it any more.

Gradually I did get used to the home. I got to know which adults to trust and which of the children to avoid. I fell into the routine and did what was expected. School was part of the routine. They agreed to allow me to return and I had to start again the following Monday. First off I had to wait outside the Headmaster's office to be given a lecture or so I presumed. Mr Harding didn't seem pleased to have me back. He either didn't know or he didn't let on that he knew, about what I'd done, except that I'd been in hospital and was living in a care home. He reminded me that I was still on his final warning and that I had to behave or else. Then he told me that I'd missed the Options Evening when you decided what GCSE's you wanted to do in the last two years.

"I'm afraid all the GCSE courses are full. We've put you down for the non-exam subjects. Better suited to children of your level of ability."

"What, even History? The teacher said I should choose it. I'm good at it."

"Can't be helped now, Vince, you weren't here, were you? Don't know what you were up to with those rather dubious gentlemen but you'd have been better off here. I understand there's been a spot of bother, Vince. You've been taken into care. Whatever the problems outside school, remember you leave them behind when you come through these gates. We don't want any more disruption from you."

That nearly did it. I was ready to tell him where he could stick his sodding school but then I thought back to the last time I'd been there in his office, with Mr Greene and Perkins.

"Heard anything about that knighthood yet, Sir?"

He was a bit taken aback.

"No, not yet. Why do you ask?"

"They had a right old laugh about it afterwards. Said there was one born every minute, and how could you seriously believe that they could pick up the phone just like that and talk to the Prime Minister."

He looked up surprised and he started to go red and cough and splutter.

"I'll get off to classes then, should I?"

He waved me away and I walked off happy. It wasn't often anyone got one over on the Headmaster.

Going to registration I was joined by Nath and Digby. They hadn't a clue where I'd been. I knew they'd think I was having a laugh if I told them the whole story, so I just said I'd had to have an operation and about being in the home. They made a few stupid comments and then Nath said that they had a new English teacher who was completely useless and couldn't control the class at all.

"You heard about Miss Williams did you? There's all sorts of rumours flying round. Someone said she's been sacked because she got caught doing it with a pupil. Imagine that eh, doing it with Miss Williams? I wouldn't mind a bit of that. What d'ya think about that Vince? Fancy a bit of that too?"

I didn't think, I just felt my temper explode and next thing I knew I'd hit him as hard as I could. Given the state of my health that wasn't very hard. When Nath recovered from the shock he rushed at me and thumped me in the stomach. I collapsed on the floor, screaming in agony. Nath and everyone else watching were amazed because I couldn't stop moaning and they had to run to find a teacher. Welfare called an ambulance straight away and I was soon back in the hospital. The doctor had a moan at me for fighting in my condition and said I could have been killed. That was twice in a couple of months, I thought. He examined me and sent me for a scan like ladies have when they're expecting. It didn't show up anything but they kept me in overnight just in case. Nobody came, but then I suppose, nobody knew.

At least being rushed off to hospital seemed to make them forget that it was me that had started the fight. The incident wasn't mentioned again. The teachers didn't seem too unhappy that I was back. Mr Milner passed me in the corridor and asked if I was out thieving again. He had a smile on his face though and laughed when I told him I was waiting till he showed me how to do it properly. Nathan was right about the new teacher. He was useless. Everybody mucked about and I felt that they were expecting me to as well. Pretty soon I found myself being drawn into my old ways. Half way through the register at the start of one lesson, when I'd been answering 'yes Sir' in a silly voice to every name that was called out, the teacher lost it. He slammed his pen on the desk and stormed over to me.

"Do you think it's clever to make stupid noises every time I call out a name? They warned me about you. Said you were a nuisance. They never said you were a moron too. Only a mindless moron would find it amusing to behave like that at your age. Why don't you grow up and stop acting like an idiot?"

He was actually shaking with rage. Everyone had gone quiet. I expect they were wondering how I'd react, if I'd just throw my chair across the room and walk out or if I'd hit the teacher as well. They must have been a bit disappointed.

"I'm sorry," I said after a bit, "I know it's stupid, I won't do it again. I'm sorry, Sir."

The teacher muttered something and went back to his desk.

After that I tried hard to stop messing about in school. Everyone noticed it. A few of the kids asked me about it. I just shrugged them off but the next time she visited I told Miss Williams.

"When he said all that, I just thought to myself that he was right, I was behaving like a stupid moron, making silly noises to try to get a laugh. There I was, Vince Viggors who'd just saved the world and nearly got killed in the process, behaving just like a little kid. I made up my mind to stop, not just then, but in all my lessons. Maybe they'll let me take some exam subjects if I can show them I'm not really a moron, like I showed you."

Miss Williams said she hoped so but not to hold out too many hopes. She wished I hadn't said anything to Mr Harding about the knighthood. She understood why I had but he was bound to be angry. He wouldn't like it that one of his pupils had seen him taken in by two strangers like that and he certainly wouldn't want anyone else to know about it. It was another reason why he might have it in for me. It hadn't occurred to me that Mr Harding could hold a grudge against a pupil. Perhaps it would have been better if I'd kept my mouth shut. That visit was also the time when Miss Williams told me about Australia. She had relatives there and she was going to spend the summer, the whole summer, with them. It had all been arranged ages ago, even before the lessons in the library began. She hoped I wouldn't mind and she'd still keep in touch after, wherever she was. You can imagine how I felt.

During the next couple of months I thought about my parents a lot, the real ones I didn't know and the false ones I did. It seemed totally out of order that I'd somehow got two lots, but couldn't live with either. I felt very lonely. Life with Sandra and William didn't seem so bad when I was no longer living there. I missed the affection Sandra had sometimes shown me and I suppose I forgot about the times I'd been locked out or told to get lost for a few hours, and about the violent rows that happened whenever William was around. More than a few times I thought about running away and going back to them. I knew though that Social Services would only take me back into care and maybe it would be somewhere even worse, like a prison even, to stop me doing it again. I even began to wonder about the story we'd come up with to tell the Professor, that I was heading for London to find a place in a squat and a job on a market. Maybe I could do that. Get lost in the big city. Start over a new life.

Even more than the home I'd been taken away from, I thought about the one I'd never known, the one I should have grown up in. I hadn't felt anything when Mr Greene had told me that my real dad had been killed in the war in Iraq, but when I was alone in my room, I started to wonder about him and felt really sad that I'd never had the chance to meet him, and get to know him as a dad. It made me feel very bitter towards Sandra and very determined that whatever else, I wasn't going back there. I wondered how he'd been killed, whether it had been a brave death, fighting the enemy or something ordinary like a road accident or cancer. I wanted to know. I wanted to know everything about my real family, what their names were, where they lived, if I had brothers and sisters, if my proper grandparents were still alive. It preyed on my mind. I thought about it all the time. In the end it got me down. The people in the home noticed and told Miss Williams how quiet and withdrawn I'd become. She suggested that I might find it helpful to talk to a counsellor or a doctor. It would be best to be able to talk to someone, not keep it bottled up. I'd been through such a lot.

"I don't want to bloody talk about it," I told her angrily, "I want to bloody know about it. Nobody will tell me anything. They tell me I was stolen, that I don't belong where I thought I did, that my mum and dad aren't my real parents and then they leave it there. No one will tell me anything else. It's like being in limbo, only knowing half the story. That boy, living there where I should be, I want to know what his name is. Don't you realise it should be my name? That's who I should be. I want to know. I have a right to know! You've got to tell me!"

I was very worked up and she looked worried. I don't think she'd seen me like that before. She spoke quietly, trying to soothe me.

"I can't give you the answers to those questions, Vince. I don't know them. They didn't tell me either. I can understand how you feel. It isn't fair on you. I'm seeing Perkins this evening. I'll talk to him about it. I can't promise anything, but I'll try."

I began to feel calmer and wondered why she called him Perkins. Perhaps that was his first name too, Perkins Perkins.

Two days later they took me out for the day, Miss Williams and Perkins. We drove into the countryside in her car and walked along the banks of a river for what seemed like miles. I found it fascinating to catch glimpses of fish and tried to catch one by holding my hands still in the water and waiting for one to swim by. The water was freezing and my hands were blue when I eventually gave up. There were cows in one of the fields we went through. I was worried they were bulls but Miss Williams smiled and said that bulls didn't usually have udders. Even if they were only cows they were big enough to be dangerous and I was glad to get out of that particular field.

After we'd been walking for an hour or so we came

to a village which had a pub and we sat in the garden to have something to eat. We each had a ploughman's but I gave them my pickled onions because I never did like them. While we were waiting for the food Perkins told me that the boy's name was Samuel.

"He's probably known as Sam."

It was a few seconds before I realised who he was on about. I thought about it. Sam, it was a nice name, nicer than Vince. I'd always hated Vince. I'd known a few Sams, they'd all been okay.

"And what's his last name? What's his surname?"

"Do you really need to know Vince?"

I nodded.

"Stevens."

"And my real dad who got killed in Iraq, what was his first name?"

"Paul. He was a sergeant."

"How did he die?"

"The light armoured vehicle he was travelling in got blown up."

"Did he suffer, I mean, was he… like… blown to pieces?"

"I don't know, Vince. I'm sorry, that's all I know about it."

"Is he still there, in Iraq? Did they bury him there?"

"No, Vince. They brought him home. Full honours funeral. He's buried in the military cemetery, the one just outside town by the Army base."

I was quiet. Miss Williams put her hand on mine and squeezed it gently.

"We're both very sorry, Vince."

It was a relief when the food came and there was an excuse for not talking.

Three days later I decided not to go back to the home after school. Instead I took a bus that dropped me near the gates of the Army camp. The fence around it had rolls of barbed wire all around the top. I found out later that it was put there when the IRA was a problem and had never been taken down. I thought it made it look like a prison, like the one where me and Sandra had visited William when he was inside. The cemetery was just outside the base. Anyone could go in. The graves were laid out in rows that looked like a pattern and everything was neat and tidy and well kept. I walked along the lines of gravestones and crosses, reading each one until I came to the one that had my real father's name. After his name and rank, it had the initials MC. It said he was in the Blues and Royals, Household Cavalry Regiment, and died on 26th March 2003. I would have been eight then, he was forty-two. I stood there for several minutes. I thought that I should have felt sadder than I did. On my way out I noticed a lady by one of the other graves. I went up to her.

"Excuse me, I hope you don't mind but do you know what MC stands for?"

"Military Cross. It's an award for gallantry, for bravery. Why do you ask?"

"It was on the grave I came to see."

"Whose is that?"

"My dad's."

The lady smiled, her eyes welling up.

"It means he was a hero."

The next day I walked into town after school and stood outside a large, modern building. I waited a couple of minutes before plucking up courage and then walked towards the automatic door that opened to let me in. The lady at the reception desk asked if she could help. I didn't know whether to tell the truth, that I wanted to find out about the death of my father or to use the story I'd thought up on the way there.

"I'm doing a project at school about the Iraq War. I need to find out about local people who were killed in it. Do you keep back copies of the News I could read through that might tell me? I'd be careful not to rip them."

The receptionist told me to go to the reading room on the first floor and ask there. She made me sign in and told me to sign out when I was finished. She said I had an hour, after that they'd be closed.

I went up to the first floor and found the room. A man asked me what year I wanted and directed me to a computer.

"Click on the month and the day, press the right and left arrows to turn the page or go back."

I was afraid I'd be recognised. Miss Williams had told me that my photo as the missing boy had been in some of the national newspapers as well as the Professor's local one, but nobody paid me any attention.

There was nothing in the records on the day my father was killed but then I realised that it might take a day or a few days for the news to get back, and they always had to tell the 'next of kin' first. It took three days. The headline on the front page said:

LOCAL HERO KILLED IN IRAQ

and went on to explain that Sergeant Paul Stevens, of Mayberry Road and of the Household Cavalry Regiment, who had been decorated for bravery in the Bosnian conflict of 1995, had been killed in a roadside incident in this latest conflict when the vehicle he was in was destroyed by incoming fire. It said an investigation into the tragedy had been ordered. It went on to say that Sergeant Stevens left a widow, Claire, a son aged eight and a daughter aged six. The family had asked for Paul to be remembered in prayers. I looked at the story for ages. My mother was called Claire. My father had been decorated for bravery. That must be the Military Cross. I had a proper sister too.

After that I clicked on a few days until I came to the edition with the funeral in. There was a picture of my father smiling, a portrait picture, just of his head, the sort you pose for. It was strange to see that face so clearly and to think he was my dad. I thought he was really handsome. There was also a picture taken at the funeral. It showed the three of them holding hands by his grave, before the earth was put back in. It gave their names too so I found out my sister was called Jessica. I felt sadness welling up in me and my eyes began to water while I was looking at the photos and reading the nice things they said about my dad. I know they always have to say nice things at funerals but that didn't mean it wasn't true. At the end it said that his death was still under investigation.

I clicked on through the next couple of weeks but I couldn't find anything. I asked the man who was working at the desk.

"Excuse me, I want to find out if there's anything about this investigation."

The man came over and I showed him the funeral page.

"Oh that case," he said, "it was reported in the paper but I remember it anyway. It was friendly fire. An American plane, the pilot thought it was an Iraqi patrol."

I must have looked blank, I didn't understand.

"Friendly fire is when you get killed or injured by your own side. It happens quite a lot. It was us and the Americans against Saddam in the Iraq War. There were a number of similar cases. Nothing got done. They said it was just a mistake. Things happen in war. He was a brave man. When his unit was being attacked by Serbs in Bosnia, he and another soldier held them off so that his comrades could reach safety. A school project is it? You look upset."

"Not a school project," I replied, wanting him to know the truth, "he was my dad."

The man, he'd said he was the newspaper's archivist, looked shocked.

"Haven't they told you? Surely someone would have told you, your mum?"

It was too difficult to explain. I made something up.

"I was too young to understand. She don't like to talk about it now. Do you have any of these left? I'd like to buy a copy of this one if you do."

"I could print it off for you. Would that help?"

I just smiled and waited. The archivist said he should charge me but in this case he wouldn't.

"Come back if you need any more information. I can see the resemblance."

"What?" I asked.

"The man in the picture, Sergeant Stevens, your dad, you look just like him."

I got up, thanked him for his help and left. I was smiling inside but I hadn't liked to show it. Me looking like my dad the hero; that was a good feeling.

Back in my room that night I kept reading the article and I spent ages looking at the pictures. My sister Jessica had fair hair, long and straight. The boy, Sam, was crying and his face was all screwed up so you couldn't really tell if he looked like Sandra or what he looked like. My mother had dark clothes on and a dark hat. She was wearing sunglasses but it didn't look like a sunny day. When it had gone quiet in the house I went downstairs to the room where they had the computers and scanned the photo into My Pictures. Then I tried zooming in to see more detail but it just came up blurry. Then I typed 'How do you get to Mayberry Road?' into a search engine and it came up with a route planner. I typed in the details of where the home was and put Mayberry Road as the destination and clicked on 'Walking'. The route came up. It was only about half an hour away.

Next morning I left the home as usual but didn't go to school. I went to Mayberry Road instead. I didn't really know what to expect. I didn't know the number of the house or if they still lived there. I just wanted to see them. I didn't know what I was going to do if I did see them and I did remember what they'd said about her, coping with depression and wondered if I should be doing it at all. It wasn't a long road and there was a bus stop half way along, so I waited there, trying not to look too obvious. I waited an hour. Six buses came along but I just shook my head towards the driver each time. A few people came out of some of the houses during that hour but none of them looked like the ones in the photo. I went to school and got a detention for being late.

The next morning I got up an hour earlier and made some excuse about having to finish off some homework in the 'early room' in school. I went to Mayberry Road again and stood at the same bus stop. After about half an hour I saw them. They came out of the house almost opposite. She was in some sort of uniform, like a nurse's, and they were both wearing school clothes. The boy was frowning and arguing about something and his mother was pleading with him to 'stop going on about it'. They got into the car in the drive, reversed out and were gone. I was there at the same time the next three days.

When Saturday came I went to Mayberry Road yet again. I was a bit worried about being at the same bus stop each time so I stood further down, near the end of the road where I could still just make out the drive. Around 10.30 they came out and stood at the bus stop. I ran as fast as I could to the one before and jumped on the first bus that came. It was going to the town centre. I bought a ticket and went upstairs. When the bus got to the next stop they got on. I was getting nervous, half hoping they'd come upstairs and half hoping they wouldn't. They stayed downstairs but when the bus got to the shopping centre I could see them get off, so I legged it down the stairs as fast as I could and started to follow them. Each time they went into a shop I waited outside, on the other side of the road. If it was a big store with lots of entrances, I followed them in but always tried to keep well behind. Eventually, in the biggest store, they went into the café and the kids sat down while she went to the counter to order. I was getting braver by then. I wanted to hear her speaking. I stood behind her in the queue. She ordered burgers and fries, shakes and a coffee. Her voice was nice, not posh but not common either. I bought a burger too and looked for somewhere to sit. The only free table was behind theirs. I heard everything they said. How she asked the boy not to grumble because they always went out as a family on Dad's birthday. That really choked me, learning it was his birthday. How could the boy moan like that when it was his dead dad's birthday? I wanted to scream that he wasn't really her son. He was a difficult child, was he? Well maybe he'd be better off with Sandra and William. Perhaps I'd be doing them all a favour if I was just to go round to their table and tell them all the truth. It would be easy. I could go and live with them, get away from the home. Perhaps the nightmares would stop.

The girl was sat facing me. She was skinny and pretty. Her eyes kept looking up at me. She had this puzzled look on her face. She whispered to her mother but I heard.

"It's him Mum, the boy at the bus stop. The boy I told you about. He's there, right behind you."

I was frightened stiff. She turned around to look. I tried to avoid her eyes but I couldn't. I saw her expression change and the look of surprise, the look of recognition, like the one on Professor Grant's face that first night in his kitchen.

"Do I know you? You look familiar. My daughter says you've been at the bus stop by our home."

She had a pretty face. It was the first time I'd seen it so clearly, so near. It would have been so easy to tell her, to see her reaction, to have her put her arms round my shoulders and hug me like a real mother would do but Mr Greene's words came back to me.

'Your mother has struggled to bring up the family on her own. She's had a hard time battling depression. We haven't told her Vince. She's got no idea about any of this. We don't think she should be told. In her mental condition she might not be able to take it.'

"I don't think so," I said, eventually, "I came here on foot."

I looked down at my food, trying to appear not interested. She apologised for the interruption and turned back to her family. I stuffed the rest of the burger into my mouth and got away as fast as I could without actually running. That afternoon, when I was watching TV, I had another flashback, only this time my sister was in it too, in the café, looking at my dead body. That night I cried into the mattress again, pillow held over my head to muffle the sound.

Chapter 16

The weirdest thing happened one afternoon when I was walking back to the home after school. I always thought of it as 'the home' rather than home, because it wasn't. There were trees along the pavement and I heard a voice.

"Hey sonny, you down there, I need you to help me. I've been here for bloody ages. Up here stupid, up the tree, I'm stuck up the tree."

I'd stopped and was looking around for who'd spoken. It was an old person's voice, an old woman's, thin and rasping. I noticed the small stepladder lying on the pavement by the tree.

"Up here, stupid, and be quick about it. Put the ladder back up and no looking up my skirt. I know all about lads of your age, all sex mad. Hurry up, I need a wee and me bladder control's not what it used to be. You could get very wet down there if you don't get a move on."

I hardly dared to look up but needed to find out where to place the steps. She was a long way up.

"What are you doing up there?" I asked. "And don't call me stupid, I'm not the one stuck up a tree."

I was enjoying it in a funny sort of way.

"Mind your own business. Well, if you must know it were the bloody cat, he'd been up here for hours. I knew he'd jump down as soon as I tried to rescue him. Couldn't leave him here though, could I? Bloody thing waited until I got all the way up before it jumped down. I'll wring its bloody neck when I catch it. I wouldn't really. I might just bloody kick it though. Hurry up sonny."

I put the ladder into position and waited.

"It's no good sonny. I can't reach it. You'll have to come up and get me."

I took out my mobile.

"I'll call the police. They'll know what to do."

"Bloody police could take ages. You'll have to do it."

"How am I supposed to get you down?"

"Don't they bloody teach you anything nowadays? Fireman's lift lad. I don't weigh anything, just skin and bone.

Bloody police always take ages. Fireman's lift sonny. Get on with it. Take care now."

I climbed up the steps. Then I pulled myself into the tree, up to the old woman. She was incredibly thin and wrinkly. When I was ready I moved my shoulder up towards her, so that she could lean across it.

"Hold me tight laddy and don't go banging my bloody head or I'll be bloody suing you for bloody damages."

"Stop swearing," I said, "I'm doing my best."

"Swearing? Bloody isn't swearing. Effing, you know what I mean, now that's swearing but I'm too much of a lady to use a word like that."

I reached the ladder and started to climb down it. She weighed almost nothing but it was still quite difficult. When I was almost at the bottom I noticed a man on the pavement, taking pictures of us with the camera in his phone.

"What are you up to?" I asked, feeling a bit miffed.

"It's a free country," he answered. "The local rag pays good money for pictures like this. They're always after human interest stories. You could be famous."

At the bottom I bent down so the woman could stand up.

"There you are then."

"Took your time. Bloody kids. Well I'll be off then, you've had your excitement for today."

With that she picked up the steps and walked into her driveway.

"Didn't even say thanks," I said to the man. "You aren't really going to send the pictures to the paper are you?"

"Course not," he replied and walked off down the road.

Next day I was on the front page, coming down the tree with the old lady bent over my shoulder. Her name was Smith. The newspaper had found her and interviewed her.

'I gave him a ten pound reward,' she was quoted as saying, 'such a nice lad.'

They called me the mystery hero and asked if anyone knew my name. By later that day they had been given it and were outside the home waiting for me after school. I told the truth and tried to play it down. They wanted me to be photographed again with the old woman.

"No way," I said, emphatically, "she didn't really give me a reward."

VINCE IS OUR MYSTERY HERO

said the headline the next day. There were several photos of me, too. Later on that afternoon, it was a Saturday, the local MP called at the home. He wanted to be photographed with the local hero; there was an election coming up. The article was in the Monday edition. According to him I was the decent face of modern youth and he said he would be inviting me down to Westminster to meet the Prime Minister. It never happened. The newspaper had asked if they could do a piece on what it was like for me to be in care. It never happened. The story was dropped. I never heard from them again but Nathan and the others had a field day.

"Picked any Granny Smiths lately?"

Stuff like that, until they got bored.

It was my fifteenth birthday. Miss Williams and Perkins were taking me out to an Italian restaurant for dinner.

"Table for four please," Perkins told the waiter.

"Felix will be joining us in a bit," he explained, 'he's rather fond of making grand entrances."

Perkins and Miss Williams were holding hands again. When Mr Greene arrived they quickly let go and the hands disappeared under the table. I figured that he didn't allow holding hands.

"That's enough of that," said Mr Greene, looking at them.

"Like two love birds," he went on, turning to me, "he's completely smitten with her. Walks around with a dazed look most of the time. Mind you, I do think he has rather excellent taste."

"I do believe you're jealous of him," said Miss Williams, smiling.

"No possibility of that, I'm afraid, other way inclined," answered Mr Greene. Miss Williams and Perkins looked at each other with surprised faces. I just wondered what he meant.

Mr Greene handed me a heavy, gift-wrapped present. It was a book, the complete works of William Shakespeare.

"Don't try reading it now. I expect you will enjoy it more when you're a little older."

I tried to make the thank you sound genuine. Miss Williams and Perkins gave me an iPod, one of the expensive ones with lots of space. I was dead chuffed. The waiter asked if we were ready to order and Mr Greene asked me what I wanted.

"Spaghetti Bolognese. I can show you how to eat it properly."

"Wonderful idea," said Mr Greene, promptly ordering four spaghettis, without asking the others. "And two bottles of your best claret and something horribly fizzy for the boy. We'll skip the starters."

I told them about the old woman and how the MP and the newspaper had disappeared as suddenly as they'd arrived.

"Had to be, old chap," explained Mr Greene. "It looked as though the national press and TV were going to run the story, so I had a word in Sir Michael's ear. He's been a friend for years, even before he became an MP. Told him that it was a bit ironic to be calling you the decent face of modern youth when you've already got two ASBOs and I can't remember how many convictions. It had the desired effect."

I was shocked, so were Miss Williams and Perkins. The table went silent. Mr Greene smiled.

"It's true, Vince, I'm afraid. The point is that you handled your assignment so well that I have high hopes that once you've finished school and university, you'll come and work with us at MI5. I can almost guarantee you a job. We couldn't have your face splashed all over the national dailies. Spies depend on anonymity. I had to put a stop to it. Seriously, Vince, I think you'd have a great future with us."

I didn't know whether to feel flattered or not. I did know that he was talking nonsense about university.

"You need qualifications to get to university," I moaned. "They've put me in the non-exam classes for next year, with all the thickos. I'll leave school with nothing. You needn't have bothered."

"Yes," said Mr Greene, "we need to talk to you about that. The Government are very appreciative of all that you've done and wish to remunerate you in some way."

"He means pay you a reward," explained Miss Williams.

"Quite so," continued Mr Greene, "anyway they have made a sum of money available to fund a good education for you, including university, when you reach that age. Until then we've reserved a place at an international college in Cornwall. It has excellent facilities in every way. Not only in terms of subjects, Vince, it offers all sorts of sports such as sea canoeing and orienteering. In the holidays it sends expeditions to places like the rain forests in Costa Rica and Borneo. As it is an international college, it takes students from all over the world and because they can't all necessarily get home every vacation, some students stay there year round. You could too. It would be better than the home. You wouldn't feel out of place, Vince. It only starts in Year 10, so everybody in your year group would be new, not just you. You've been accepted, a place is yours. It would be a wonderful opportunity. What do you think?"

I didn't know what to say.

"Professor Grant put us onto it. We explained that we were thinking of financing your education and he suggested the college. One of his former students is the Head of Science there and they keep in touch. That's not all, Vince. The Professor also wishes to make amends. He is completely alone. He has no family. He intends to rewrite his will in your name. You would be the sole beneficiary."

Miss Williams interrupted again to explain in plain English. He was going to leave all his money to me.

"He's quite a wealthy man, Vince," said Mr Greene. "As well as the will, he is also going to set a sum aside for you when you reach the age of 21. All in all you will be very well taken care of. It's only what you deserve, Vince. We are all very grateful to you. The most important thing is that this will be your chance for a new beginning, a way of transforming your life and your expectations."

He paused, waiting for me to say something. I had no

idea what to say. It was too much to take in, another big change after everything else. I was just starting to get used to the Home. I didn't particularly like it there but at least it was there, near my parents, both lots. I knew that Cornwall was hours away. Perkins broke the silence.

"They're having an open day next week. We could go down and have a look around. You could come too, Karen. We'll make a day of it. Leave it till then to make a decision, Vince. Keep an open mind."

I nodded in agreement. At least it meant I didn't have to make a decision then and there.

Just then, the spaghetti arrived. Mr Greene instructed everyone to watch me carefully.

"Damned tricky stuff, long spaghetti. Has a mind of its own. Just follow Vince."

I demonstrated how to do it. They probably knew already but it was a bit of a laugh. Miss Williams and Perkins pretended that they hadn't done it like that before and Mr Greene curled far too many strands around his fork and then, just as he got it to his mouth, half of them dropped down to form a long tail that he sucked up with the longest, loudest slurp ever. Almost everyone else in the restaurant heard and looked across.

"I said it was damnably tricky stuff," Mr Greene explained, as the rest of us started laughing. He winked at me. I knew he'd done it on purpose.

While the others were having coffee, I told them about the cemetery, Mayberry Road and the café in the department store. Mr Greene told Perkins off for having told me about my real family and Miss Williams told Mr Greene off, but much more sharply, for not realising that he'd left me in no-man's-land, knowing a little but not enough.

"I stand corrected," he said, raising his eyebrows to me. "You can understand the pressure she's put me under to get you into the college. Still, Vince, you did the right thing, not telling your real mother. It would have put her under intolerable strain. Maybe in the future there might be possibilities, but not now. Anyway, don't you see what I mean about joining us? You found all that out so easily and quickly, you're a born detective, Vince. You'll make a super spy!"

Later that night while I was getting ready for bed, I read the instructions for the iPod and glanced at the Shakespeare. I picked it up. There was a tape thing on one of the corners that stopped it from coming open. I pushed it up to look inside. After the first thirty pages or so I found that a hole had been cut into the paper and in that, curled into a bundle held by an elastic band, there were five brand new ten-pound notes. It made me smile.

The following day Miss Williams phoned me and said how disappointed she'd been by my response to the offer of the college. She went on a bit about what a special place it was and how it had every possible facility under the sun. I didn't like to say so, but that only made it worse because it made me even more sure that I wouldn't fit in. I didn't want anywhere special, just an ordinary school where I could be myself. She made it sound a bit better when she said that there were no bottom sets or non-exam groups and that had to be good for me compared with what I'd have to suffer if I stayed put. I told her that it was too far away and she asked what difference that made, so I said that I might never see her, stuck all the way down there. She answered I shouldn't be thinking like that because she had to apply for jobs wherever they came up, and that could mean anywhere. I might be nearer to her in Cornwall or further away, there was no telling. Then she told me that she had an interview coming up but she couldn't say where and I figured it must be because of what she'd agreed with Mr Harding. After that phone call I didn't know what to think about anything.

The following Tuesday Miss Williams called for me very early at the home, even before most of the live-in staff were up. She was quite smartly dressed and I wondered if I should have made more effort myself but she said I was fine. Then we drove across town to fetch Perkins. It was quite a long drive even to get to the start of Cornwall and almost as long after that to reach the college. We had to stop twice on the way. I was quite pleased to be having a whole day with Miss Williams even if Perkins was there, because she was going off to Australia right after the term finished and that was only a few days away. When we got to the college though, she said she had a headache and just wanted to go off on her own somewhere quiet and I had to go round with Perkins instead. She said she wanted me to get to know him better anyway, and it was the perfect opportunity. I wondered about that and if it meant she was getting serious about him.

We were shown around by a 6th Form student who looked kind of Chinese and spoke like an American. His parents had homes in Singapore and New York and he was meeting up with them in Mexico for the summer. He raved on about how great the college was and how much I would like it. As we walked around, he pointed out things like the drama studio and the radio station, as well as the classrooms. One of the buildings was really old and looked like a castle, but the others were all really modern. One of them had a flat roof with a lawn on, with benches for sitting. None of the kids were wearing a uniform but none of them looked like chavs either, and there was no litter or graffiti anywhere. Later on we were expected to try out one of the college's outdoor activities for ourselves. They were all new to me but Perkins said we should choose rock climbing because he'd done a bit of that before. We had to change into the right sort of gear and then a mini-bus took us and some others to a beach a couple of miles away where there were cliffs, quite high and steep. It looked dangerous but the climb itself wasn't too difficult. There were lots of places to put your hands and feet and even a bit of railing in one place. It took quite a lot of effort though and made my wound ache. It felt tender for days afterwards. I tried not to look down, except when I got to the very top. I don't suppose there was any real danger because of all the safety ropes. It made me think of the last time I'd had to go climbing. Half way up I called down to Perkins not to shout out any more stupid remarks because I didn't want to fall off again.

They gave us sandwiches and drinks before we left. People were standing round and talking quietly. A teacher asked me what school I was at and when I told him he looked blank. Perkins told him it was a local comp and the teacher said that was jolly good because they ought to have more working class students, then he walked straight off to talk to someone else. Before we went out to the car Perkins texted Miss Williams and she was waiting for us by the time we got there. Perkins gave her a kiss on the cheek. She looked at me. I knew what she was going to say. I'd been dreading it.

"Well, what did you make of it, Vince? Are you going to accept?"

I knew she really wanted me to say yes but the only part of the afternoon I'd enjoyed was the climb and that was mainly because I had to concentrate so hard I couldn't think about anything else. The rest of the time I'd hated it. I didn't think that I could ever feel happy there.

"I don't think so, no."

They both looked horrified.

"I wouldn't fit in. I felt completely out of place all afternoon. It isn't for someone like me. I bet none of them kids live in council flats. None of them would have ASBOs. None of them would muck about in lessons. That Chinese kid flies round the world every year. I've never even been on a plane, well except like… you know. They'd make fun of me. It's all wrong. I'd never fit in."

"No Vince, it's you that's wrong," said Miss Williams, her voice sort of angry and sad at the same time. "Don't you see Vince that it was the council flat where you didn't fit in, with Sandra and William? You weren't their child. Your dad was the war hero, not the man in prison. You didn't fit in there but you didn't let it swallow you up. You resisted. You might not have realised it, but you did resist. The notebook Vince, remember the notebook and never forget it. It was your way of saying that you didn't fit in, that you had more to offer, that you could do better with your life. Remember how surprised I was, how incredulous that you could produce such work. It was the real you coming through and this college is the opportunity for the real you to grow and shine. It will be difficult at first, I know. You will feel out of place to begin with. You're bound to, but it won't last. You'll get used to it, you'll make friends, you'll settle in. You'll thrive in this sort of place. It will bring out the best in you."

Her voice was becoming louder and more intense.

"I don't think I'll ever speak to you again if you say no to this, Vince. It'll be like turning your back on everything we've achieved together. I'll be so angry. It'll be such a waste. You have to agree Vince. You must say yes."

She stopped and sniffed. Her eyes were watering. Perkins handed her a tissue. I didn't like to see her like that. I was a bit concerned that she might really mean it about not speaking to me again. I could understand why she wanted me to accept.

"All right then," I said, "I suppose I'll give it a go. Just a go, though. I'm not staying if they make fun of me."

They smiled and I got a hug, but it would have been better from Miss Williams.

Chapter 17

Those summer holidays seemed to drag on forever. More than ever I felt in limbo, waiting for college to start and my new life to begin, living through the last few weeks in the home. There wasn't even any school to help pass the time. I got friendly with the guy who came round every so often to cut the lawns and tidy the garden. He wasn't long out of school himself. He told me he'd spent two years hanging around, doing nothing and getting in trouble, until he decided that if he didn't do something to change he'd end up an addict or in prison, or maybe both. So he borrowed the money to buy a ladder and a bucket and set himself up as a window cleaner and never looked back. He'd branched out into gardening as well because he hadn't got enough windows to fill all his time. When I told him about the college and what it was like, his eyes lit up and he said he wished something like that had happened to him. It made me feel a lot better about going.

It was him who suggested I should grow something. We marked out a little plot together at the end of the back garden and he helped me dig it over so that the turf was buried. Next time he came round he had a plastic tub of what was called 'living salad' that he'd bought in the supermarket. He told me that I didn't have enough time to grow stuff from seed but I could separate all the little plants out and grow them on instead. I didn't like to tell him I wasn't big on green stuff but I did as he showed me. Next day the little plants were all limp and lying down but I kept watering them, and after that they perked up and grew quickly. I suppose I got the bug and asked if I could make the plot bigger by digging up more lawn. I went round the supermarket myself and spent my own money on the same sort of tubs, only with different sorts of herbs growing in them. After a few weeks I was picking stuff and taking it into the kitchen for the cook to use. Slugs were a bit of a problem. Not long after starting I came down one morning to find that some of the plants had been eaten and several slimy trails on the soil. I didn't like to touch the slugs but I scooped them up with a trowel and squashed them. I found out that slugs came out mostly at night so from then on, before I went to bed, I hunted round with a torch and found hundreds, well, quite a few of the little blighters. I stopped squashing them though, not because I felt particularly sorry for them, but because it wasn't a nice thing to have to do. There was a roundabout at the end of the road with trees and grass in the middle. I used to put the slugs in a box overnight with some grass for food and then take them and empty the box in the roundabout. I figured that if they had any sense they'd stay put and if they hadn't they'd get squashed anyway, only without me having to do the squashing.

Miss Williams sent postcards from Australia regularly, pictures of kangaroos, koalas and the Great Barrier Reef where she'd gone snorkelling and seen real live sharks in the distance. She said she got back on the boat in double quick time. She also e-mailed me some photos that people had taken of her, including some on a beach, only she was wearing a t-shirt and shorts, not a bikini, which was a bit of a let-down. I was also pretty gutted when her last card said that she wouldn't be back before I left for college but she did promise to see me very soon after. Perkins came round regularly though, and took me out in his car. It was very old and had a canvas roof that you could put down when the weather was good. Perkins said it was a vintage model and worth a lot of money, and I couldn't understand why he didn't just sell it then and buy a new one instead. When I suggested it while we were driving along he looked as if he was going to have a fit and almost drove it off the road. I grew to like Perkins more and more, but it was a long time before I got to know what his first name was.

In the last week of that summer holiday I went back to see Sandra. She opened the door with a cigarette in her hand and a large bump in her belly. The baby was due in a few months. William was back inside prison, having broken the terms of his parole. She told me the child wasn't his but she wasn't worried, she'd decided she wasn't going to let him back this time. She was fed up with the violence and didn't want it growing up scared like I'd been. She said she was sorry about what she'd done, taking me home from the hospital like that. Then she asked if they'd told me where her real son went. She'd been wondering what he was like and if he might want to go and live with her. That really came as a kick in the teeth, to think that I meant so little to her that she could just put someone else in my place. Maybe she said it without thinking. Perhaps she was just lonely. It still hurt. I had to think how to answer, whether to tell her or not. The boy had grown up thinking his dad was a hero. What would be the point of him knowing that his dad was a villain? It wasn't his fault he'd been brought up where he was. It wasn't just me whose life had been affected, we'd both been deceived. Better to leave him be. Later on I realised it was the first time that I'd had thought kind thoughts about Sam. Until then I'd only felt resentment towards him.

"They never told me," I answered. "It would make things difficult for him anyway, wouldn't it? Whoever he's with, he thinks she's his real mother and she thinks he's her son. It wouldn't be fair."

I also made one further trip to Mayberry Road. I didn't really know why, I just found myself going there. I waited for a few minutes at the bus stop and then I came to my senses. The girl would recognise me, the mother would be suspicious. She might see the resemblance with my father. 'Maybe in a few years,' Mr Greene had said. I got on the first bus that came.

I didn't go to see the Professor. I was still having bad dreams at night and flashbacks in the daytime too. Professor Grant was always in them. I was worried that seeing him again in person would make them worse. I did write, though, to thank him for the money and to say I was going to the college. Perkins suggested I should. I even put in that I'd go and see him sometime.

Perkins took me down to Cornwall in the car. On the way he told me to look in the glove compartment. There was a small package inside, wrapped up with a ribbon.

"A going away present from Felix and myself. Hope you like it."

I untied the ribbon and undid the package. Inside was another finger.

"It's not quite as versatile as the first one. It's only got a radio inside. It's tuned to Radio 1. I hope that's all right."

I was dead pleased. I put the finger over the end of the stub and spent quite a long time turning my hand around to look at it. Then I worked out how to turn the radio on. The station was playing the Kaiser Chiefs.

"Cool," I said, "I predict a riot."

I had to explain it to Perkins.

We had to wait in a long queue of cars to get into the college, even though a field was being used as an overflow car park. Everybody was arriving at the same time. Some of the kids obviously knew one another because they were running up and hugging or shouting greetings. Others looked a bit sheepish and worried and I guessed they were the newcomers like me, the Year 10 kids. We had to make a couple of trips to unload everything. We'd gone out and bought a load of new clothes the week before and Perkins had even bought me a laptop, which was great because I'd never had one of my own. He said that it would be important for my school work because the lessons were online as well as in classrooms, and I would have to e-mail my homework instead of handing in an exercise book.

I was to be in something called Blake House, but actually it was three houses, and my room was on the middle floor of the second one. It wasn't very big but it had everything I needed, and a separate door that led to my own private toilet and shower. When we'd unpacked a few things we were supposed to find the main reception and register but I told Perkins he might as well go before that, as it was such a long drive back. Actually, I was worried that it would make me look weedy if I had an adult with me to register. Perkins left saying he would be in touch and I sat on the bed, alone again. I felt a chill feeling come over me and had another flashback. I suppose I was completely used to them by then, even if they were horrible. I knew not to fight it, just to let it happen. I'd even started to keep notes on which events happened in each flashback. I'd got this little notebook that I kept in a pocket and I'd worked out a set of numbers, each one for a different thing. I had to write it down quite quickly before I forgot all the details but it seemed to help. After a few minutes, when I felt calmer, I got up and checked in the mirror that I was looking all right. Then I made my way across to the main school building where we'd been told to go. Almost all the pupils registering still had their parents with them. It made me feel stupid for making Perkins go and very lonely too. When I got to the front of the queue the man asked for my surname.

"Viggors," I answered. The man looked down a list.

"Vince Viggors?" the man continued.

I don't know what made me do it. I hadn't thought about it before.

"No, not Vince, I'm called Sam. Please put me down as Sam. That's my real name. The Vince was just a mistake."

The man looked up from his papers.

"All right Sam, it's a bit strange but I'll make a note of it so that it gets changed on all the electronic registers before school starts tomorrow. That way the teachers will call out your proper name. Will that be okay?"

I smiled and nodded.

All the kids in my building were new to the college. We were supposed to gather in the lounge at a certain time for tea and cakes and so we could go round and meet each other. Mostly though, we were too nervous and just talked to the people we happened to be next to. Some of the kids looked really miserable and I figured that maybe I was more prepared for this than them. It wasn't the first time I'd been separated from my loved ones and sent off to a strange place. Some of them hardly seemed to know any English, either. One of them was standing next to me and managed to tell me that he was from Chad which was somewhere in Africa. He seemed to latch onto me and tried to ask me something about the rest of the day. While I was explaining, as best I could, several other boys and girls started to gather around to listen. An adult came up as well, a few minutes later.

"Sam isn't it? Listen, Sam, I'm the Senior House Master here at Blake and it's my job to make sure everyone settles in well. You seem to be taking this in your stride. You obviously know how to look after yourself. Do me a favour, Sam, take care of this little lot will you? Make sure they know where to go, what time to do it, that sort of thing. It would be a great help. I always need a few special helpers I can depend on at the beginning of the college year. Will you do that, Sam?"

I nodded and smiled again.

'Bloody hell,' I thought, 'maybe it won't be so difficult after all.'

That evening, however, I wasn't so sure. At tea I found myself sitting at a long table and next to a girl who spent the whole time talking to a girl opposite and completely ignoring me. Not that I would have found it easy to talk to either of them. They may as well have been from a different universe. The girl opposite seemed to have spent the summer flying between different parts of the Mediterranean in her father's own private jet and the girl next to me came from Florida. When I asked her if she'd been to Disney World she just turned and looked at me as though I was stupid, then turned back again without speaking. Later I found the games room and was joined by some of the foreign students that I'd been asked to look out for. Most of them seemed to have come from very rich backgrounds too, and when they asked me about my home I found myself coming out with an excuse about having to make a phone call and getting away as quick as I could.

Back in my room I felt utterly alone. There was supposed to be a disco later on but I couldn't face it, so I watched telly instead and had an early night. I couldn't sleep and I found myself dwelling on all that had happened that year, the meetings with Miss Williams, the fat policeman in his car, the excitement of the break-in, Professor Grant, the secret passage, the car boot, the plane, the terror of the crash. Mainly though, I thought about how everything that had happened afterwards seemed so completely unfair, like the whole world had it in for me. And I thought a lot about all my parents that night too, Sandra who'd stolen me, William who'd beaten me, Paul who'd died without ever seeing me and Claire who might not be able to cope with the knowledge that I even exist. I wondered if I'd lost them all forever and the thought made me almost choke with sadness. It was just too much. And Miss Williams? After all our adventures together she'd almost disappeared out of my life, her whole summer on the other side of the world with just a few postcards to show and a message that she'd see me some time in the future. I found myself saying 'please let it be soon', over and over. I suppose that's what some people would call praying. It was almost as if she was the only family I had left. I felt quite desperate because I was afraid that I was going to lose her too.

When I woke up next morning it was very early and still dark outside. It took me a while to collect my thoughts and work out where I was, but as soon as I had, the overwhelming feeling of sadness returned. I tried telling myself that I was bound to be lonely in a new school surrounded by strangers and that all the other new kids would be feeling the same, but I knew it wasn't true. Everyone else would have a family somewhere, someone to go back to, someone who loved them, someone to call on their mobile. I didn't. I was completely alone. I had no one, no one to love me, no place to go back to. It was a devastating feeling. I lay there for some time, frightened that the feeling might never go away. Then I remembered what Miss Williams had said about having a choice in whether to do good things or bad, and it dawned on me that this was another situation where I had a choice. I could take the easy way out and give in to the sadness, tell them that the college wasn't for me and ask to go back in a care home, or I could stay and try. I could try to overcome the loneliness, try to get over the flashbacks and try to make a go of the college. It wouldn't be easy, I might fail anyway, but it was worth trying. It had to be worth trying. Two years in a place like this had to be better than two more years of Mr Harding and Nath and no GCSE's at the end.

There was only one choice, really. I made myself get up and quickly washed my face in cold water. Then I put on a t-shirt, some shorts and my trainers and went downstairs. No one else was up and I wondered if it was allowed, but I opened the door, let myself out, went down the steps and started to run. I only intended to go round the grounds a couple of times, just enough to work up a bit of a sweat and to take my mind off things, but when I got to the main gates I carried straight on through and out into the countryside. Then I really ran. I ran down lanes, up hills and across fields wet with dew. I hopped stiles, jumped streams and climbed fences. My wound hurt and I got a stitch but I didn't care because out there, running in the cool morning air, I felt the darkness inside me starting to lift, and for the first time in months I began to feel happy.

I got as far as the coast. The track took me to the very edge of the cliffs, a sheer drop to the rocks and sea below, the view breathtaking. The sea was a grey-blue colour and choppy with big waves. Out on the horizon there were at least four big container ships and I wondered how far they had come, which continents they'd visited, whether I'd be able to travel too one day. Down in the valley, away from the coast, there had hardly been a breath of wind, but high on the cliffs it was blowing so hard and cold that my ears stung and all I could hear was its roar. The track continued away to the left and I followed it for a few minutes until I saw a village come into view, the houses clustered round a tiny harbour, with a breakwater stretching out into the sea. A few fishing boats were returning from their night's work, seagulls following in the wake. I waved at the fishermen and a couple of them waved back. Then I ran on and downwards until I reached the first houses. It was calmer there out of the wind, and I caught the lovely smell of the seaside. The gulls were screeching and a couple of them flew up towards me and seemed to hover motionless in the air, just a few feet away, almost within touching distance. I'd never realised before how big they were.

I was tempted to stay longer, to explore the village, but being late on the first day wouldn't have looked good. Besides, there would be plenty of time for exploring later. There would be so much to investigate in a place like this. I remember that it was just then, when I was thinking about exploring, that it all just sort of clicked into place. How nobody there knew the old me, the kid off the Forest Estate, the 'two ASBO' Vince. Nobody knew about my past; the awful things I'd done and the bad things that had happened.

This was a place where I could put the old Vince behind me; make him a thing of the past. I could start again. Like father, like son? Well yes, maybe, but my father wasn't William, the villain, my dad was Paul, the war hero. My future wasn't decided, anything was possible. Vince was gone. I was Sam, the new me. It was a great feeling.

I ran back all the way, happy to be alive and really looking forward to the day ahead. On the way up the stairs to my room I passed the girl I'd sat opposite to at tea the previous evening. I was drenched with sweat and still puffing hard but she looked at me and gave me this raised eyebrow expression look, like she was surprised and impressed. Then she smiled. Breakfast was nearly over by the time I got down but she was still there by herself and she beckoned me to go and sit next to her. When she asked me where I was from I was flustered for a bit. I knew I wanted to put the past behind me but I couldn't just blot it out or invent something out of the blue, so I told her about the estate and the home and she didn't seem bothered. While we were talking I could see this little crowd of kids gathering, waiting for me a few yards away, the boy from Chad and the others. When I told her how the teacher had asked me to look after them she seemed even more impressed. A bit later, when I shuffled my little band of followers over to the main hall, she came too. There was going to be an assembly and then we would be put in our tutor groups and given our timetables.

The hall was big enough for the whole school to fit in, with space for the staff on the stage behind the Headmaster's table. While we waited I could see the other pupils eyeing us up, the Year 11s trying to look cool and the sixth formers who were just talking quietly. After a few minutes the teachers took their places and the room went still. The Headmaster stood up at the table and began to speak. After some stuff about all the school had to offer, he welcomed the newcomers and said he was confident we would be as successful as all those who'd gone before us. Then he introduced the new teachers. Each of them had to stand up as their names were called. Most of them looked a little embarrassed. One definitely didn't. The new member of the English Department, Miss

Williams, was looking straight in my direction and smiling her beautiful smile.

Lightning Source UK Ltd.
Milton Keynes UK
UKOW04f1504191114

241866UK00001B/32/P